Miss Pearly's
Girls

Also by ReShonda Tate Billingsley

More to Life

The Stolen Daughter

ReShonda
Tate Billingsley

Miss Pearly's Girls

KENSINGTON PUBLISHING CORP.

www.kensingtonbooks.com

DAFINA BOOKS are published by

Kensington Publishing Corp.
119 West 40th Street
New York, NY 10018

ISBN: 978-1-4967-3539-3
First Trade Paperback Printing: March 2022

ISBN: 978-1-4967-3540-9 (e-book)
First Electronic Edition: March 2022

10 9 8 7 6 5

Printed in the United States of America

For Grandma Pearly,
the inspiration for this story, minus the secrets

Miss Pearly's Girls

Chapter 1
Maxine

The creaking wicker rocking chair suddenly stopped. Maxine Bell Cartwright leaned forward and inhaled. The aroma of fried chicken was wafting out through the open screen door and onto the back porch. That scent was better than the relaxing bubble baths she took every Sunday evening and her stomach growled in anticipation. When it came to Southern fried chicken, her mother could show the Colonel and Mr. Church how it was really done.

Maxine's nostrils weren't the only ones being tantalized. The smell made Petey Lawrence stop in midmow. He wiped his brow, ridding it of the sweat that dripped from his hairline, brought on from the brutal August Arkansas sun. He sniffed, then a wide smile spread across his young face when he glanced up at Maxine.

He flipped the lever on the handle and the whir of the lawn mower slowly subsided. "Oooh, Miss Pearly is at it again," Petey said.

"It's Sunday, so you know Mama is in her element." Maxine lifted her long, salt-and-pepper curls, which made her look a lot older than her fifty-two years, from her neck and tied the hair in a bun. Then she fanned herself with her hand. "The air is out in there, so I don't even understand how she's standing it inside that kitchen. I'm sure that cooking oil raises the temperature another ten degrees."

Petey laughed. "My granny said the AC has us spoiled." He walked over to the edge of the back porch, picked up his orange watercooler, and took a long gulp.

Maxine dismissed Petey's comment with the wave of her hand. "Tell Mother Channing that Jim Crow said she's allowed to have air conditioning now."

Petey was shaking his head before she finished her sentence. "Un-huh, you want me to tell her that and then have to hear an hour lecture on how high her light bill is? No, ma'am. I'll just let her go on believing what she wants to believe."

That brought a smile to Maxine's face because those words sounded just like what Mama Pearly had been saying when they'd first bought the AC unit for her back in 2010. Even after they'd installed the unit in the dining room window, it had still taken two years to get Mama Pearly to stop complaining about the cost of electricity and just turn the darn thing on.

Once she'd done that, though, Mama Pearly had quickly gotten spoiled and enjoyed having a cooler house, especially in the middle of these savage summers. But it seemed that Mama Pearly hadn't yet convinced her best friend, Caroline, or Mother Channing to everyone in Smackover, of the benefits.

Petey took another gulp, his thirst from his hour of mowing their acre and a half obviously taking its toll. " 'Bout that chicken; you think Miss Pearly got an extra piece for me?" Petey asked. His eyes were wide as he rubbed his stomach like it was waiting on an affirmative answer.

"We would both be insulted if you didn't stay and eat supper," Maxine said before she leaned back in the chair and resumed her rocking. Outside of Walter and her mother, Petey had become her most-welcomed companion. Sometimes he would sit for hours and listen to her tell stories of growing up in Smackover. Sharing stories with him brought them both joy.

"Yum, my belly is doing a happy dance," Petey replied as he hopped around, doing a little jig. "Let me get back to work so that when we sit down to dinner, I don't have to think about nothing else but your mama's good home cooking." He yanked the chain to turn the lawn mower back on. It sputtered before the motor roared and Petey went back to his task, with a little more pep in his step now.

Maxine smiled at the sight of the boy as she watched him push the thirty-pound machine. He reminded her of her own son, Walter Jr., at that age. Only Junior, as they called him, would've rather performed open heart surgery on a bull than do manual labor. Not at the age of fifteen. Despite trying to always make sure he had chores, Maxine hadn't been able to keep up with her son. Junior was always off somewhere, exploring the acreage, dissecting animals, digging up bugs. He was completely disinterested in anything that didn't serve his own needs. By high school, chores were for everyone but him as his complete focus was on anything related to science. It had paid off, though, as her baby was now considered one of the top pulmonologists in Philadelphia.

Maxine set her journal where she'd been reading notes from today's sermon aside, preferring instead to watch Petey and think about her son. When Petey rounded the corner of the house to tackle the one acre of land there, Maxine called out, "You need any help in there, Mama?"

"No, baby, I'm good."

"Really? I know you've got to be suffocating in that kitchen," she said, though she didn't make a move to go help.

"I got the fan on, plus I'm just about done," her mother replied.

"Okay," Maxine said, leaving out what she was thinking—that that fan was doing nothing except moving that hot air around. "Just let me know if you need me." When her mother said nothing else, Maxine turned her attention back to her sermon notes. She read the first line, like she'd done the last dozen times she picked up the journal. But no matter how hard she tried, she couldn't make it to the next line. It was this blinding heat that kept her mind from focusing. She had to do something to get more comfortable so she could study and review her notes from that good word that her husband gave this morning.

What could she do, though? She already had on her sleeveless housecoat, something that she really didn't like to wear. Normally, she wouldn't be caught dead in anything sleeveless, but during last summer's heat wave, she'd cut the sleeves off her favorite flowered housecoat, and now she only wore it on days like today.

She glanced down at her housecoat and a small smile crossed her face as she remembered Mama Pearly a few years ago, when she'd come home from shopping at Flora's Boutique in El Dorado and she'd shown her mother her purchase.

"Who did you buy that for?" her mother had asked with a deep frown.

"It's for me, Mama. Don't you like it?"

Her mother had huffed and puffed before she said, "Yeah, I like it. For someone who's eighty years old."

Maxine hadn't been insulted or shamed by her mother's words. Everyone in town had been calling her an old soul since she was a little girl.

The sound of the chicken sizzling in the pan mixed with the aroma that already had her stomach lurching. Without even going into the house, she knew her mother had fixed a grandiose meal, despite the fact that she was only cooking for a trio. Their large family had been reduced to just Mama Pearly, Maxine, and Walter Sr. (and, occasionally, Petey). Yet, especially on Sundays, her mother couldn't seem to adapt to the fact that she wasn't cooking for a dozen folks, which left them with leftovers for just about the whole week.

"I'll let the chicken cool down. Collards will be ready in a bit," Pearly said, appearing at the screen door. Her petite frame was draped in the red-and-white apron Maxine had given her last Christmas and she'd worn just about every day since. Her jet-black-dyed curls were still fresh from her Saturday trip to

Miss Wanda's Cut-n-Curl and framed her plump face like an oval picture frame.

"I can't believe you're sitting out here in all this heat," Pearly said, pushing the screen door open and stepping out onto the back porch that stretched from one end of the house to the other.

"It's cooler than the house, Mama. Especially with all that frying that you're doing."

Pearly grinned. "I know you're not complaining about that."

"No, I'm not." Maxine chuckled. "You know how much I love your fried chicken. I just can't sit in there with the temperature inside probably near one hundred and twenty degrees. Why we can't call someone else to come fix the AC is beyond me."

"Because I don't want anyone but Henry Taylor working in my house and he'll be back in town tomorrow. Besides, it's not that bad, but you're right. It is a little bit cooler here out back." She glanced at Maxine. "You'd probably feel better if you put on a hat. You're frying out here just like my chicken in there. You know you easily get sunburned and those peach cheeks are gonna turn scorching red."

Maxine had gotten a horrible sunburn once when she was nine years old and Mama Pearly had been scared of the sun ever since.

"I'm fine, Mama. Henry Taylor didn't build this big ol' porch covering for nothing." When the worried look didn't leave her mother's face, she changed the subject. "But please tell me you scaled back a little bit on dinner. You know Walter went to the revival in Shreveport," Maxine said.

"I know." Pearly folded her arms and nodded. "And we should have gone with him."

"That wouldn't have made sense, Mama. It was just Walter and the deacons. And how would you have made that trip all the way down there with the way you were feeling yesterday? You didn't need to be on the road like that."

"I feel just fine." Her hands went to her thick hips as if she was offended Maxine would even suggest that she was sick.

"Well, you weren't feeling that way yesterday, so it's good that we just stayed right here."

"Hmph," Pearly huffed.

"What's wrong?"

"I'm just trying to figure out something."

"Something like what?"

"When did you become the mama and me your child?"

Maxine chuckled, Pearly did not.

Pearly said, "Anyway, my son-in-love still needs to eat when he gets back. Plus, I'm sure Petey wants a plate."

"Of course he does. Just thinking about it already has him cutting the grass a little bit faster."

Pearly leaned off the porch to see if she could see Petey, but she could only hear the whir of the lawn mower. She turned her attention back to Maxine, stood for a moment, shifted her weight from one foot to the other, inhaled, then said, "Petey sure does a good job" as her eyes surveyed the fresh-cut grass in their backyard. "He's a hard worker." She paused, and Maxine could tell there was something her mother wanted to say. Finally, it came out. "Leslie called me today."

"Did she now?" Maxine said. Suddenly, her attention was back on her journal as she resumed her rocking. And now, she was able to make it to that second line of her notes.

"Yeah, she calls me just about every week."

"Does she now?" Maxine said as if she didn't already know this.

"Yeah. We didn't talk long, but she seemed downright giddy about something."

"Did she now?" Maxine repeated, without lifting her eyes as she studied the third line of her notes in her journal.

Pearly's shoulders sank, the way they did every time she talked about her daughters to one another.

"When's the last time you talked to your sisters?"

Out of habit, Maxine did what she always did whenever her

sisters were mentioned; she sighed, then rolled her eyes. "I have no desire to talk to my sisters. You know that."

"Stop being ugly," Pearly said, her voice tinged with sadness. "I keep telling you, family before everything." She took a long, deep breath, then released it. "Lord, I don't know where I went wrong with you girls."

Maxine pressed her lips together so the words she was thinking wouldn't come out. She would never disrespect her mother, but she'd long ago given up on her mother's dream of "one big happy family."

There was something evil that hung over the Bell sisters; at least, that's what Maxine believed. A force that brought out the worst in them all, especially when they were together. So, they were at their best when they kept their distance and lived their own lives. That was their reality—even if their mother refused to accept that fact.

"It just makes me so sad to see my girls hating one another." Her voice was soft and peppered with a thousand pains.

Maxine filled her cheeks with air, then blew it out. She closed her journal and glanced up at her mother. "Mama, we don't hate one another, but we don't get along. Never have and probably never will."

"And I will never understand why." A mist covered her eyes.

Maxine paused the sway of the rocking chair. "I just don't need the toxicity, Mama. Stella is in her own self-centered world. Star and her moods have always been exasperating."

She stopped, and Pearly gave her a hard stare before she asked, "And Leslie?"

Maxine stared back and then shook her head. "Well . . . I just can't do it. I can't do it with any of them. The only thing I have in common with my sisters is that we all love you, and that's all that matters. And now that we've gone through this for at least the four hundred and thirty-third time, I'd really appreciate it if you dropped it."

Pearly's eyes narrowed. "You don't have to listen, but one day you'll hear me," she said, her voice stern. "When all is said and done, family is all you got."

"Okay, Mama," she said, her tone meant to put a period on the conversation. "You probably should go check on your collards." Maxine leaned back in the chair and the squeaking began. Her body was stiff, her eyes straight ahead onto the yard that Petey had just tackled. The rocking, her stance, a dismissal to her mother.

Pearly crossed her arms, tapped her foot, and, when Maxine said nothing more, Pearly huffed, then let the screen door slam behind her as she turned and walked back inside.

Maxine's shoulders slouched a bit. She hated disappointing her mother in this manner, but what else was she supposed to say to her except the truth?

She pushed aside her journal, her attention no longer on her sermon notes. Instead, she rocked, and once again took in the fragrance of Sunday dinner before her gaze roamed to the cows grazing in the pasture across the street. Between that sight and the sounds of Petey's lawn mower and the birds chirping, she was back in that zone where she was before her mother had come out.

Maxine marveled at how her home brought her such peace. To her, Smackover was the definition of serenity. That was a drastic difference from how her sisters felt. They hated Smackover; not the town so much as all of its country ways. Even from the time they were kids, her sisters had talked about how they couldn't wait to leave.

As soon as they graduated high school, both Stella and Leslie were on the first Greyhound out of town. Star had been anxious to leave, but not eager to go too far. So, she'd moved an hour and a half away to Hot Springs.

But as for Maxine, she would never leave. There was nothing out there that was better, nothing out there that was greater than this place that would always be home.

*   *   *

"Ma-xine . . . Maxine!"

Maxine sprang up in the rocking chair and tried to get her bearings. Had she dozed off?

"H—help me, Ma-xine . . ."

"Mama?" Maxine blinked as she tried to focus on the voice. Was it real? Had she been dreaming?

Then she saw movement from the corner of her eye. The screen door wide open . . . and her mother clutching the side of the doorframe. Pearly's eyes were wide and filled with terror.

Maxine jumped up and sprinted across the porch, the wooden planks creaking beneath her heavy steps. "Mama, what's wrong?" Instantly, her mind went to the suffocating heat inside the house. Was her mother having a heatstroke?

Maxine crouched down and reached out for her mother, but an arctic blast swept over her when she saw the blood pooling at her mother's feet.

"Mama!"

Mama Pearly's chest was slowly heaving up and down as she tried to catch her breath. She glanced down, almost in slow motion, and mumbled, "Lord, Jesus" when she saw the blood. Then her eyes rolled into the back of her head and she slumped to the floor.

Chapter 2
Stella

"I brought you some hot wings."

Stella Bell's eyes made their way down to the plate that was piled high with chicken wings dripping in buffalo sauce. She looked at the wings, then at the face of the man holding the plate.

"Wings? Really, Lincoln?"

"What?" Lincoln said, his eyebrows bunching together in utter confusion.

"Out of all the choices you had at that buffet table, you bring me wings?"

"But you love wings."

She pointed to her tweed boucle outfit. "This is Chanel. Do you know *anyone* who eats hot wings while wearing Chanel?" she snapped.

"Do I know anyone who wears Chanel?" he asked with a matching attitude.

"You know me!" Then she glanced around at the men and women dressed in professional attire, milling throughout the ballroom of the Belmont Hotel at a reception for the Atlanta Falcons. Nothing about this exclusive affair said "hot wings." In fact, Stella made a note to question the caterer as to why they'd even served them. "And probably half of the women in here are wearing Chanel," she added.

"Oh, I'm sorry," Lincoln said, throwing up the hand that wasn't holding the plate of wings. "You're in siddity mode. My bad."

"No, I'm in work mode, and I'm not about to walk around, greeting clients, potential sponsors, and taking care of business with buffalo sauce dripping from my lips."

Lincoln grinned, then lowered his voice. "Well," he began, so softly that Stella had no choice but to lean closer to hear him above the chatter and laughter that filled the ballroom. "If you did get any of this sauce on your lips, I'd be happy to lick it off for you."

Stella rolled her eyes, but before she could tell Lincoln that his comment wasn't appropriate because she was working, her friend Jodi sauntered over.

"Lincoln, what are you doing here?" Jodi asked. Her disdain was evident as her eyes went from Lincoln's Kangol hat to his baggy pants, down to his boots. "And in Timberlands at that."

Stella raised an eyebrow and turned her glance to Lincoln. She was waiting on the answer to that question as well, because this was something she'd wanted to know from the moment she turned around after speaking to the Falcons' VP of marketing and saw Lincoln standing at the entry, decked out in all his gear. Though the guest list was handled directly by the marketing department and not her as the publicist, Lincoln couldn't possibly have been invited to this exclusive, private event.

He flashed a dimpled smile, his chocolate skin glistening against his light blue paisley cuffed shirt. "You two aren't the only ones with connections," he said as he slid half a wing in his mouth, sucked off the meat, and pulled out a dry bone. "These are pretty good, but nowhere near as good as mine."

Stella stifled her groan. For Lincoln to be so sexy, he lacked class, which was reason number 327 why they could never officially be together. She said, "Let me get back to work."

"Work? Doing what? This doesn't look anything like work to me." He glanced around the room at all the people mixing and mingling, all decked out in designer fashions. Though this Sunday evening reception was supposed to be informal, the marketing team had made sure this event was top-notch, decorating the entire room in red and black—the Falcons colors—and laying out a buffet that should've been in a magazine spread. Even the two dozen or so professional football players who were there were dressed like they knew they were coming to an event in Atlanta's most exclusive hotel—unlike Lincoln, who'd shown up like he was going to an Ice Cube concert.

"It looks like you're up here, hobnobbing with the big dogs," he added.

"I'm working," Stella repeated. "I have several clients here, one of whom we're trying to secure a huge sponsorship backing for, so I'm trying to stay focused on closing that deal."

"Yeah, let my girl handle her business," Jodi said, her eyes still filled with disgust.

Stella knew that Jodi was just trying to have her back, like she always had in the seventeen years of their friendship, from their days at Spelman. But Jodi's comments to Lincoln were more than just backing up her friend. Jodi made no qualms about the fact that she didn't think Lincoln was good enough for Stella, and she let both Lincoln and Stella know that every chance she had.

She tossed her long, blond curls over her shoulder and turned her attention back to Stella. "You go back to work; I'll be at the bar."

"No doubt trying to scam up on some free drinks," Lincoln said as she turned to walk away.

Jodi stopped, glanced back over her shoulder, and turned up her nose. "Whatever, at least I'll be able to get a drink. Stella, you might want to join me when you're finished because Lord knows your struggle-boyfriend can't afford to buy you a glass of water." Then she sashayed off.

Lincoln's cavalier smile faded fast, replaced by the irritation he felt. "Look," he began, with his shoulders hunched up so high they almost reached his ears, "I'm getting real tired of your girl always disrespecting me."

"Did she lie, though?" was what Stella wanted to say, but instead, she took a deep sigh. "So you never answered the question; what are you doing here?"

He relaxed, and the sexy smile returned. "I hadn't seen you in two weeks because you've been," he made air quotes, "so busy. I just came to check up on you. See how you were doing. Because you seem to forget that you've got a man."

While a man demanding a title in her life would be attractive for most women, Stella hated having this conversation with Lincoln, especially here.

Still, she answered. "We've talked about this," she said matter-of-factly. "I'm on lease. Nobody's purchased me, so therefore no one needs to be 'checking up on me.'" She knew that would shut him up because while Lincoln wanted it to be clear that she was his girl, he was clear that he wasn't ready to be a husband until his catering business took off. At this point, though, Stella wondered if it ever would take off.

He'd been working on his dream since she met him at a client event five years ago. Back then, he wanted to open a five-star restaurant in a strip mall downtown. She'd laughed when he first told her that, thinking a five-star restaurant in a strip mall was a joke. But he'd been serious, and had never been able to figure out why that dream hadn't materialized.

By the fourth year, all Lincoln wanted was a food truck. Now, he was just settling on a catering business. But to date, none of those three dreams had panned out.

Lincoln made enough money to support himself by bit-acting jobs in between catering gigs. But his sparse income didn't put him in the same stratosphere as Stella financially. Reason number 328.

"See, there you go with that leasing-versus-buying mess." He stopped a passing waiter and took some meatballs from the tray, then turned back to her. "I keep telling you I'm just trying to get my life together and then I'll be able to buy you," he said, stroking her hair.

Stella slapped his hand away. If his sex wasn't so good, she would dump him right now.

"Would you stop? How many different ways do I have to tell you that *I'm working*," Stella said, glancing over her shoulder, hoping no one had overheard their exchange. In fact, she needed to step away from Lincoln because she didn't want to even be seen with him. "These are my clients."

He squinted, his eyes scanning the room again. "These look like NFL players to me."

"Many of whom are my clients," she said through gritted teeth. "You know that!"

"Oh, yeah. I forgot. Miss Atlanta Falcons. Always on point." His voice was filled with sarcasm.

This conversation wasn't going the way she needed it to, so she flipped. Decided she'd get further by being nice. "Listen, I really do have business I have to finish up here, but why don't you just go on back to my place, whip up one of your specialties, and we'll hook up for dinner later tonight?"

That brought a smile to Lincoln's face. "Now you're talking," he said. "But umm, how am I supposed to get in to your place?"

Without hesitating, she said, "The code is 91783."

"Who can remember all those numbers?" Lincoln replied. "Just give me your key, I'll go make a copy and this will solve all our problems." He flashed a grin, even though he knew before he asked his request would be denied.

"We're not," Stella began, and then, Lincoln joined in, "on key level."

He said, "You say that all the time, but we really need to be."

He flashed that sexy smirk that had been her kryptonite from the moment they'd met. Not this time. Not while she was working.

"Well, whatever. You know the deal, so it's up to you. I'm going to mingle with my clients now."

He picked up a wing and did the one-swoop, suction mess again before he discarded the bone on his plate. "Well, like I said, I'm not just here for you. I'm an invited guest."

She inhaled, ran her fingers through her honey-brown curls—her relaxing technique—then forced a smile. As she did, she saw two players she'd just signed contracts with to be their personal publicist looking her way.

They held up their glasses and smiled, acknowledging her, and she did the same. That sealed it. She wasn't going to say another word to Lincoln about their situation. She was too professional for that.

The players often joked with her about how she blew off all their advances. Her calmness as she turned men away was her trademark and she wasn't about to blow that now.

"Enjoy your evening," she said before she began to walk away.

"So really? It's like that?" Lincoln said.

Stella didn't even look back; she wasn't worried about him getting out of line because though he was a little rough around the edges, he wasn't ignorant.

Stella sauntered over to the bar, where she saw Jodi still standing.

"Ewww," Jodi said after Stella joined her. "Like for real, what is he even doing here?"

Stella shrugged, deciding not to repeat the conversation she'd had. She motioned for the bartender. "Cranberry and vodka, please." Stella usually didn't drink at these working social events, but after that encounter with Lincoln she wanted something before she started mingling with her clients.

"Coming right up."

"You know what?" Jodi continued as the bartender stepped away to make her drink. "He can't be putting it down *that* good. You need to kick him to the curb."

"I really do." Stella sighed, and then she pressed her lips together. So often, she'd been tempted to go deeper into this conversation with Jodi. But even though Jodi was her closest friend in Atlanta, Stella never let on how lonely she really was.

It would have been too hard to explain. She'd created a new life where she was so successful. Living in a million-dollar condo in the Buckhead section of the city, working in a coveted position, and mingling with celebrities and athletes who most people only saw on television. Her career gave her all the accouterments she'd desired as a child, and she'd left those days of wanting more behind. Now, she lived completely opposite the country bumpkin lifestyle she'd grown up in. She'd shed her past, claimed the life she was meant to live, and called herself victorious.

Yet there was a heaviness that hung over her, one that sifted through her condo and kept her awake at night. It was a combination of loneliness and guilt . . . and Lincoln helped her move past that. The nights they spent together, she didn't think about how she'd abandoned her family, she didn't feel remorse about the life she left behind, the scandalous things she'd done to create her new reality. Lincoln was good for her in that way.

But how could they be together on any permanent basis when she only felt comfortable with him in her bedroom?

"Allow yourself to envision us together," he'd told her just last week.

Stella shook her head. No, there was no future with someone she was ashamed to be seen with in public.

"What you need to do," Jodi's voice cut through Stella's thoughts, "is give that Donovan Caradine a chance."

"I'd love to give Donavan a chance, but," she paused to thank the bartender for her drink as he set it in front of her, "I don't think his wife would like it."

"Well, yeah. And then there's that." Jodi shrugged and sipped her drink.

Stella quickly downed her vodka, grimacing as the liquor warmed her throat and eased down inside her.

"Hey, there's Harlow Wilson, the guy I'm supposed to be schmoozing with to get him to financially back our initiative,"

Stella said as she spotted Harlow across the room talking to Mason McClean, one of the vice presidents of the Falcons' organization.

Jodi waved her away. "You know you don't have to babysit me. Go do your publicist stuff. I'm just gonna slink off and try to find a baller looking for someone to adopt." She paused. "Unlike you, I don't mind being the side chick," she added with a wink.

"Girl, bye." Stella laughed at her friend, knowing she didn't mean a bit of what she said.

As she moved away from the bar, Stella composed her steps, curving her way through the crowd. Harlow had been her main target for the evening; they were trying to secure his support for the diversity initiative the Falcons' organization was starting. But right when she was just feet away, her cell phone vibrated. Stella glanced down to see her sister's picture fill the screen. Without hesitation, she pressed Ignore and continued over to Mason.

"Hello, Mason dear. How are you?" Stella turned her charm up to high.

"Well, if it isn't the beautiful Stella Bell," Mason said, his words thick with his Southern accent.

"Stella Bell? I love that name," Harlow said with a wide grin.

Though they hadn't formally met, Stella had done her homework and knew everything there was to know about the owner of the Texas Land and Cattle Company. "Stella, this is Harlow Wilson," Mason said.

Stella extended her hand.

"Hello, Mr. Wilson. It is a pleasure to meet you."

Harlow took her hand and kissed the backside, and it took everything inside her not to roll her eyes. If there was a poster child for the State of Texas, it would be this man. Though his stomach was screaming to burst free from his white, button-down shirt, Stella had seen his corduroy jacket and ostrich boots in the Neiman Marcus catalog, and together those two items cost more than her car.

"The pleasure's all mine. Mason here has been telling me great things about you, Miss Bell," Harlow said, his eyes doing a slow roll down her body. She didn't miss how his glance lingered on her Pilates-toned legs.

"Well, I like to have great things told about me." Stella leaned her shoulder in just a bit, a flirtatious trick she'd learned from her mentor, Aungelle.

Aungelle had been a master at professional flirting. She was the one who taught Stella to paint the aura of femininity, while remaining a boss chick. It had paid off and been one of the reasons their PR firm, First Impressions, had snagged the lucrative Atlanta Falcons' contract.

Stella smiled as her phone vibrated in her hand again. Although Harlow paused, as if he was waiting for her to answer it, Stella didn't even glance down as she pressed Ignore once again and continued her conversation.

"The Falcons have been doing some amazing work on the social justice front," Stella said to Harlow. "You will not be disappointed when you come on board."

"Ha! I like how she's talking like the deal is already done," Harlow said.

"That's why we love her," Mason replied, a proud grin across his face.

Stella's phone vibrated again. This time all three of them glanced down at the device in her hand.

"Well, somebody desperately wants to get in touch with you," Mason said.

"My apologies," Stella said, holding up her phone. "If you'll excuse me, this is my sister. She's called multiple times, so let me check to make sure everything is okay."

"No problem," Mason said, holding up his hand. "We'll be right here when you get back."

"Yes, we will," Harlow leered.

Stella smiled, but her lips turned downward the moment she stepped away. "Yes?" she snapped, answering the phone as soon as she rounded the corner.

"Well, hello, dear sister." Star's singsongy voice filled the phone.

"What do you want, Star?"

"Dang. I haven't talked to you in three months and that's how you greet me?"

Stella took a deep breath. First Lincoln, now her sister. She was definitely going to need another drink. "You haven't talked to me in three months because you haven't called me in three months, and we both know why."

"Well, I'm calling now." Star laughed.

"Look, I can't talk right now. So whatever it is that you need from me, you'll have to call me later."

Stella hung up, closed her eyes, then released one of those long, cleansing breaths she'd learned from her yoga coach. She turned her phone off before she tucked it inside the pocket of her jacket. There would be no more interruptions as she closed the deal with Harlow Wilson. That was what she wanted to focus on; not on Lincoln and definitely not her over-the-top sister.

Chapter 3
Maxine

This was a pain she never could've imagined. Maxine was a godly woman and she knew there would come a time when all of them would cross those pearly gates. But she wasn't ready for her mother to take that journey.

Since Leslie left town eighteen years ago, it had just been Maxine, her husband, and her mother. What would she do if that changed? How could she possibly go on?

She'd been at the hospital for over three hours. They'd come into the ER, and within an hour, they were moving her mother to a room and Maxine hadn't heard anything else.

Maxine wrung her handkerchief as she paced across the tile floor in the sparsely furnished waiting room of El Dorado Memorial Hospital. The hard-weathered chairs and two end tables were evidence that this place wasn't designed for anyone to get comfortable. The room was empty, with the exception of a frail, elderly woman who sat in the corner, teary-eyed as she rocked back and forth. The sterilized smell, which Maxine had lived with daily for twenty-two years as a nurse, now made her stomach queasy.

There hadn't been many times when Maxine wished she'd lived in a bigger city, but this was one of those times. The hospital wasn't bad, but it was small compared to Mercy Hospital in Little

Rock. There, they had a staff that was four times the size and twice as qualified as the people at El Dorado Memorial.

On top of that, suppose her mother needed a specialist? Maxine had worked here at El Dorado Memorial for ten years before she retired in 2018. She couldn't remember anyone on the medical staff ever being referred to as a specialist.

A groan pressed through her lips at that thought, and she squeezed her handkerchief tighter. She had to make sure that her mother had the absolute best care.

"Sweetheart, why don't you come and have a seat?"

Maxine turned to her husband, Walter, startled, almost like she'd forgotten that he was there. Maybe that was because he'd met her here, after the EMTs had rushed her mother here to El Dorado, twenty minutes away.

"Come on, sweetheart," he said in his smooth tone that was her balm. "You haven't sat since you got here."

"I know, I'm so worried."

"And I understand, but wearing out your legs isn't going to make your worry go away and it's not gonna help Mama Pearly."

He reached his hand toward her, but she shook her head, even knowing that he was always her calm in the storm. Not just because his six four, 260-pound presence made her feel safe, but he was one of those powerful Baptist preachers who knew how to articulate strength and pass on hope in every word he uttered.

But right now, while she needed every bit of his comforting words, they aggravated her.

"Should I play Scrabble too, while I wait?" she snapped at him. "Or maybe a good ole game of bid whist would be better, and I could see if that sad old lady over there wants to be my partner."

After thirty years of marriage, Walter was used to what her mother called some of her "ugly ways." So he simply pushed himself up and strolled to the other side of the room, blocking her path.

"Let's pray," he said, taking her hands into his.

Maxine's instinct was to snatch her hands away. Instead of praying, what she wanted to do was cry out and ask what kind of God would even have her mother in the hospital fighting for her life. She wanted to demand that God come down and perform one of His miracles.

But she knew better than to say anything like that. If there was one thing the good Reverend Walter Cartwright didn't play with, it was being blasphemous toward God.

"Why don't you just pray for me?" she said as she pulled away and maneuvered around her husband. "I can't even think straight."

"You don't need to think. Just be still," he said, stopping her.

Maxine opened her mouth, but then snapped it shut. What would be the point of arguing about this when all she should be doing was praying? So she took a deep breath and relaxed her shoulders as she moved to stand in front of her husband. She let Walter take her hands this time, then together, they bowed their heads.

Walter was devoutly religious; he prided himself on what he called an unrelenting personal relationship with God, enhanced by a lifelong studying of the Bible. But even with all of that, he wasn't one of those long-winded preachers.

". . . and Lord, we know Mama Pearly is a fighter. We pray that you give her the strength to pull through. Amen."

"Amen," she said with him, then exhaled. She had to admit she felt a little relieved. Prayer always did that for her.

But the feeling didn't last. As soon as Walter released her hands, she moved away from him, pacing the same path she had before. "What's taking the doctor so long? Shouldn't they know something by now? I just need to know something, anything."

"You know as soon as they have something they can tell you, they'll come out and talk to you," Walter replied. He paused, then tilted his head up a bit, as if he were weighing his next words, as his eyes followed her. "But sweetie, with your mother having been admitted, don't you think it's time to call your sisters?"

That made her stop, spin, and face him. She narrowed her eyes and glared at her husband. "Call them for what?"

He kept his voice steady. "So they can know what's going on with their mother."

Maxine rolled her eyes and resumed her pacing. "You think they care what's going on with Mama?"

"I don't know, but we have to give them the choice to care . . . or not."

She shook her head and turned away from Walter. "I'm sure they're too busy with their lives to care about what's happening down here in Smackover."

"I'm not talking about Smackover; I'm talking about your mother."

"Well, Smackover or my mother, they don't care." She waved her hand, dismissing her husband's thoughts.

"Come on," Walter said as he eased toward her and took her hand, stopping her once again. "You know better than that. Just because they don't show their concern in the same manner as you doesn't mean they don't care."

She gave him a long side-eye. "Are you talking about my sisters or your siblings?"

He lowered his eyes, saying nothing.

Maxine smirked. "That's what I thought," she said. Of course, Walter would preach reconciliation. He and his eight siblings were so close, they all still talked via phone at least once a week and got together once a month, even though they lived in differ-ent parts of Arkansas. Even though he'd been part of the Bell family for more than two decades, there was no way Walter would ever be able to understand their family dynamics.

"What do you think can be wrong with her?" Maxine said, changing the subject, but she didn't give her husband space to an-swer. "I know she hadn't been feeling well this week; that's why we didn't go with you down to Shreveport. But I just thought it was a summer cold. I've been taking her to Dr. Warren for her regular check-ups, and she said everything was fine."

"You know your mother. Do you think she would have said anything differently?" Walter asked.

"Damn," Maxine cursed under her breath, which was the only way she ever let a curse word slip through her lips. Of course Walter was right. If anything was wrong with her mother, she would never let anyone know. That's the way Pearly Bell was; she cloaked herself in secrecy and tried to raise her daughters to be the same.

"Family business stays in the family," was a mantra Maxine had heard all her life.

Was that what her mother had done? Had she kept her business to herself, forgetting that Maxine was her family, the only family that really mattered?

The thought that her mother was sick and hadn't told her made Maxine's knees weaken and she lowered herself into the chair next to Walter. If her mother had been going through something and hadn't told her . . . just the thought devastated Maxine. She couldn't stand the idea that her mother had been going through something alone.

"I should have pressed her," Maxine whispered.

"You know your mother," Walter said.

She didn't respond. She hadn't really been talking to Walter anyway. But her thoughts continued. She should have taken it upon herself to be all in her mother's business. As her only child—at least the only child who cared—shouldn't she have known what was going on with her mother's health?

The questions lingered until Dr. Samuel Woods, the chief of surgery, appeared in the doorway.

"Dr. Woods," Maxine jumped up from her chair, "is my mother okay?" The nurses had told her Dr. Woods was handling her mother, but that was the only information she'd gotten so far. The fact that Dr. Woods—the closest thing El Dorado Memorial had to a specialist—was on the case was cause for concern by itself.

"We've got her stabilized," the doctor replied. The elderly white man pushed his tiny spectacles up the bridge of his large nose. "But I have to be honest. It's not looking good."

Those words made Maxine tremble, and then she felt Walter right by her side.

Dr. Woods glanced down at his clipboard. "Are you aware of what's going on with your mother?"

"No," Maxine said, trying to keep her voice steady. "Did the heat trigger something? It was really hot in the house." When the doctor hesitated, she added, "I have her power of attorney, so I should know."

He nodded, but still didn't say anything.

Maxine added, "Plus you know me, Dr. Woods. If there's something going on with my mother, I need to know."

Dr. Woods released a heavy sigh. "We have your power of attorney on record?"

"Yes," Maxine breathed, but the doctor still hesitated. "Dr. Woods. Please, what's going on with my mother?"

"Well," he began, tucking his hands into the pockets of his lab coat. "Miss Pearly didn't want anyone to know," he said. Lines of concern now creased his forehead.

"Dr. Woods," Maxine said his name like it was a demand, "we're beyond that." Now her tone carried a warning. She was prepared to tackle this man to the ground and either seize his notes or choke him to death, it didn't matter to her. Either would work as long as she found out the truth about her mother.

He didn't respond for a few seconds, then finally said, "She's heavily sedated because . . ." He paused like it was difficult for him to utter the words. "Your mother has stomach cancer."

"Stomach cancer? Wha- . . . when?? How long?"

Dr. Woods sighed. "She's known a while. I asked her had she

told you all. She assured me that she would. As in most cases, it was diagnosed at a late stage." He took another deep breath before continuing. "Unfortunately, it is now at Stage 4."

"Oh. My. God," Maxine said, falling into one of the chairs.

"Stage 4? Is that the worst?" Walter asked.

Dr. Woods nodded.

Maxine was stunned into silence.

"I'm so sorry, Maxine," Dr. Woods said.

"Doctor, can my wife go see her?" Walter said.

Dr. Woods expression was filled with sympathy as he said, "Yes. But like I said, she's heavily sedated, so don't stay long."

When Dr. Woods exited and turned left, Maxine bolted from her seat and out of the waiting room and turned right. She scurried down the hall with her husband right behind her. Maxine pushed open the door and stared at her mother for a moment. The privacy curtain was pulled back because her mother was the only person in the room. The low light made it hard to see, but Maxine instantly noticed the wires peeking out from her mother's hospital gown. The IV in her wrist punctured her mother's wrinkled skin as it pumped medications into her veins.

Maxine felt her throat tense up. She eased to the bed and, with tears in her eyes, kissed her mother's forehead. All she wanted to do was sit at her mother's side and hold her hands, and try to figure out how she hadn't seen this coming.

"Mama . . ." Maxine mumbled.

She didn't know how long she'd been standing there, looking down at her mother. It was only Walter's gentle touch, rubbing her back, that kept her from releasing the wail she felt building inside.

"M . . . Maxine?" The sound of Pearly's weak voice caused Maxine to clutch her mother's hand tighter.

"I'm here, Mama," she said. With her fingers, she stroked her mother's cheek as she struggled not to cry. "Mama . . . you're gonna be okay. We're going to get through this."

Pearly moved her chin toward her chest, as if she was trying to nod. Then, she said, "My girls" Her voice was just above a whisper.

"What did you say, Mama?"

"Pl . . . please get my g-girls." And then the sound of the beep sped up. Pearly arched her back and her eyes rolled into the back of her head.

"Mama!" Maxine cried. Her eyes went to the machine; it took her just seconds to study it, evaluate it, figure out what was going on—her mother's blood pressure was spiking.

The doors swung open and a nurse rushed in. Dr. Woods was right behind her.

"We need you to wait outside, please," the nurse said as she began adjusting the blood pressure cuff on her mother's arm.

"Mama!" Maxine shouted, still holding on to her mother's hand.

"Maxine, you have to go," Dr. Woods said as he opened her mother's right eye and shone a light into it.

Walter stepped to Maxine's side. "Come on, sweetie. You know how this goes. We can wait outside."

Maxine nodded, then sobbed as her mother's fingers slipped from her grasp. Her sobs deepened as she let Walter lead her out. He held her tightly as the door closed and Maxine pressed her face to the small window, trying to study every action of the doctor and the nurse.

This time, Walter didn't ask for her permission as he took her hand and began to pray.

Chapter 4
Leslie

Leslie Bell felt like her heart was going to jump out of her chest as joyful tears trickled down her face. This was a wonderful day for an outdoor wedding: warm, but not terribly so. The early August sun was shining brightly as a pleasant breeze from the north rustled in the surrounding shrubs, cooling the guests and family members as they took their seats on either side of the walk leading to the gazebo. Rose petals lined the walkway and sheer ribbons draped the railing and banisters.

Nona appeared at the end of the walkway, elegant in a radiant, light-yellow, beaded gown that was cinched at the waist, accenting her hourglass figure.

Though she was an accomplished author, no way could Leslie have penned a story this amazing. But if she had written the perfect wedding scene, this was exactly how it would have played out. Here, in a plush garden, surrounded by pink zinnias, orange marigolds, and white azaleas. Their fragrances sweetened the air, adding only more enchantment to this day.

Leslie beamed as the first chords of the music that Nona would enter to rang out. Nothing about this ceremony was conventional, so it was no surprise that Nona would be sauntering down the aisle to Gloria Estefan's "Here We Are."

Nona was model beautiful on a daily basis, but today she was simply exquisite. She'd forgone the veil for a halo of yellow roses, which sat atop her head, making her look almost angelic.

Leslie adjusted the beaded belt on her off-white pantsuit and moved into her place, under the large flower arch, as the minister motioned for everyone to take a seat.

As Gloria sang about how there was nothing she could do to keep from loving you, Nona made her way down the aisle. Her eyes were also covered by a mist of happy tears.

"We are gathered here today," the minister began once Nona had stopped in front of him. Leslie inhaled her nervousness as he continued, "to celebrate this union of love between Nona Louise Sanchez and Leslie Ann Bell."

Leslie glanced over at Nona and resisted the urge to reach up and dab at her tears.

"If there is anyone who sees fit as to why this union should not take place, speak now or forever hold your peace," the minister continued.

While Nona eased her head back toward the audience, Leslie didn't bother to turn around. She knew no one would object. Most of the white folding chairs on the left side were empty. That meant that she was among friends . . . her family had not been invited. They were not a part of her life. This life. They didn't even know Nona existed.

"You can continue," Nona told the minister with a wide smile as joyful chuckles rose behind her. "There are no objections as everyone is here in love."

There was light applause as Leslie matched her bride-to-be's smile.

"That's what I like to hear," the minister replied, flashing a huge grin, "everything done in love. That is the Lord's command and the only way it should be."

The rest of the ceremony was a blur as Leslie wanted to revel in the journey that had brought her to this place. At thirty-six, she had given up on love. After one-too-many broken hearts, from men leaving her because she "had issues," to men telling her, she "didn't know how to show love," Leslie had decided that true love wasn't in the cards for her.

So instead, she'd buried herself in her thriving career as one of the country's top romance authors. Because there would never be any way she could know love, she crafted stories of love.

Then she met Nona, who had dragged her kicking and screaming out of the closet. From the moment they met, they had chemistry and a connection. Nona had been instantly attracted to her. But they became friends only, because after all, Leslie was "straight." Over time, their friendship flourished, and after years of searching for a place to belong, she found that with Nona.

Nona had been patient as she wrestled through her confusion, supportive as she worked on finding herself and loving in spite of Leslie's resistance. Until one September evening, Leslie had given in and given her relationship with Nona a chance.

Now, because of Nona, she'd met her soul mate and found her purpose in life beyond her career. Leslie had never been happier.

"I now pronounce you wife and wife. The brides may now kiss."

The minister's words brought Leslie back to the present, this moment she wanted to remember forever. She gently leaned in and the two kissed as the crowd erupted in applause. When they stepped away from their kiss, they both laughed, their happiness on full display—and for once, Leslie didn't care who saw it.

Leslie took Nona's hand as they moved past the three rows of chairs to the open part of the garden where a spread had been set up with all their favorite foods. The caterer had done a magnificent job, blending their cultures—everything from tamales to queso cups to fingertip rips and tiny cups of banana pudding. It was obvious the thirty guests were enjoying it as they immediately swarmed the buffet table.

"I am so happy," Nona said, kissing Leslie as they watched

Nona's cousins pile their plates high with food. "I know you wanted to elope, but thank you for giving this day to me."

Leslie smiled. If she could see that joy on Nona's face on a regular basis, her wife could have whatever she wanted. "I want to spend the rest of my life making you happy."

Their moment was interrupted as their friends and Nona's family rushed over to them with their greetings and best wishes. They chatted with several guests before the photographer approached them.

"Beautiful ceremony," he said. "Can I get some pics before you eat?"

Nona nodded and took Leslie's hand as they moved into position.

After taking a few pictures with Nona's family, Leslie stepped to the side so the Sanchez family could have a few family photos for themselves.

She beamed as she watched her wife surrounded by her loving family, and when Nona's mother hugged her daughter, Leslie's smile faded a bit.

"I can't believe you don't have any family here."

Leslie turned toward the voice and her smile returned. Her friend, Charlotte, hugged her before she continued.

"I really wish there was someone here for you."

"You're here," Leslie said.

"You know what I mean."

"I do. And didn't you hear the minister say this is all in love? That's all we want here today," Leslie replied.

Charlotte shrugged, a sympathetic expression crossing her face. "I know, and I'm just saying. Nona's whole side was filled with her family and friends." Charlotte pointed to the left side of the garden area.

"Well, that's why we weren't supposed to do sides," Leslie said. For a moment, her eyes settled on their wedding planner, still scurrying around, making sure that every champagne glass was filled, the hors d'oeuvres continued to be refilled, and that the trio of musicians kept on delighting the guests.

The woman was taking care of everything—except for the one request Leslie had. She didn't want bride and bride sides when it came to where the guests would sit. But their planner had either messed up or hadn't cared what Leslie wanted. Finally, Leslie finished with, "But today I'm not focusing on any negativity. I'll forget about the wedding planner and you forget about my family."

Charlotte flashed a wide smile. "You're right. Today is about happiness, and I'm so happy for you and Nona. And to think, I was just trying to hook you up with an expert for book research."

"Well, you did good . . . on both counts." Leslie's eyes caught Nona in midlaugh and her heart swelled with more love than she ever thought was possible. "That one meeting led to my happily ever after."

Charlotte turned serious as she stared at her friend. "I think about those days when I was so worried about you." She shook her head. "You were in such a dark place."

Leslie leaned back and looked at her friend. "Didn't we just agree that today was only about positive thoughts and things?"

"I know. And yes, but you've come such a long way and I just want to acknowledge that."

"Thank you."

"And I guess I should acknowledge Nona too. And what she's done."

Leslie nodded. "She's done so much. First, she was my resource, then my unofficial therapist. And now, what could be better than her agreeing to be my wife. Now, I can die happy."

"Awww." Charlotte hugged Leslie, then stepped back. "Listen, I can't take all of your time. You need to mingle with everyone here."

Leslie glanced at her watch. "Yeah, we only have about an hour left." She kissed Charlotte's cheek, then moved through the crowd, taking selfies, dancing, and then heading over with Nona to cut their two-tier cake.

After most of the crowd had dispersed, Charlotte approached Leslie and Nona just as they were saying goodbye to Nona's sister.

"I'm about to head out. This was amazing. I am so honored to have witnessed this," she said.

"Well, we really appreciate it," Nona said, hugging her.

"Oh," Charlotte said, digging into her purse. She pulled out a cell phone and, with a wide smile, handed it to Leslie. "I almost forgot. Can you believe that you made it all day without checking your messages and social media? You get a blue ribbon."

"Yes, I know she must love me. She went all day without her phone," Nona said, and they all laughed.

Leslie shrugged. "I was a little busy today."

They laughed again, and Leslie had to admit that she couldn't believe she hadn't thought about her phone either. Charlotte and Nona were always teasing her about how much time she spent each day checking every social media account, reading emails, and texting with her agent.

"Well, thank you for taking very good care of my phone. But before you leave," she pulled Nona to her, "can you take a pic for us to commemorate this day?" Making this request made Leslie pause. How far had she come in so many ways? For the first two years they dated, Leslie refused to take pictures. The drastic contrast in their skin tones, which was so obvious when they stood side by side, reminded Leslie of the relentless teasing—most of the time from her own family—that had on most days, left her crying alone in the bathroom. How many times had she been called Tar Baby, or Darkie or Midnight? Nona's complexion, the shade of wheat, had initially driven her to those dark times. Not anymore, though.

"We just paid a wedding photographer fifteen hundred dollars and she wants to take a picture with her iPhone." Nona giggled as she snuggled closer to Leslie.

"Say cheese." Charlotte snapped the picture, then handed the phone to Leslie. "See you two later. Have fun on your honeymoon. Love you both."

"Love you too," Leslie said as Charlotte darted off. Before she tucked her phone away, she checked her call log, and the string of missed calls caused her eyebrows to shoot up.

"What's wrong?" Nona asked.

At first, Leslie was silent.

Nona added, "You're frowning, and we agreed, no frowning on our wedding day."

Leslie glanced up, her frown deeper now. "It's my sister. She's called several times."

"Which one?"

"Maxine." Leslie paused. "You think she somehow found out about the wedding?" She shook away her own question. "No, how would she?"

"Maybe she did; maybe someone told her."

"Who? Nobody here in Houston knows her." She studied the call log again, this time counting each of the twelve missed calls.

Leslie contemplated checking her voice mail. It wasn't like she and Maxine spoke very often. At least nine months had passed since their last call, which ended with Maxine berating Leslie for "telling family business in one of her books" when Leslie created a character with an ornery, judgmental pastor's wife. Maxine had been livid. The crazy part was Maxine hadn't even read it; she'd just heard some people gossiping at church about it, and that set Maxine off. That conversation had ended with Maxine demanding a retraction—as if that was even possible—and Leslie telling her sister where she could put her veiled threats. So, surely Maxine calling now and this many times only meant one thing: something was wrong.

"Call her back and see what she wants." Nona paused, as if she didn't want to say the next words. "Something might be wrong."

It was only because she and Nona had the same thought that

Leslie decided she had to make the call. The only thing—she didn't want to talk to Maxine, not after the last time.

She wondered if her mother knew what Maxine wanted. Deciding that was best, she dialed the house phone, then closed her eyes and said a quick prayer to a God she often ignored that her mother, and not Maxine, would answer.

She held her breath as the phone rang and rang before the antiquated answering machine came on.

"You have reached . . ."

Leslie hung up before her mother's voice could complete the instructions.

"She didn't answer?" Nona asked.

"I called my mom, not Maxine."

"But you didn't leave a message?"

Leslie shook her head. She didn't know why she was making such a big deal out of this, but as soon as she had that thought, she knew why. No one back in Arkansas knew her truth. And as far as Leslie was concerned, she wanted to keep it that way. There was no need for her to have any communication with anyone who shared her DNA unless her name was Pearly Bell.

Nona leaned in and kissed her. "Just call, babe."

Leslie inhaled. "You're right, I just need to do this. Get it over with. It's probably just drama, like the last time." That thought gave her the push she needed and she dialed her sister's number.

Leslie was a bit startled when Maxine answered on the first ring, and her nerves shot up to the moon when she took in her sister's tone. "Leslie!"

Leslie braced herself. "Hey. I saw I had several missed calls from you."

"Yes, I've been trying to reach you all day."

"I, um, I've been kind of busy, but what's up?"

"It's Mama."

Those words felt like someone had taken a sledgehammer and punched Leslie in the stomach.

"Mama? Is she okay?"

"She is for now. She passed out and she's in the hospital, but she's stable now." The tone of Maxine's voice sent shivers through Leslie's spine.

"What's wrong with her?" Leslie's voice was just above a whisper.

"I really don't want to tell you this over the phone."

Leslie gripped her phone tighter. "Stop treating me like the baby," she snapped. "Just tell me, Maxine."

"All right." A beat, then, "It looks like Mama has stomach cancer." She paused, but when Leslie didn't say anything, Maxine continued. "It's advanced. She's in the hospital." She sniffed. "You should get home sooner rather than later."

Their previous fight was forgotten. Their history had been pushed aside.

Oh yeah. This was bad.

Maxine continued. "I don't want you getting on the road tonight. The drive from Houston to Smackover is tough enough, and you won't be able to get to see her until tomorrow anyway."

Leslie hesitated. "I'll be there." She hung up without saying goodbye.

When she was sure Leslie was ready, Nona walked around to face her wife. Her eyes were wide with fear when she asked, "What's going on? Is there something wrong with your mother?"

"She . . . she's been hospitalized." Leslie began shaking. She clutched the back of a chair and then eased down into the seat as thoughts of what her sister had said swirled in her mind. Seconds ticked by, then, "Oh my God, if something happens to my mom . . ." She looked around the garden, where she'd just shared the happiest moment of her life. And now this. Now, this could possibly be the beginning of her mom's end.

"I–I need to get to Arkansas." She was frantic, then her eyes settled on Nona. "Oh my God. No. Our honeymoon."

Nona clasped Leslie's hand inside hers. "Calm down, sweetheart. No worries. Turks and Caicos isn't going anywhere. Remember, you insisted on insurance, so we'll just reschedule. We need to go to Arkansas."

For a moment, Leslie stared at her wife. *We?* There wasn't going to be any *we*. There was no way that *we* were going anywhere.

But those words never left her mind. She only had enough strength to collapse into Nona's arms and weep.

Chapter 5
Stella

Being pretty came at a price. And these Loubitons were demanding payment. Stella couldn't wait until she got inside her house because these five-inch stilettos were made for one hour and she was four hours past that expiration time. Her feet were screaming for mercy.

Part of her wanted to just get home, kick off these shoes, relax, and then enjoy the evening she hoped would be filled with the peace of solitude, something she only craved after one of these evenings.

But Lincoln had sent her a text reminding her that he was waiting at her place with his infamous shrimp tortellini, a bottle of cabernet sauvignon, and—himself—for dessert, all her favorites.

That was how he always managed to get her: through promises of food, wine, and sex. There was a never-ending battle between her brain and her body . . . and her body always won.

This was her fourth time giving Lincoln the code to her place, and she changed it right after he left every time. He hated when she did that, but it was what it was.

The soles of her feet protested with each step she took up the walkway. As she limped toward the front of her condo, she glanced up and almost moaned out loud.

"Evenin', Stella."

Stella waved to her nosy neighbor as she lumbered up the steps to the entryway.

"Hi, Mrs. Miriam."

Mrs. Miriam was actually housesitting for her nephew, a well-known record producer who was always on the road. She didn't do anything but stay home all day and take care of his dog, so she spent her time in everybody's business.

Mrs. Miriam approached the railing of her first-floor balcony, the miniature schnauzer cradled in her arms like a baby. "Someone is at your place, just in case you didn't know."

"Thank you," Stella replied. "I know. He's my friend."

"Well, if you ask me, that handsome young man needs to move out of the friend category." She chuckled. "You and that high-yella skin and him with that good, curly hair. You two would make some beautiful babies."

"Good day, Mrs. Miriam." Stella rolled her eyes, wanting to dismiss this woman and her words. How many times had she heard comments like, "high yella" and "redbone." Everyone assumed that her looks, particularly the fairness of her skin, had opened wide the doors of opportunity that she'd had to kick down. She'd worked hard, and people like Mrs. Miriam dismissed her education, her focus, and her determination.

Stella's mind was on the discussion that awaited her inside. She had already told herself she would not be discussing the event because she wasn't going to have her night topped off by getting into a nonwinnable debate with Lincoln. She'd gotten Harlow Wilson to commit to their diversity project, Mason McClean was happy, and her bonus this time would be approaching fifty thousand dollars. Not bad for an evening of schmoozing with Harlow Wilson. Stella didn't want that euphoria ruined. She was going to do what she did best with Lincoln; she'd eat that great meal he'd prepared, and then she'd let him devour her.

Stella unlocked her front door, and when she stepped inside, the aroma wrapped around her like a long-lost lover.

"Hey," Stella called out as she stepped into the foyer. She swore her soles sighed when she eased out of her shoes.

"Back in the kitchen, bae," Lincoln called out.

She stood in place, just for a moment, as she wiggled her toes, then removed her jacket before she draped it across the back of the sofa and walked down the long hallway. Her steps always slowed as she passed the Mixtiles gallery wall she'd filled with pictures of her new-and-improved life that began on her first day at Spelman. The more-than-a-dozen photos told the story of her years at college: trips to the homes of classmates, four spring breaks to places she couldn't really afford but had scraped and saved to attend to keep up with her rich friends. To, finally, her graduation from Spelman, before she began documenting her professional life. Her first job working publicity for Tyler Perry Studios, the first day she and Aungelle opened their company, the day she signed the Falcons' contract. Her eyes settled on the last picture on the wall, the only picture from her past: a 5-x-7 of her mother holding up Stella's first-place spelling bee ribbon in the sixth grade. Stella stood in front of her mother in the photo, pride all over her face. A smile crept up on Stella's face as she recalled her mother in church on the Sunday after the spelling bee.

"Giving honor to God and my church family, I just want to let you all know about my amazing Stella," her mother had said during the church announcements. Mama Pearly had dressed in her Sunday best: her pale pink suit with the lace collar, stockings, and a matching pillbox hat. She was grinning like she'd won the lottery as she held up the oversize yellow first-place ribbon.

"My baby girl won the spelling bee for the whole state of Arkansas," she announced to applause.

Stella had sat proudly in the pew, beaming as she clicked the heels of her white patent leather shoes together. She and Star were also clad in their baby blue Easter dresses, but for once the

academic attention was on Stella and not Star. Star wasn't bothered by the shift in attention; she was consumed with the itchy
collar on her dress. She'd been fumbling with it when they were
trying to take this picture after the announcement, so Mama
Pearly had made Star sit down while she and Stella took the
photo that now hung on her wall.

Stella sighed, pushed aside the memory, and rounded the corner to the kitchen. As soon as she entered, she inhaled again and
moaned, but this time it wasn't from pain. "Oooh, Lincoln, you
sure know how to put a smile on my . . ." Stella's words trailed off
as her eyes stopped at her kitchen table.

"What's up, sis?" Star sat with a huge grin, looking like she had
received a personal invitation to be sitting in Stella's home. She
wore a burgundy velour jogging suit, and her auburn braids
bounced around her plump face as she spoke.

"Star? What are you doing here?" Stella looked at her sister
and then shifted her glance to Lincoln. "What is she doing here?"

Lincoln kissed Stella on the cheek. "Well, we'll get to that in a
moment." He paused and looked back and forth between the two
of them. "But why don't we start with, why didn't you tell me you
had a twin sister?"

Stella ignored his question and turned back to Star. She folded
her arms across her chest as she glared down at her sister. "Why
are you in Atlanta? In my home? In my kitchen?"

"That's what I called to tell you when you so rudely hung up on
me earlier." Star leaned back and propped her feet up on the
chair across from her. "Me and Ty were passing through and we
were tired. So, we wanted to see if we could crash at your place."

In that moment, Stella wished she had never purchased a
three-bedroom condo. Wished she had never listened to the Real-
tor who'd told her that the bigger condos had a greater resale
value. Wished she could lie to her sister and tell her that she
didn't have room for her in her home or her heart, although the
latter was the truth.

"How did you get in?" While she meant the question for Star, Stella swiveled, and with more attitude in her body than her tone, she directed the question at Lincoln.

He shrugged. "I thought she was you at first."

Stella rolled her eyes. "Really? So you left me working, but you thought that somewhere in between me talking to one of my clients, I dashed off and got my hair braided?"

Lincoln shrugged. "I didn't go through all that. I just know that you women will throw on a wig and change up your look. I thought you were trying to do some freaky kind of role-play stuff because," he pointed between the two of them, "you two look just alike. You can't blame me for thinking she was you."

"No, she can't," Star jumped in. "Because identical twins always fool everybody." She smirked.

Stella leaned back, and stared down her nose at Star. Was she kidding? They may have had identical facial features, but that was where their identicalness ended. Star had a good forty pounds on her, so even with the trick of their faces, how had he confused Star for her when he knew her body intimately? He knew doggone well she wasn't that big.

Stella's eyes roamed over her sister's outfit. Nor would she ever wear velour in August. Scratch that: wear velour, while she was walking, talking, and breathing of her own accord.

Lincoln threw up his hands and returned to the stove, where he checked the simmering food.

"She's your twin sister. What was I supposed to do? Leave her on the doorstep?" he said.

He sounded like the very idea was ludicrous when that was exactly what she would have done if she'd been home.

Star raised an eyebrow at her sister. "Really, Stella?" she said, as if she'd just read her twin's mind.

Stella wanted to tell Lincoln the fact that he didn't know she even had a twin sister should have told him that she wouldn't want to come home to see her sitting in the kitchen.

"What are you even doing in Atlanta?" Stella asked, turning her attention back to Star.

"You know what? Have I told you how good it is to see you, sis?" Star said, though she didn't make any kind of move to stand and hug her sister. When Stella didn't respond, Star sighed. "Ty had to make a drop in Athens. It was a turnaround trip. We've been on the road nineteen hours and we were getting too close to being exhausted. So I told him we could crash here."

Stella spun around, as if she was searching for her brother-in-law. "Where is Ty?"

"He's in the guest bedroom upstairs, knocked out already. I told you we were tired."

Stella closed her eyes, thought about her yoga instructor again, and inhaled, then exhaled.

While she'd been shocked to see Star sitting in her home, she wasn't surprised to hear that *Ty had to make a drop*, whatever that meant. Mentally, she rolled her eyes. It wasn't that she didn't like her brother-in-law; but he was always hustling up on some kind of plan. She wasn't in touch with Star too much, but it seemed every time they connected, Star was caught up in some kind of get-rich-quick scheme with her husband. He'd sold it all, from vitamins to coffee to a cell-phone pyramid scheme with a prominent pastor.

But nothing had worked . . . no. actually, there was something that worked very well with Ty. He was good at getting her sister pregnant. That dude had super sperm that made him a gold medalist in making babies. Her sister had five children, more than halfway to having the starting lineup for a baseball team.

Even now, Stella shook her head at the thought of Star having five children, including a set of twins. Her oldest was off somewhere in Los Angeles, trying to be a rapper. But the other kids— a sixteen-year-old, a set of twin boys, and a two-year old—all lived at home. Stella couldn't even imagine.

"I mean, if you're just that against helping your sister out . . ." Star rose dramatically from her seat. "I can go wake Ty and we can just sleep in the truck." Star stared at her sister, waiting for her to say something. When Stella stayed silent, Star sighed. "Fine, I'll just get Ty. But can we at least borrow a blanket or something?"

Stella threw up her hands in frustration. "Why do you have to be so extra?"

"Me?" Star grinned before she backtracked to where she'd been sitting. "You're the one who took me through all this." She plopped back down in her seat, then turned her smile away from Stella. "So Lincoln—that's your name, right?"

"Yes?" His response was tentative as he gave Stella a sideward glance.

"You might need to run to the store and get some more food." She smacked her lips. "Because once he wakes up, my man won't be tired anymore and he'll be able to eat that whole pot. This that real shi-shi, poo-poo kind of eating. We're usually a lot more regular than my bougie sister, who, by the way, used to be just as regular as me. But anyway, we're starving, so whatever you're cooking is fine 'cause that smells off the chain."

Stella inhaled, then thought about yoga again as Lincoln chuckled.

"Regular?" he said. "I call Stella bougie all the time, too, but I knew my girl had a little *regular* in her."

"Oh, she got a *whole* lot more than regular. She's quite a bit country too." Star laughed. "She just tries really hard to hide it behind all her fancy clothes and her expansive home here."

Stella glared at Lincoln as he laughed.

"Really?" She fumed. "The two of you do know that I can hear you, right?"

"Awww, chill, babe." He leaned in for a kiss, but when Stella turned away from him, the kiss he meant for her lips landed on her ear. It was as if he didn't notice. He just said, "I'll be back. Gonna run to the store to get more shrimp."

Stella didn't reply, just stood in place with her arms still folded even after she heard the door slam behind him.

Star said, "His *girl*?" Her tone was filled with surprise. "Hmph. I didn't know you had a man."

"I don't," Stella replied, finally dropping her arms. "He's just a friend."

Star tsked as she shook her head. "Does he *know* that he's just a friend? 'Cause the way he's all posted up barefoot in your place like he lives here, you're gonna have to give him some kind of eviction notice."

Stella huffed, then sat down across from her sister. "So," she started as she began to remove her David Yurman bracelet and rings and said, "because you're just passing through after one of Ty's drops, I'm wondering if you have my money?"

The groan was instant. "Just once I would like to talk to you and you not start talking about money." Star held up a finger. "Number one, if I had your money, we would be staying at a hotel because you're not the most welcoming hostess and I would rather not have to crash here." She put up another finger. "Number two," she looked around the condo, "it don't look to me like you're hurting for that pitiful little five hundred dollars you let me borrow, and number three. . . ."

"Wait a minute, before you go into another lie, I'd like to address point number two. I don't care if it's only five dollars, it's the principle of it," Stella said. "And yes, it was just five hundred dollars, but it was three hundred the time before that and eight hundred the time before that, not to mention. . . ."

Star frowned. "Hold up," she interrupted Stella. "You're actually sitting back and keeping score?"

"Score? This isn't a game. That's your problem; you think we're playing some kind of game when this is about money."

"Money that went to take care of your nieces and nephews."

"Whatever, Star." Stella gathered the necklace and bracelets she'd just removed.

"Listen, you're talking down to me and judging me, but everybody can't be all as high-and-mighty and as perfect as you," Star said, leaning in and jabbing her index finger in her sister's direction.

"Oh, here we go." Stella looked up to the heavens.

"Yeah, here we go. 'Cause you think because you went to that fancy college, and got yourself a good job, that you're better than everyone else."

"I've never said anything or done anything to imply that I'm high-and-mighty, as you say, or better than anyone else."

"Imply?" Star laughed. "You don't *imply* anything, you just come right out and do it. Look at you now. Here you are, holding on to, what? Five thousand dollars' worth of jewelry," she said, pointing to the necklace and bracelets in Stella's hand, "and you're harassing me about five hundred dollars?"

"Harassing? Is that what you call it? Asking for my own money that you promised to have back to me in two weeks twenty-two weeks ago, is harassment?"

"Yes." Star nodded. She leaned back in her chair like that simple word proved her point. "It is. Because I'm not in the position to give you back that money and you don't even need it."

"How do you know what I need?" Stella was indignant.

"I know you don't need five hundred dollars."

They faced off, each glaring at the other, and it was Stella who blinked first. She turned her gaze away, glancing down at the jewels she held.

"Okay, Star," she said, her tone weary, "I've had such a long day and I'm tired, certainly too tired to engage in one of your rage fights again."

Star pressed back in her chair, this time like she was trying to put as much space as possible between her and her sister. Her glare was full of daggers. "See, you don't even know me now. I'm not even like that anymore."

In an instant, a moment flashed in Stella's mind: back in Smackover, in the bedroom they shared, Star standing just feet from her, trembling with rage—*You wore my letterman's jacket?*—

Stella had no chance to respond before Star reached for the lamp on the table between their twin beds and with the motion of a star baseball player, pitched it across the room, sending it crashing into so many pieces that they would find little remnants of the porcelain in the carpet for months to come.

Stella blinked herself back to the present. "Whatever you say," Stella said.

"Yeah, whatever because—"

"Pick up the phone, Trick, pick up the phone!" The rap lyrics blared from Star's phone.

As her sister reached for her cell, Stella said, "You are really too old for that." She shook her head.

Star eyed her caller ID. "Dang, it's Maxine." She glanced up. "Does she have some kind of superpower to know we're fighting?"

Stella smirked at the memory that came with Star's words. Maxine had always treated them like little kids, scolding them, bossing them around. Stella had resented that treatment, although now that she was older, she understood it better. The thirteen years' difference in their ages, even more with Leslie, had put a lot of responsibility on Maxine.

Stella watched Star as she accepted the call, then sat up straight in her chair. "Hello," Star said, looking like she was bracing herself for their big sister's chastisement for either her posture or their fighting.

"Wait, Maxine," Star said, and the way her eyes widened made Stella now sit up in her chair. "You're speaking too fast. Slow down. What's going on?"

The tone of her sister's voice made Stella scoot to the edge of her seat.

"Oh my God," Star cried. "Oh no. Oh no." Her wails filled up the room and bounced in and out of Stella's ears.

But Stella was frozen, not understanding, as she watched her sister's distress. Star slid down in her seat. "Nooo!"

Stella jumped up, pushed her chair back, and raced around the table. She grabbed the phone from her sister and with one hand pressed the cell to her ear and with her other, tried to help her sister up, but Star had crumpled to the ground.

"Maxine, it's Stella. What's going on?"

There was a moment's pause. "I didn't know you were with Star," Maxine said.

"Yeah, she's at my place. What's going on?" Stella repeated.

"Oh, Lord, Mama, not my mama!" Star wailed louder, sending Stella's panic into overdrive.

"It's Mama," Maxine said.

"Jesus, don't take my mama!"

Stella could barely hear over her sister's cries.

She spun toward Star, who was laid out on the floor. She snapped, "Would you shut up so I can hear?" Turning back to the phone, she asked again, "What's wrong with Mama?"

Maxine's voice was solemn, but Stella heard the panic in her words.

"She collapsed at home, but now she's in the hospital. Stomach cancer. And it's advanced. It's spread to several other organs."

Stella fell down into the chair where Star had been sitting. "Oh. My. God. Is she going to be okay?"

"She had some internal bleeding, but they temporarily stopped it. They've got her stabilized now and are keeping her heavily sedated." She paused, and Stella could tell that her sister was trying to keep it together. "But you guys probably need to get home sooner rather than later."

Stella hesitated for a second before she said, "Maybe I should talk to the doctor."

"Why?" Now, Maxine's tone was tight. "Do you think I'm making up something just to get you here?" Maxine huffed her exasperation. "As if I would do that! You know what? Come or don't come. I did my part. At least I picked up the phone to let you know."

"Maxine, calm down," Stella said. "I didn't mean it like that at all." Stella took a deep breath. "I'll get Star together and we'll be there tomorrow."

"Fine," Maxine said before the phone went dead.

"Do you have another wet towel?"

Stella cut her eyes at Ty as he sat on the sofa, Star's head resting on his lap. His wife's wails had sent him barreling down the stairs and he'd been comforting Star for the past hour.

"Really, Star?" Stella said, just as Lincoln came back into the living room.

"I got you, bruh," Lincoln said, as if he'd anticipated her sister needing another towel over the six she'd already used. "And it's warm," he added.

"Thanks, man." Ty grasped the towel and dabbed Star's forehead. His muscular arms held her with a gentleness that impressed Stella.

"Mammmmaaa," Star cried, sounding as if no time had passed since she'd heard the news. "Jesus, please don't let anything happen to my mama."

"You've said those exact same words to Jesus about two hundred times already. You may want to switch up the message, so that He doesn't get bored," Stella said.

"Just because you don't care that Mama is dying . . ." The moan Star released sounded as if it rose from deep inside her soul.

"First of all, who says she's dying? She's in the hospital and Maxine didn't mention the word *dying* at all."

"Yeah, because they put people who are well in the hospital," Star said, guiding Ty's hand to dab her eyes with the towel.

Stella held up her hands, surrendering. "I don't want to argue with you." She grabbed her phone from the coffee table. "I need to make some calls to have someone cover this event for me to-morrow. And then I'll head out in the morning."

Star slowly lifted her head, moving as if there was a boulder on her shoulders. Ty helped her to sit up, then he pulled up her braids, wrapped them in a bun, and tucked the ends in to keep her hair from falling. He moved like he was a seasoned pro. Then, he dabbed her face again before he pressed his lips against her forehead, holding her there for a moment.

Star gave her husband a weak smile, as if she didn't have the energy to appreciate him fully. But when she turned to Stella, she had more than enough energy to growl at her sister.

"We're leaving tonight! After we eat, we're getting on the road. We're going to Hot Springs first to get the kids, and then we'll go on to Smackover in the morning."

"Okay," Stella said with a shrug.

"Good. I'm glad you agree. So how long do you think it'll take you to get ready?" Star asked. "Because we really do want to head out after we eat."

"Okay, but what does that have to do with me being ready?" Stella asked, confused.

Now, Star was the one who gave her a frown filled with confusion. "Aren't you riding with us?"

For a second, Stella stared at Star, not believing her words, and in the next moment, she burst out laughing.

Star kept her eyes on her sister as she sat straight-faced, as if she were patiently waiting for Stella to recover from any joke she thought she heard.

Suddenly, Stella stopped. "Wait . . . are you serious?"

Star folded her arms. "Why would I not be serious?" she said, her neck swerving with each word she spoke.

"Because, umm," Stella's eyes moved between Star and Ty, "aren't you guys in a big rig?"

"And? It has a cab," she said, sounding like Stella should have known that. "We'll change out and get our Tahoe when we get to Hot Springs."

Ty said, "Calm down, baby. I don't want you to be any more upset than you already were. Remember, your blood pressure."

But before Star could respond to her husband, Stella said, "Oh, you guys have an SUV?" Her eyebrows were raised in surprise.

"My man does work," Star snapped as Ty rubbed her back. "It's a 1983, so it probably isn't up to your standards, but it gets us from point A to point B; in this situation that means it will get us from our house to Mama's house and that's all that matters." She paused but didn't give Stella time to respond. "Anyway, you're gonna need to pack light 'cause Ty's hauling chickens back to Hot Springs. So you don't want your stuff in the back trailer with the animals."

That declaration even caught Lincoln by surprise. He looked at Stella like he was trying to envision her in a big rig.

"So you want me to ride in an eighteen-wheeler with chickens?" Stella said. "Girl, bye. I'm flying home."

"That's crazy," Star shouted. "Do you know how much a last-minute ticket is going to be?"

"And that's why I work, so that if I ever need to buy a last-minute ticket, I can. So that I won't be forced to ride in the cab of a chicken-carrying eighteen-wheeler," Stella scoffed.

Star pressed her lips together and narrowed her eyes. "You can be snotty all you want, but Ty earns an honest living. He doesn't discriminate in his cargo, and I think that's something to be lauded, not disparaged."

Stella didn't reply, but Star lifted the towel that had just been on her forehead and shook it in Stella's direction.

"Every time I ask you for money, you always make it seem like it's such a big deal, but now you have no problem paying for a last-minute plane ticket."

"Are you really going to sit there and tell me how I should

spend my money?" But then she added quickly, "You know what? We don't need to do this right now. Thank you for the offer, but I'm good."

"It really is no big deal for you to ride with us," Ty said. Since middle school, when Stella and Star met Ty, he'd been mediating their arguments. He had this uncanny ability to get Star to calm down. Maybe it was because, from day one, he made Star feel beautiful; when anyone else had something to say about Star being overweight, he made it known that he adored every inch of her.

But those teenage days were far behind them now.

"You could give us that money and just ride with us," Star added.

"I'm not doing this with you, Star," Stella said.

"Fine. Waste your money. 'Cause by the time you make it to the airport in Little Rock, rent a car, and drive down to Smackover, we'll be chilling, already having dinner. And you better hope Mama ain't dead by the time you get there."

"Would you stop saying that? Mama is going to be fine."

It was as if those words made Star remember. She pressed the back of her hand against her forehead and fell against the sofa.

"Oh Lord, Mama. I don't know what I'm gonna do if I lose my mama," Star cried.

"Baby, it's going to be okay," Ty said, gently easing her head toward his lap again. He stroked her hair as he repeated, "Mama Pearly is going to be fine," over and over again.

His response didn't surprise Stella. Ty had been Star's protector since the day they met, while walking home from school on the first day of eighth grade. Ty had been the new kid in class, sent to live with his grandfather in Smackover because he'd been running with a group of boys who'd been breaking into homes and stealing scrap metal in Mississippi. After Ty was almost shot by a homeowner, Ty's mother had sent him away before he ended up dead.

But it didn't take him long to find trouble in Smackover. The first incident happened the day after he met Star. They'd agreed to meet up after school to walk home together. When Ty came out of the school, he found Star surrounded by a group of girls, though there had only been one speaking.

"Hey, Miss Piggy," this girl named Tremeka, who looked like she'd flunked three grades, said as she taunted Star about being the fat twin.

Ty had run over, jumped in, and talked about Tremeka, her mama, her daddy—who'd been shot the year before after a game of dominoes—her cousins, and all her relatives so bad, that girl had taken off running in tears, and he'd consoled Star on the way home. That was the moment when Ty fell in love with Star Bell.

Ty verbally assassinating that girl should have been a lesson for the kids in middle school, but apparently some boy hadn't heard. A few weeks later, in science class, Star had pushed him because he smacked her on the behind. Well, the boy swung back, hitting her dead in her eye. After school, Ty had been waiting for him, and he'd beat him so badly, the boy's mother had to rush him to the hospital, where the ER doctor gave him nineteen stitches across his forehead. That was the day Star fell in love with Ty Owens, and they'd been inseparable ever since.

After that, nobody in Smackover, or anywhere else they traveled, ever messed with Star.

"Baby, let's get out of here," Star said, raising her head. She turned to Lincoln, who was standing near the kitchen door, looking like he was unsure whether he wanted to get in family drama. "I wanted to get a taste of some of your good cookin', but my blood pressure's already high. Sitting here foolin' with my sister will have me in a hospital bed right next to Mama."

Stella wanted to tell her sister that maybe if she shed about fifty pounds, her blood pressure would go down.

As she watched Star and Ty gather their things, Lincoln eased up behind her.

"Babe, you all right?" he whispered.

"Yeah, I'm fine," she said.

With his backpack hooked on his shoulder, Ty paused and turned to Stella. "You sure you don't want to ride with us?"

"No, thank you," Stella said. Then, she added again, "But thank you for the offer."

He shrugged. "Okay. Well, we'll see you there." He gave one of those brother handshakes to Lincoln, mumbled his goodbyes, then gave a nod to Stella.

Star rolled her eyes as she walked out without saying goodbye and letting the door slam behind her.

Lincoln wrapped his arms around Stella. "Well, that was something."

She whipped around and glared at him. "Now do you see why I'd rather forget I have a twin?"

He shrugged and nodded at the same time as he moved back toward the kitchen.

Stella followed him and said, "And the way she was just acting . . . that's my sister on a good day."

Lincoln lit the fire back on his meal, then turned to face Stella. "Watching the two of you was deep. I've never heard of identical twins who hated each other."

That made Stella pause. "I don't know that I hate her. In fact—" She stopped herself from saying more. Then she added, "We . . . we just don't get along."

Stella couldn't believe that she had almost shared too much with Lincoln. She didn't discuss her family or what happened between them with anyone. That was the one lesson she had taken from Smackover . . . and her mother.

Family business stays in the family, her mother had always said right after she'd told them, *When all is said and done, family is all you got.*

Along with the single suitcase of belongings she'd taken with her when she'd left Smackover for Spelman, she'd taken her mother's lessons.

"Well," Lincoln said, "let's at least sit down to eat."

"No." Stella shook her head. "Can you put the food up and see yourself out? I'm going to go make my flight arrangements and go to bed."

"But babe. I'm here; I know you want to talk about your mother and—"

"No, I don't."

"But—"

"Thanks, Lincoln. Be sure to lock the door." She turned away, not giving him room to respond as she made her way upstairs.

Chapter 6

Maxine

"This is ridiculous that we still can't see Mama."

Maxine knew she shouldn't be snapping at her husband, but where else was she supposed to direct her frustration?

"Patience, sweetheart," Walter said as he read through some paperwork while intermittently watching her to make sure she was okay.

Maxine had gone home last night—only at the doctor's urging. But she'd been up and back here at the hospital before visiting hours. Not only would they not let her back into her mother's room, no one had any more information than they did yesterday. If Walter hadn't been with her, Maxine would've snuck back and planted herself right by her mother's bedside. But he was here, reining her in with a watchful eye, so once again she simply paced across the dank hospital waiting room, wishing she was anywhere but here.

The lone, elderly woman was back in the corner, resuming her fervent rocking. Two other people had arrived, a young Hispanic couple who'd rushed their infant daughter in. They were mumbling prayers in Spanish. Maxine's initial inclination was to go pray their comfort, but she fought the urge because right now, her focus needed to be solely on Mama Pearly.

This waiting room, and others like it throughout the hospital, were the areas Maxine hated most when she worked here. The small "Quiet Room" off to the side was the place she had watched as doctors delivered devastating news to thousands of families over two decades. Just the thought that she could soon be on the receiving end of those kinds of horrifying words had sent an unyielding panic throughout her body.

"It's not about making me happy, sweetheart." Walter's tone was as gentle as always when he faced her. "It's about making your mother happy. She wants her girls here. She *needs* her girls here."

Maxine stopped, folded her arms, and said, "Mama may have wanted them, but she doesn't need them here. They haven't been here all this time."

His smile was warm as he said, "Honey, you've got to let all of that animosity go, at least for right now. Everything at this time is about your mother. She needs all her girls and she needs them all united."

Maxine scoffed. Her husband's words were laughable. They hadn't been united since they were younger, if even then. They were oil and water. The Hatfield and the McCoys. Cain and Abel. "And if there is a good side to what is happening here, it's that all of you will be together and you can address some of these issues," Walter continued when she didn't respond. "You ladies can work on all of this while everybody's here, together . . . as sisters."

Maxine waved his words away. "Trust me, we are not going to be able to work anything out because we are sisters only by birth, not by heart. We have nothing in common. Stella thinks she's too good for everybody. Star is just in her own little trifling world with that husband of hers, and Leslie?" Maxine paused for a moment and swallowed, most hurt by her youngest sister. "Who knows what's going on with Leslie? There are times when I think she'd prefer it if none of us existed."

"Okay, you've taken a good inventory of your sisters. How do you think they would describe you, my love?" Walter asked, the right side of his lips lifting into that smirk she hated.

"Oh, they wouldn't give me the credit I deserve, of course," Maxine said. "They wouldn't give me credit for anything. Not the fact that I was the one who had to take care of them. Growing up, Mama worked all the time. So I was the one there, making sure they did their homework, making sure they had a home-cooked meal. I did all of that as a teenager and a young woman, giving up my life. There were so many times when I couldn't hang out with my friends because I had to take care of my sisters."

Walter's patience with this rant, which he'd heard countless times, was to be commended. Usually, he interjected right away, but today he let her continue.

"Do you think any of them appreciated the sacrifices I made?" Maxine shook her head, as if the anger of what happened all those years ago was still fresh. "No. Not a one of them. They've always been ungrateful," she said.

Walter sighed. "Well, my advice hasn't changed, so I'm going to say this to you again. At some point, you're going to have to let that bitterness go. But I've been thinking about something lately. I've been saying you need to work this out with your sisters, but you may need to have this discussion with your mother. She was the one who placed all that responsibility on you," he said.

Maxine cringed, thinking that Walter didn't know anything. But how could he when, even after thirty years of marriage, he knew so little about the Bell sisters?

When her shoulders slumped, he said, "Don't look at it as a burden, sweetheart. Look at it as a way to bring everyone together and make your family stronger."

Inside, she huffed, and outwardly, she said, "Some folks from the church are supposed to be coming up here."

"Good. We can use all the prayer we can get," he said.

"Yeah, and I hope they'll come with some holy water for when my sisters get here." Walter chuckled, but Maxine didn't. She said, "You know what?" She paused, then grabbed her purse from the chair next to where Walter sat. "I think I have some in my purse."

"Would you stop?" Walter said as he gently grasped his wife's arm. He stood, pulled her closer, and kissed her forehead. When he leaned back, he stared straight into her eyes. "I know you're stressed, but I want you to calm down and know that I got you. You're strong, but I got you. And we'll get through this together, okay?" He smiled and kept his eyes on her until she half-returned his smile.

"We'll get through this . . . with your sisters." She rolled her eyes and he chuckled. Then he said, "When are they arriving?"

"I don't know. Leslie is driving up from Houston. She said she was leaving this morning. Star said she and Stella would be here today also." She shook her head. "I still can't believe the two of them were together."

"Did you ask why they were?"

"No. That wasn't my focus, and even if it were, I wouldn't have been able to ask because Star was being her normal overly dramatic self and falling all out like we done already put Mama in the ground." She released an exasperated breath. "So now she's going to come here with all that drama. And all those badass kids." Maxine shook her head like the very thought of them had her irritated already.

"Language, sweetheart."

"I'm sorry." Maxine exhaled and resumed her pacing. She was ashamed to have cursed, because she took great pride in how she always behaved as a proper first lady. She never had any challenge in that role, except when it involved her sisters—well, there was that one time when she had stepped out of character just a bit, but no one had blamed her for going after Ramona Harrison after she tried to make a move on Walter. Other than that, she always kept her pristine demeanor—unless her sisters were involved.

Maxine paused, brushed down the sides of her cotton paisley dress, and stood erect, as if she was composing herself back to her first lady stature.

"I truly didn't mean to call my nieces and nephews that . . ."

Walter smiled and nodded.

"Even though it's true," Maxine mumbled. "Those kids have no home training and they're drama-filled, just like their mother. And my mother doesn't need that drama. She needs peace and quiet so she can rest and heal. I don't want her dealing with all their mess." Maxine walked over to the window that faced the parking lot. She inhaled, then exhaled the breath building inside her. "I—I'm just not in the mood to deal with my sisters."

She paused and continued staring outside.

"We have peace around here," Maxine continued, her back still to her husband. "Every time they come, it doesn't end well . . ."

It never would because it never had.

"Maxine!"

Even though their three-bedroom house couldn't have been more than 1300 square feet, Mama Pearly yelled like they were on opposite ends of an eight-bedroom mansion.

Maxine groaned, and paused, her hands in the air above her head. "Yes, Mama?" She looked at herself in the mirror. All she'd wanted was some time to herself to style her hair.

She waited for her mother to respond, but then, a moment later, her mother appeared in the doorway to her bedroom. Her expression bore bad news before her voice spoke it.

"I need you to keep an eye on your sisters. Clara and I were about to head to Camden for the church revival."

"Mama!" Maxine exclaimed, spinning around in the chair she'd dragged in front of her prized vanity table, which her fa-

ther had built himself for Maxine's thirteenth birthday. "I'm supposed to be going to Evelyn's birthday party tonight. You promised I could go."

"Not this time, sweetheart." Her mother clipped a pearl earring in her right ear. *She had on her white ushering suit, which meant she already knew she would be ushering for this revival prior to breaking this last-minute news to Maxine.*

"Why can't they stay by themselves?" Maxine asked.

"I'm not leaving two five-year-olds alone to watch a two-year-old."

"But Mama . . ."

"Maxine, this is not open for debate." *Her mother's voice was stern as she clipped on the other earring. Maxine blinked, but that wasn't enough to hold back her tears. This couldn't be happening now. Not when she'd finally gotten the attention of Eric Robinson, one of the cutest boys in school. He was the first and only boy to act interested in her. And he was going to be at Evelyn's* Purple Rain *birthday party, but now it looked like she would not.*

Her mother saw the tears in her eyes and sighed. "Maxine, I'm doing everything I can, but you've got to help me. You still have to take some responsibility."

Her mother peered at her; her expression and her words silenced Maxine. Made her look away, like she always did when her mother said this. Maxine wanted to cry out, remind her mother that she had promised that Maxine was going to live a normal teenage life. But that hadn't happened. And it seemed it never would.

When her mother turned around, Maxine pushed herself up from the vanity table and followed her mother into the living room, the whole time trying to press down the rage building inside her. None of this was fair. She hadn't chosen motherhood, yet it had chosen her. She hadn't asked for these kids, yet she was constantly playing mother. Why did she have to do any of this?

Of course, she'd never, ever utter those words. Not only because she'd been raised to be respectful, but her mother had done so much for her.

"Bye, my loves," Mama Pearly said, kissing the twins as they sat cross-legged on the floor, their eyes riveted to Tom and Jerry. Then, she moved to Leslie and smiled. "Are you going to take your fingers out of your mouth long enough to give Mama a kiss?" She tickled the two-year-old, and Leslie giggled. "And why are you taking your socks off?" she asked as she slipped Leslie's sock back on.

Finally, Mama Pearly turned to Maxine. She sighed as she took her hands. "I know you're upset," Mama Pearly said, "but this is life." She kissed Maxine on the cheek and left.

Maxine moved to the door and watched her mother pull the car from the driveway. She stood fuming, even after the car was long gone. When she finally turned away from the screen door, she stomped over to the TV and slammed it off.

"Hey!" Star said. Even though she was only five, she'd already taken on leader-of-the-pack tendencies.

"I wanna see cartoons," Leslie cried as she pointed to the TV.

"You're such a crybaby," Maxine said, snatching Leslie up by the arm. "You ruin everything for everybody." She jerked Leslie and flung her back onto the sofa like a rag doll.

"Owww," Leslie cried.

"Stop it, Maxine," Star shouted, rising to her feet. "You're hurting her." Star rushed to her baby sister's side. Leslie whimpered and held her arm.

Star studied the spot where Maxine had grabbed Leslie; then, with a scowl, she faced Maxine, fists in the air, poised and ready to do battle. "You put a bruise on her arm," Star growled.

"Shut up," Maxine snapped. "Nobody's talking to you."

"I don't care. You're a meanie." Star challenged her sister.

"And I'm not gonna let you put any more marks on her."

"Why not? She's so black it's not like anybody will see it. She's nothing but a tar baby with red hair." Turning to Leslie, Maxine spat, "You freak of nature!"

Leslie whimpered as she sat on the sofa, clutching her arm and hiding her face in a pillow. Though she probably had no idea of the meaning behind Maxine's words, just the tone was frightening her enough.

"You're so mean," Stella said, finally speaking up.

"I don't care. It's true."

That memory pained Maxine. There had been so many days like that. Her rage manifesting itself onto Leslie. For years, Maxine had regretted and held a silent shame for the way she'd treated all of her sisters, but especially Leslie. She'd never be able to count the number of times she'd verbally abused her, and Maxine had prayed about ways to make it right—with all of them. But God hadn't answered. And now, their estrangement was solidified. It was no longer just because of her. They were adults now, and each responsible for their own actions.

"Sweetheart?"

Maxine turned toward her husband.

"You didn't hear what I said?"

She shook her head. "Sorry. My mind drifted."

"I was just trying to let you know . . ." He pointed toward the hall.

Maxine looked in the direction he pointed and saw the elderly woman walking toward her. She wore an old, floral dress that stopped just above her nude knee-highs. Her hair, which was like a web of silver yarn, encased her head. Her face was wrinkled, the lines telling the story of a dozen griots.

"Hello, Mother Channing," Maxine said.

The woman pulled Maxine into a deep embrace, and a flowery perfume assaulted Maxine's nostrils.

"Hey, baby. I'm so sorry to hear about Pearly. I've been praying from the moment I heard and all the way here," Mother Channing said. "Clara is parking the car. And Jessie Mae is still on the first floor. She's on her way up, but her arthritis has her moving slow and she was taking too long to get out the car." She hugged Maxine again. "We are going to form a mighty, mighty prayer circle to pray your mama through this."

"I appreciate you all for coming. I really do," Maxine said. "Mama can't take visitors right now, though. But I'm sure she'll be able to feel your presence."

Mother Channing threw up her hands toward the ceiling. "Yes. In the Mighty name of Jesus," she said, her back bent and her eyebrows knitted.

If elderly women had ride-or-die friends, Mother Channing and her crew were that to Mama Pearly. They'd been friends for more than six decades. "Are your sisters on the way?" Mother Channing asked.

"Yes," Maxine said. "They're all coming."

"Okay. It will be good to see everybody." She dabbed her puffy eyes. "Hopefully, Pearly can get out of here by Sunday and the whole family can come to church like old times." She adjusted Maxine's collar as a sad smile spread across her face. "Your sisters used to cut up something terrible in church."

Maxine nodded. "Yes, ma'am, and then you started rewarding them with a butterscotch candy." The memory of how that one piece of candy could make Stella and Star behave brought a smile to Maxine's face.

"And you too. Even though you were always acting like you were too old, you loved when I'd slip you a piece of candy too."

"Yes, ma'am, and Mama would fuss at you every time."

She chuckled. "It's amazing what that little piece of candy did. You girls loved you some butterscotch." She inhaled. "Oh Lord. I hope Pearly is gonna be all right. I can't lose my best friend." Her voice trembled.

Maxine patted her hands, giving Mother Channing permission to release her emotions. She sobbed.

Walter did what he always did. He pushed himself up from his chair and stepped to the women right when he was needed. He held out his hand for Mother Channing.

"How about you accompany me down to get some coffee in the cafeteria?" he said.

She wiped her eyes and tried to suck up her tears.

"Yes, coffee. I need that. This hospital is where my Frank died. So it's just . . . it's always hard on me to be here."

"You know you don't have to stay," Maxine said. She enjoyed Mother Channing's company, but the woman was seventy-five years old; she didn't need the stress.

"Oh, I'm not going anywhere," Mother Channing replied. "We are here for you, baby, and we wouldn't have it any other way. Pearly needs our prayers right now. We need to set up a Holy Ghost convention right here in the waiting room."

Maxine smiled her gratitude. Maybe having people here would keep her mind off everything that could go wrong with her mother. And her sisters, once they arrived.

"Well, come on, let's go get some coffee," Walter said, extending his arm.

"Okay." She took his arm and turned to Maxine.

"You keep an eye out for Clara and Jessie Mae."

"Yes, ma'am."

As they left, Maxine exchanged glances with the young couple. She felt led to ask, "How's your baby?"

The mother—who looked like she couldn't be more than eighteen—swallowed, then covered her mouth to keep a sob from escaping.

"She's in surgery," the young man said. "She . . . she had an aneurysm. I didn't even know babies could have aneurysms."

Maxine's hand went to her chest. "I am so sorry. I'm going to pray that everything works out and you can take your little one home soon."

They nodded their gratitude as he pulled the mother close and she released her sob.

Maxine excused herself so she wouldn't invade their moment. She was just about to go see if she could find a doctor or nurse for an update when Dr. Woods entered.

"Good morning, Maxine."

"Dr. Woods, finally. Can you tell me what's going on with my mother?"

"Your mother is still heavily sedated and she will be for the next few hours." He paused and glanced at his watch. "You really should go home and rest. I have strict orders that Miss Pearly can't have any visitors today."

"Dr. Woods, that's not going to work for us. Plus, my sisters are on their way."

He sighed. "Okay. I know you girls are just as stubborn as your mother. But I'll tell you what, go home, give her some time to rest, and come back around five. That'll give you two hours before visiting hours end."

Maxine looked like she was about to protest, but Dr. Woods held up his hand to stop her. "That's the best I can offer."

Maxine's shoulders slumped and she said, "Fine."

Dr. Woods thanked her for her cooperation, then excused himself just as Walter, Mother Channing, Clara, and Jessie Mae entered.

After greeting her mother's other two friends, Maxine filled everyone in on what Dr. Woods had just said.

". . . So, let me get you back to the house," Walter said when she was done.

Mother Channing nodded her agreement as she patted Maxine's hands. "And we're headed to the church, where we're going to convene all the prayer warriors in town."

That brought Maxine a sliver of comfort. She only hoped this time God was listening.

Chapter 7
Leslie

Silence was a third passenger in between Nona and Leslie as they drove from Nacogdoches to Shreveport. Leslie could tell that Nona wanted to engage her; she'd started conversations about everything from Leslie's next book to whether or not they should get a dog. But Leslie had left her conversation back in Houston. Going home left her with few words.

Leslie sat in the passenger seat, gazing out of the window, taking in the countryside as they drove along Highway 59. She took in the rural sights along the way: the clotheslines brought back memories of summers when she had to hang clothes by herself. The cows grazing reminded her of how her nephew, Walter Jr., tried to ride a neighbor's cow bareback and she was the one who got in trouble. Though she stretched the recesses of her mind, Leslie couldn't retrieve any happy memories.

"You okay?" Nona finally asked.

Without glancing her way, Leslie reached across the console and intertwined her fingers with Nona's. That gesture pacified Nona for the moment.

When they finally exited Interstate 20, Leslie looked over at her wife and spoke the words that had been on her mind. "I *really* don't want to go back."

Nona nodded her understanding and simply replied, "But you'd never forgive yourself if you didn't go."

Leslie gave her a slight nod before her gaze shifted back to the window. Her shoulders slumped when she said, "You're right. I have to be there for my mom, but everyone else . . ." She paused. "You don't know my people."

After a moment, Nona said, "That's true. But that's because . . ." She left it there, waiting for Leslie to finish her sentence.

But Leslie stayed silent. It was hard for her to talk to anyone about her family and the way she'd grown up. She'd given Nona the facts—that she had three sisters—but that was all she'd said, and she'd only done that after they were in a committed relationship. She did share with Nona her undying love for her mother, but that was the extent of it.

"What is it that you hate so much about this place? This place that is your home?" Nona asked.

Leslie thought about the question for a moment. "Home. That word should fill you with warm memories, shouldn't it?"

"I'd hope so, that's what I'd want for you."

With her eyes still outside, Leslie shook her head. "Home for me is a place where I don't belong. I've never fit in." Leslie swallowed, trying to push down the rising bile that always came when she was forced to remember.

"I'm so sorry."

Leslie shrugged, grateful that Nona didn't press to find out more. But she wouldn't; she knew her so well. "It is what it is, right? I mean, I can't reach back and change those years."

"No, you can't, but maybe you can create some new memories, good memories at home. Maybe not with this trip, but another time."

"Another time," Leslie repeated. "I hope, I pray for another time."

"Because of your mom?"

Leslie swallowed, the disdain of going back replaced by genuine fear for her mother. Since she'd received the call, she hadn't wanted to really think about what her mother collapsing, her mother in the hospital, her mother having cancer, really meant. "My mom," Leslie started, "she's wonderful. She showered me with so much love growing up, at least she did when she could. She was always working. She didn't have a choice. Our father died before I was born, so she had to work a couple of jobs to take care of four children."

"So you were home alone a lot?"

"Oh no, not at all. I think I told you, I was the youngest."

Nona nodded, but didn't speak as if she knew Leslie was finally opening up and she didn't want to interrupt.

"Maxine was left in charge, but Stella and Star could pretty much take care of themselves. I guess that's why Maxine resented me the most. She hated having to take care of me and that . . . that wasn't a pretty sight." Leslie was silent as she thought back to the countless nights when she begged Mama Pearly to let her accompany her to the light company. It was where Mama Pearly worked every night from eight until she was finished cleaning every office in the three-story building she had to clean by herself. Usually Mama Pearly would drag into their home after three in the morning, hours after Leslie had cried herself to sleep from Maxine's taunts, teasing, and overall torture. "Yeah," Leslie sighed, pulling herself out of her memories. "It wasn't good with my sister."

"So what are you saying?" Nona pressed for the first time. "She was mean to you?"

Leslie chuckled. "Yeah, I guess you can call someone who tortures her little sister, who's fifteen years younger . . . I guess you can call her mean."

"But why?" Nona asked.

Leslie shook her head as she pushed back a tear. "Maybe it's because my daddy died in a car accident on his way to the hospital when I was born and they blame me. Maybe it's because they were just embarrassed by having such a dark little sister. Or maybe she's just evil."

"Was it just Maxine? Your other sisters weren't mean like that, right?"

"No. I mean, we all have our issues, but no one has a heart as black and as hard as Maxine."

"Wow," Nona said. And then she was silent, as if she was shocked by her wife's words.

As if she had to give Maxine some redeeming quality, Leslie added, "Maxine did calm down some after she got married, and especially once she had my nephew, Walter Jr."

"Did she treat him that way?"

"Oh no, she loved on him. That was when I realized that it was really just me she hated. She would go from loving and nurturing with him to downright vicious with me."

"Wow," Nona repeated.

Leslie wondered if Nona finally had had enough. She could continue if Nona wanted her to, which surprised Leslie. Maybe she needed to do this because she was heading home. Maybe she needed to talk about her demons before she had to face them.

The two sat in silence for a few moments before Nona said, "This explains a lot, babe. I'm so sorry you had to go through that."

"So, you're not upset that I didn't tell you this before?"

"Not at all," Nona said. "I love you, and just hearing this now, I wouldn't have wanted you to relive this or share it before you were ready to."

"Thanks for understanding."

"Of course. This is what we do, right? We're married now." Nona smiled and Leslie tried to do the same, but her lips just wouldn't curve up.

Nona said, "Now I understand why you were such a loner when we met."

"I've been a loner from way back. I never really had any friends in school; I was always afraid that I'd meet a girl who was just like Maxine." She paused, then blew out a breath. "The names she called me." Another pause. "*Tar baby* was her favorite."

Nona gasped.

"But that wasn't the only name I was called. There was *Knight Rider*, and *Blackie*, and the one that hurt almost as much as Tar Baby—*Midnight*."

Nona stayed silent, her eyes straight ahead on the road, as if she was processing all that Leslie had just revealed. Not that Leslie expected Nona to say anything. What could anyone say?

Nona switched lanes, but she never let go of Leslie's hand, as if she knew her wife needed her protection right now.

Finally, Nona said, "Do you think you were a loner just because of the way Maxine treated you?"

Leslie cocked her head. "I don't know. I mean, I never really analyzed it before. I was too young to figure it out all those years ago, and since then, I've done my best not to think about that time."

"I get it. But I was wondering if part of you being a loner had to do with you not walking in your truth back then." When Leslie stayed silent, Nona pulled back. "Well, really, the only thing that matters is that you're doing it now," Nona said. "Life is too short to live in anything other than our absolute truths."

When Leslie still didn't say anything, Nona squeezed her hand, before she pulled her grasp away. "Why don't you try to rest? I have the GPS and it will get me the rest of the way."

It was only because this discussion had made her so weary that Leslie agreed. She adjusted the seat, leaning back, and then wiggled, until she found that comfortable space.

But even as she closed her eyes, she knew she wouldn't sleep. This discussion and her revelations had stirred up too much inside, and now the memories came rushing back.

Leslie knew she was about to get in trouble before Maxine even spoke. It was just the sight of her sister standing in the doorway, her eyebrows furrowed, that rage filling her eyes, that was a constant whenever she looked at Leslie.

"Quit bouncing that ball in this house!" Maxine shouted, speaking as if Leslie was hard of hearing. "I'm not gonna tell you again." Maxine wiped her hands on the hand towel she had tossed over her shoulder. "Take it outside."

"It's raining," Walter Jr. whined.

"Then find something else to do," Maxine said.

Leslie rolled her eyes, though she didn't do that until Maxine had turned her back and was headed back to the kitchen. As soon as Maxine rounded the corner, Junior resumed bouncing the ball.

"I told you we were going to get in trouble," Leslie said. As his aunt, she had been given the responsibility to make sure Junior was doing what he was supposed to, which was a never-ending job because he was the definition of hardheaded. He was nine now, and though she was six years older, he never listened to her.

"Shut up, you ain't my mama," Junior said, dribbling the basketball on the hardwood living room floor.

"I don't want to be your mama either." She reached for the ball and Junior yanked it out of her reach, giggling as she almost fell.

"Fine! Do what you want. I don't even care." Even as those words left her mouth, Leslie knew she didn't mean them. If Junior got in trouble, she would be in more trouble. That's why when the ball got away from him, bounced across the room, and hit a vase sitting on top of a corner table, knocking it over and shattering it into a million pieces, Leslie freaked. She dove for the ball before it bounced away and did any more damage.

The ruckus made Maxine come running back in.

"What in the world is going on?" Her eyes went to the ball in Leslie's hand. "I thought I told you to stop bouncing that ball in here. You just don't listen. Why can't you get some-

where and sit down like Junior? And you're supposed to be the responsible one."

Leslie glanced over at her nephew, who had dove onto the sofa, pulled out a book, and was actually sitting there pretending to be reading.

"It wasn't me, Mama," Junior said.

"I got the ball before you broke something else," Leslie snapped. *"You're such a damn liar."*

Before Leslie could take a breath after speaking those words, she felt the sting of Maxine's palm across her face. *"Watch your filthy mouth! Now sit your black behind down somewhere and act like you got some sense."*

Even though she held her hand to her face, trying to massage away the sting of Maxine's slap, Leslie wasn't sure which hurt more: the slap or the black comment. She'd heard it from Maxine—and others—at least a million times, probably even more when she considered that Maxine had been belittling her darker complexion since before she even understood the meaning.

But the quantity of times didn't soften the impact. Whenever Maxine spat that word at her with such venom, it pierced Leslie all the way down to her soul.

"And don't you dare cry," Maxine growled. *"Or I'll give you something to really cry about."*

Leslie ran into her bedroom, and it was only behind her closed door that she allowed that first tear to fall. Then a river followed. Why did Maxine hate her so much? She sobbed as she sat on the edge of her bed, but then, just moments later, she crouched down and got onto her knees.

This had become so familiar to her. She was six years old when she'd first decided to do what she'd seen her mother do so often. It was the night when Maxine had called her Tar Baby in front of some of her friends, who'd come by to celebrate Maxine's twenty-first birthday. All she'd done was ask for a piece of cake, because it was her birthday too.

Instead, she'd been mortified when Maxine and her friends had laughed and laughed, sending her running, once again, to her room. There, she had cried and, for the first time, dropped to her knees, praying to a God that she didn't quite understand, but who she hoped could help her.

Now, she took her hand away from her still-stinging cheek, and she pressed her palms together. "Dear God," she began, the way she always did. "Mama said You never make mistakes. But I don't understand what I did to make Maxine hate me. I hate her, too. Please God, take me away from here so I don't ever have to see her again. Amen."

A tear seeped through Leslie's closed eyes, but she didn't move to wipe it away. She didn't want Nona to notice because she didn't want to talk anymore about her family. But she couldn't stop her thoughts and the questions she'd always had about her sister.

Like when Prairie View A and M University had knocked on her door with a full engineering scholarship, she'd taken it, even though she hated engineering, just so she could get away from Smackover . . . and Maxine.

But why hadn't Maxine done the same? Leslie used to wonder if Maxine was bitter about never having left their hometown. It had always been curious to Leslie about why Maxine had chosen to stay and go to the local community college and get an associates in nursing. Why she'd chosen to get married so young, have a baby, and then move her struggling husband in with their mama while he built a church? If she was going to be mad at anyone, she needed to be mad at herself, and no amount of now-masquerading as an esteemed first lady could ever mask that hate in her heart.

As the car slowed, Leslie's eyes fluttered open and she sat up. Her eyes grew wide when she noticed Wrangler's Convenience Store. Had they already exited the freeway?

"We're in Smackover?" Leslie asked.

"Yep. You've been asleep two hours."

"Wow. I'm sorry, I didn't mean to make you drive all this way." It was like the air had shifted and a suffocating presence was seeping in through the car vents.

"It's okay, hun," Nona said as she maneuvered their car in front of Wrangler's. "I'm just going to run in the store and get an energy drink. Do you want anything?" Nona asked.

Leslie was just about to tell her that she'd go in with her, when she saw one of her former classmates walking in the store with another woman who looked like she could be her twin.

She fell back in her seat. "Nah. I'm good. I'll just wait here."

"Okay." As Nona leaned in to kiss her, Leslie coughed and turned her head.

"Sorry." She tapped her neck. "Something is in my throat." She coughed again, then feigned a smile. "Can you bring me a water?"

Nona leaned back, studied Leslie for a minute, then simply said, "Okay."

As she exited the car, Leslie slid down in the seat. Why couldn't Nona have stopped in Monroe? El Dorado? Anywhere but five minutes from the home where she grew up.

Leslie put her hand over her face as she kept an eye on her classmate and the other woman. They were already at the counter checking out, so Leslie turned to reach in the backseat to get a blanket to cover herself. Maybe if she pretended she was sleep, they wouldn't notice her.

She grabbed the blanket, pulled it to the front, swiveled around, and locked eyes with Shelton Rockford stepping out of the store. He was thirty pounds heavier and bald, but how could she ever forget the first boy she ever kissed?

Their eyes stayed connected as he approached the car.

"Damn," she whispered.

He tapped on her car window, but she didn't move. "Leslie?" Her eyes were still on him.

"Oh my God, girl, it's Shelton."

Leslie held her breath for a moment, wishing she could close her eyes, tap her heels together three times, and be any other place but here.

When she stayed frozen in place, he tapped the window again. "Roll the window down. Get out and let me see you." His enthusiasm was hearty.

In an instant she measured her options, then sighed and gave in. She opened the door and stepped out. "Hey, Shelton," she said, without any enthusiasm.

His eyes drifted from her Tory Burch flip-flops to her skinny jeans to her fitted Black Power graphic T-shirt.

"Dang, girl, look at you. My famous ex. My mama got both of your books on display, talking about that was supposed to be her daughter-in-law."

Leslie wanted to remind him that he'd kissed her on a dare, took her virginity with a bet, and, when he really started to like her, his mother was the only person he let know because as he had told her behind the gym one Wednesday afternoon, "Being seen in public with you would mess up my rep." When her eyes had filled with tears, he'd tried to clean it up by hugging her and saying, "I didn't mean nothing by it. You know you're pretty for a dark girl."

"I heard about Miss Pearly. That's why you in town?" Shelton said.

She nodded, though her eyes didn't stay on his. Her glance darted between Shelton and the front door of Wrangler's. "It is."

He studied her in amazement. "Dang. I haven't seen you in fifteen years." He frowned. "You cut all your hair off?" he added as if he'd just noticed.

"I did." She glanced back at the store. She could see Nona now standing in the checkout line.

"Bet. It's kinda butch-looking, but I guess if Halle Berry can pull it off, so can you." His grin was wide, and she saw nothing but pride in his eyes, as if he had rewritten history and had forgotten that he had never wanted to be seen with her in public.

"So," she began as Nona walked to the counter, "it was good to see you, Shelton. Tell your mother hello."

Leslie reached for the door handle, but before she could dip back into the car, she heard, "Is that Midnight?" The offensive nickname floated over her shoulder.

She bit down on her lip. Inhaled. Exhaled. Then twisted and was transported back fifteen years. She stared into the face of the girl she'd hated since she was eight years old. "Leslie," she snapped. "My name is Leslie."

Seeing Tisha Harding still made Leslie nauseous, even after all these years. Tisha giggled as her eyes roamed up and down Leslie. "Girl, I know your name." She turned to the woman with her. "This is my cousin, Trina. Trina, this is our old classmate, Leslie, but everybody calls her Midnight, cause you see she is black as—"

"Nobody calls me Midnight," Leslie cut her off. "My name is Leslie."

Tisha smacked her gum as she tugged at her too-small Wonder Woman tank that was riding above the flabby pouch in her stomach.

"Dang. Leslie done went to the big city and got her some juice."

"Tisha, chill. Damn," Shelton said, obviously aggravated. "We too old for that."

"My bad." Tisha threw up her hands innocently. "I was joking around with the big-time author." She turned back to Leslie. "My *husband* has become high-and-mighty in his old age. He seems to forget he's the one who gave you the nickname."

Shelton looked away to the front of the store, then to his car, and finally his glance dropped to the ground. Another time, another place, Leslie might've been hurt finding out that the girl she hated most had married the guy she loved. Now, she wanted to wish them well together and then get as far away from these people as she could.

"Who's your friend?" Tisha asked as Nona stepped to the driver's side of the car.

Leslie hesitated, then said, "That's Nona. Nona, these are some of my classmates." Nona tilted her head at Leslie, then gave an unsure wave, probably noticing the exasperated expression on Leslie's face. "But we really gotta get going," Leslie continued.

"Well, it was really good to see you," Shelton said, finally able to make eye contact again. "We're proud of you and we're praying for Miss Pearly."

That comment wiped the smile off Tisha's face and she shot daggers Shelton's way. Leslie motioned for Nona to get in the car, which she did.

"You guys take care," Leslie said, jumping in the passenger seat and slamming the door.

At first, Nona was silent. She didn't say anything, until they were back on the street. "I thought you said you didn't have any friends here."

"I don't, and before you ask me anything else, can we just get to the motel, please?" Leslie said. Her exasperated tone caused Nona to raise her eyebrows, but she remained silent as she pulled out onto the freeway.

Leslie hated talking to her wife this way, but explaining to Nona the details of what she'd been through seemed pointless. She had one goal in returning home: get in and get out.

"I'll just drop you off at the hotel, let you rest, and go check on Mama," Leslie said.

Nona's mouth dropped open. "Drop me off?" she said, as if those words were foreign. "So, you don't want me to come with you?"

Leslie sighed. From the moment they'd left Houston, she was waiting for the right moment to have this discussion.

"Babe . . ." Leslie began. "You know . . . my family . . ."

"I know you haven't told your family about us," Nona said. "And though I don't agree with it, I'll honor it . . . for now. But I didn't come all the way down here to sit in any hotel."

Leslie glanced at Nona and shook her head. "There's no way I can do this now. Not with my mother in the hospital. My focus has to be on her, and if I were to tell my sisters . . ."

"I get that. That's why I said I'll honor your wishes. Look, you can introduce me as your friend . . . your best friend who didn't want you to drive down here alone."

"I don't know . . . I don't know if anyone will buy that."

"Why not? Aren't we friends? I promise you, we will be just fine. But babe, I love you. So I'm not going to let you go through this by yourself . . . We're a team now. For better and for worse."

A hesitant smile crept up on Leslie's face. She didn't say a word as she took Nona's hand, raised it to her lips, and gently kissed it, feeling as if a seven-hundred-pound boulder had just been lifted from her shoulders. Every day, Nona made Leslie love her more.

Chapter 8
Maxine

The frustration of four decades simmered to the top as Maxine crawled on the blue-and-white-tile kitchen floor, scrubbing the crevices with the small brush. She was determined to get the grout up. The floor, and every other part of this house, needed to be spotless.

Maxine heard the approaching sounds of her husband's footsteps behind her, but she didn't stop her scrubbing.

"You already keep a spotless house, sweetheart. There's really no need for you to be killing yourself like this," Walter said as he leaned against the doorframe and watched her.

When they'd returned from the hospital, Walter had tried to get Maxine to rest, but she'd immediately begun her frantic cleaning spree. Walter hadn't been able to stop her when she was using her bleach mixture to clean the baseboards, and he wouldn't be able to stop her now. She wasn't about to give her sisters anything to talk about.

Maxine dropped the brush into a bucket of water, pushed herself up, and moved over to the counter, where she grabbed a duster and began running it across the top of the china cabinet.

"So you really think someone is going to be looking up there?" he asked.

"You know they're going to have something to say." Maxine stretched to make sure the duster reached all the way to the back of the cabinet. "They already have something to say about us living in Mama's house."

Walter hooked his fingers on his overall straps and shook his head. "We pay the bills here. We take care of this house. But honestly, I think that's you. I don't think any of them even care. That's something that you inflict upon yourself, darling."

As if her husband's words didn't matter, she moved from the china cabinet to the crevices in the large oak dining room table.

"Oh, trust me, they will complain about something," she said without looking up. "Which is crazy, because none of them even want this house. They'd be just as happy if we sold it and put Mama in a nursing home."

"Has anybody ever said that?" Walter asked.

She paused and glanced over her shoulder. "No, but I know my sisters."

Walter sighed, like he wasn't in the mood to go back and forth with his wife today. "You've been so stressed over the last few days, and I was hoping you would get some rest before everyone arrives because once everyone gets here, it's going to be nonstop for you."

Maxine replied by scrubbing harder.

"Leslie is supposed to be here around three. So is Star and her family. I don't know about Stella. I haven't talked to her anymore. Star says she's supposed to be flying into Little Rock and then driving down." Maxine paused and looked at the clock on the wall. It was a quarter to one. "They're probably already en route." That caused her to scrub faster.

"Okay. I'm going to let you get back to your useless cleaning." Walter threw up his hands as he turned and exited the room.

Maxine retrieved the glass cleaner from her cleaning basket, sprayed it on the doors of the china cabinet, then furiously wiped off the liquid.

An hour and a half later, Maxine stood back and admired her work. The house was drill-sergeant clean, and none of them could possibly find anything to complain about.

Just as she was about to get a moment's rest in the recliner in her living room, there was a knock at the door.

Maxine took a deep breath, brushed down her apron, and rushed to the front of the house. She pushed the screen door open.

"Hey, sis," Star said, leading the way in. She had her two-year-old, Lil Ty, on her hip.

"Hello, Star." Maxine gave her sister a half hug. Out of all of them, Star was the one she could tolerate the most. Star didn't care if you had a problem with her; if she liked you, that was all that mattered.

"Hey, sweetie pie," Maxine said, reaching for her nephew. He clutched his mother tighter.

"Let me lay him down. He's cranky from the drive." She lay the toddler on the sofa and he instantly hiked his behind in the air and went to sleep.

Star's oldest daughter, Cheyenne, entered while Star was covering Lil Ty up. The fifteen-year-old's face was buried in her iPhone, her pink hair a shocking contrast to her espresso skin. Her ripped jeans exposed too much thigh and her T-shirt had the words "Un-Feminine" across the front.

"Hey, Maxine," Cheyenne said.

Maxine's mouth fell open in shock. "Did she just call me by my first name?"

Star laughed as she kissed Lil Ty and stepped back to face her sister. "That's her thing now. Some of that new-age teenage stuff. She calls everybody by their first name."

"You know that's insane, right?" Maxine said. "And why is her hair pink?" she asked as if Cheyenne wasn't standing right there.

Before Star could reply, Ty and their other two children, Jordun and Jabari walked into the room.

"How ya doing, Maxine?" Ty flashed a sorrowful grin, then pulled Maxine into an embrace. "I'm so sorry to hear about Mama Pearly." He released her and turned to Walter, who had just walked in. "Hi, Walter."

"Good to see you all. Hate it's under these circumstances," Walter said, shaking Ty's hand.

"Uncle Walter, you got something for us?" Jordun said, excited as he pointed to his twin brother. "Me and Jabari turned seven last week."

"Well, of course I do." Walter reached into his pockets and moved his hands around, as if he was searching for something. This was a routine he'd done with them all their lives. He pulled out two bills. "Yep, here's five dollars for you. And five for you." He glanced over at Cheyenne, who had taken a seat on the sofa with her earphones in and her head still buried in her phone.

"Cheyenne, you don't want any?" Walter asked.

She didn't even glance up.

"Cheyenne." Star waved her hand in front on her daughter's face. "She has those air pods in and her music blasting."

"Aren't those things like two hundred dollars?" Maxine asked.

"Yeah, but Cheyenne works at McDonald's and we let her spend her money on whatever she wants."

"And you're always complaining about money and yet you let her spend her money on that?"

Star held up her hand. "Don't start, Maxine."

"How was the drive here?" Walter patted Ty on the back, as if he wanted to change the subject.

But before he could answer, Star asked, "How's Mama doing?"

"She was stable when we left her last night," Maxine said. "We went up there this morning, but they weren't allowing visitors because she was sedated after surgery. We can go back in a few hours." She closed the front door. "I wanted to clean and get ready for you all. Mama cooked up a big meal yesterday . . . almost like she knew y'all would be coming."

The thought made a lump swell in Maxine's throat and caused Star to race over and throw her arms around her sister.

"Oh, Maxine. I'm so sorry," Star said. "I know you must've been scared out of your mind to see Mama pass out."

Maxine inhaled, pulled herself together, and said, "Mother Channing came by yesterday and put the food up. So I figured I'd warm it up for everybody this evening because I know y'all got to be hungry."

"Nobody's thinking about food right now," Star said. "I need complete details on what happened, what's wrong, and when is Mama coming home." Star paused, and when she continued, her voice quivered. "I already lost my daddy. I can't lose my mama too."

Maxine squeezed her sister's hand. Even though it had been over thirty-five years since the car accident that had claimed their father's life, the pain of losing him never went away.

"Anyway, visiting hours end at six, so I was thinking we could go see Mama, then come back here and eat," Maxine said. "Do you know how far Stella is out?"

"I texted her," Star said. "She's about thirty minutes out. Leslie should be here any minute now."

"Well, why don't you tell them to just meet us at the hospital?" Maxine said. She turned at the giggles she heard behind her and saw Jordun and Jabari crawling under the dining room table. While she loved the laughter of children, the last time the boys were here they'd broken one of her beloved ceramic collections. "You think the kids will be okay here?" she asked, wondering if she was talking to her sister or if she was asking herself that question.

"Oh yeah." Star turned to her oldest and removed her earphone.

Her daughter glanced up, surprised. "Hey, what are you doing?"

"I need to tell you something. We're going to the hospital. Watch your brothers."

Cheyenne frowned as she glanced up. "What? Seriously, Star?"

Star waved off her complaints. "Do what I said. Your dad and I will be back in a bit."

"What about Maxine? Can't she watch them?"

Maxine's eyes widened in shock. She knew she was an old soul, but she couldn't possibly be that old, where she missed how it was okay for children to talk to parents this way.

Cheyenne punched the sofa and raised her voice. "Oh my God. This sucks." She stood and stomped toward the front bedroom.

Maxine tensed up and Walter stepped to her side. "Not your fight, honey," he whispered.

Maxine shook her head as she removed her mother's red apron and grabbed her purse. "Let's just get to the hospital."

A knock on the door made them all pause.

"I'll get it because I'm the house slave around here," Cheyenne said, stopping and opening the door. "Hello," she said.

"Hi." Leslie stood on the front porch, shifting uneasily.

"May I help you?"

Star approached the door. "Cheyenne, if you don't move out of the way. That's your auntie, Leslie."

"I don't know her," Cheyenne said, her eyebrows elevated.

"Our baby sister," Maxine said, from the dining room, where she hadn't moved since she picked up her purse.

Leslie managed a smile as she stepped through the front door. "It has been a while since I've seen you."

Cheyenne just gave her a blank look.

"Yeah, you were four the last time I saw you."

"Okay," Cheyenne said, turning to walk away. "Sorry, I can't stay and chat. I have to go change into my slave clothes."

Leslie bunched her eyebrows together and looked from Maxine to Star.

"Ignore her. She stays doing the most," Star said, hugging her sister. "You look good."

Leslie greeted the twins, then, Ty and Walter.

When she turned to Maxine, Leslie hesitated, then took a step toward her. But before she could reach out, Maxine said, "You cut all your hair off." Her eyes were open wide, as if she couldn't believe a woman with sense would do that kind of thing.

Leslie stepped back and her hands instinctively went to the back of her head. "About four years ago," she said.

Then, nothing. No one said anything as everyone shifted from one foot to the other.

"Well." Maxine finally broke the awkward ten seconds. "We're about to head to the hospital, so you're just in time. Did you drive? You want to ride with us or just follow us?"

Leslie shifted again, then said, "My . . . um . . . my friend drove with me here so I didn't have to make the drive alone."

"Why didn't you bring your friend in?" Walter asked.

Leslie shrugged. "I wanted to come in and make sure you guys were here first."

"Well, you can introduce her to everyone at the hospital," Maxine said. "We need to get going."

Leslie nodded. She seemed relieved. Maxine hated that there was always tension between them, but at this point she didn't even know how to fix it.

Chapter 9
Stella

"What part of Arkansas are you going to again?" Lincoln's voice boomed through the Apple CarPlay system in the Hyundai Sonata.

"Smackover. It's a small town at the bottom of the state," Stella replied as she exited the highway onto the rural road that led to her mother's house.

"I can't believe that's a real place," he said, "nor that you never told me that's where you're from." He paused, as if he expected her to explain herself. When she said nothing, he continued, "We've been together two years and you've never talked about this . . . about your twin . . . about your past."

Now his tone was filled with hurt, and Stella's eyebrows rose. It wasn't as if they were on a I-need-to-know-your-background level, so she didn't get him being in his feelings about where she'd grown up.

"Well, it's a very real place," she said, deciding not to address his emotions. "But let me keep my attention on these country roads. I'm about twenty minutes out from my mom's house."

"I really should be there with you," Lincoln said.

While Stella would've welcomed his company on a road trip—they'd taken one once to North Carolina and she'd had so much fun—no way would she bring him around her people. If she ever brought a man around her family, it would have to be a Denzel-Idris-Robert Smith-level type of man in looks, occupation, and finances.

"I know we go back and forth," he continued when she didn't respond. "But you mean the world to me." He paused, then inhaled like he was trying to gather strength to continue. "About last night," he continued, "when I said, 'I love you,' I meant it."

Stella gripped the steering wheel. She had hoped they wouldn't talk about last night. She'd asked Lincoln to let himself out, but instead he'd put up the food, then come into her bedroom, crawling in bed next to her as she slept. She'd wanted to be upset, but his presence comforted her. And when she'd shifted to turn over and make love—because that's what they did in bed—he'd stopped her and just held her.

"Let's just be," he said, his thick arms pulling her close to him.

She'd lain there, feeling safer than she had in years. Right before she dozed off, she heard Lincoln mutter, "I love you, Stella."

She'd snapped to attention, glad that her back was to him. She'd released a soft purr, pretending to be asleep, although she did snuggle closer to him. She hadn't liked his words, but she was pleased when his arms tightened around her.

"Did you hear me?" Lincoln said, tugging her away from his love confession last night.

"I'm sorry. What'd you say?" she replied, knowing exactly what he had said.

"I said, when I told you, 'I love you,' I meant it. And when you get back to Atlanta, I want us to talk about what it is you want. I want to know how I can break down that wall and prove to you that I'm the man for you and figure out what we need to do to go to the next level."

"You're the one who always says you're not ready," she replied.

"Maybe I wasn't. Maybe I convinced myself of that because I

didn't think it's what you wanted." He paused. "But I want to be with you. I want us to be together."

Stella wanted to protest, tell him that wasn't happening, but she had felt something last night that she hadn't in a long time. Secure, though she wasn't about to confuse security with love.

Stella didn't do love. She'd already tried that once in college. She and Ethan Bowers. It was wonderful because he checked all the boxes on her list, which were wealth, good looks, intelligence, and ambition. But even though the two had fallen in love, his old-money family didn't think the Spelman girl was good enough for their Morehouse son because she didn't come from a pedigree family. In fact, because they'd never met anyone from her family at all, nor would she talk about her family, they crafted their own stories and decided that whatever her background, it wasn't worthy of their son. They'd sent Ethan to study abroad and he'd chosen his parents' wishes over her.

That was the end of love for Stella, but still she said, "Okay," to Lincoln, knowing she'd never be able to give him what he now seemed to want.

"Okay?" he said, as if he was asking her a question, as if he couldn't believe she agreed.

Stella felt his smile through the phone. He continued, "And you know, all you have to do is say the word and I'll be on the next flight to Smackover."

She laughed. "They don't have flights here. You have to fly to Little Rock and drive down."

"Well, whatever. Just let me know you need me and I'm there."

Need you? Stella thought. That was a new concept. Since she set foot in Atlanta, she'd tried not to *need* anyone. "Thank you. I really appreciate that, but I'm good," Stella said. "I shouldn't be here long. Just want to see about my mother and then I'll be back."

"Well, whenever you return, I'll be right here waiting."

Stella stifled her groan, then welcomed the incoming call.

"Hey, that's my other line," she said. "Let me grab it, it's my sister."

"Okay, babe. Remember, I'm only a phone call away. Love you." He hung up without waiting for a reply. Thank God.

Stella pushed the Talk button. "Hello."

"Where are you?" Star's voice was curt.

"Almost there."

"Well, just meet us at El Dorado Memorial Hospital. We're already on the way," Star said. Then, like Lincoln, she hung up the phone before Stella could say another word.

Sometimes, the way they were bothered her. It hadn't always been this way, and as she drove, Stella tried to remember when the disconnect between her and her twin sister began.

Mrs. Glover passed in front of the fourth-grade class, a disappointed look on her face.

"I am not happy with the quality of work you boys and girls submitted." She walked over to the first desk and set down the two-page paper. "I must say that I am thrilled beyond belief with my star student, though."

Stella smiled, filled with joy as Mrs. Glover finally acknowledged her. Stella picked up the paper from her desk, then lost her smile when she saw the name at the top of the page. "Mrs. Glover, I'm Stella, that's Ella." She pointed to the seat next to her.

Mrs. Glover retrieved the paper. "My goodness. You'd think halfway through the term, I would know the difference. It's adorable the way you two dress alike, but I'm going to have to figure out a way to distinguish between the two of you," she said, handing the paper to Ella.

Good luck with that, Stella thought. From their butterscotch skin to their honey-brown curls, the girls truly were one embryo split into two. It was hard for anyone, other than their mother and Maxine, to tell the difference between them.

Mrs. Glover pushed her wire-rimmed glasses up on her petite nose and turned back to face the class.

"Ella Bell, please stand." Ella eased from her chair. Any other student would've been worried that they were in trouble when the teacher called on them to stand, but the confident expression on Ella's face proved she knew better. "Class, once again, Ella got five stars on her paper." She squeezed Ella's cheek. "Such a bright young girl, headed places."

Ella waved to the classroom like she was in a beauty pageant. Several kids snickered, others rolled their eyes.

"Perhaps you can work with your sister," Mrs. Glover said sliding another paper onto Stella's desk.

The big C minus glared at Stella and wiped the grin off her face.

Mrs. Glover wagged her finger in Stella's face. "If you would put half as much effort into your schoolwork as your sister, you wouldn't be bringing home these type of grades," she said. "I'm extremely disappointed in you, Stella Bell."

Stella lifted the paper and it trembled in her hand. In that moment, she felt something she'd never felt before—she was sick of her twin sister. She was the one who had studied hours for this test. Ella hadn't studied at all.

For years, every teacher, every relative, even her friends, compared the two of them, and for all this time, Stella's irritation had festered inside. Everyone always raved about how smart Ella was, when she was the one who worked hard.

Now, with Mrs. Glover's words, Stella's irritation bubbled over as she stared at the red C minus across the top of the paper.

Ella slid back into her seat, then caught her sister's eye. She tapped her A plus as she held up the paper in a braggadocio manner in Stella's direction.

Stella rolled her eyes, and inside the volcano of emotions erupted.

That afternoon, as they walked home from school, Stella was surprised that it was just the two of them. Usually, they walked home with three other kids who lived in a trailer down the road, but today, Stella was glad they were alone.

The two walked silently for a while, Ella in her own world as she sang some New Edition song. Then, when they were about halfway through their mile-walk home, Stella said, "I think Mrs. Glover likes you better than me."

"Nuh-uh. Why do you say that?"

Stella stared at her sister to see if she was kidding. How could she deny this when Mrs. Glover made it so obvious? But Stella explained anyway. "She's always raving about you, and most of the time you don't even try."

"I can't help it." Ella shrugged as she kicked a large rock along the path. "It just comes natural, I guess."

"Whatever." Stella stomped alongside her sister, her bottom lip poked out in frustration. "I'm sick of her mistaking me for you."

"Everybody does that 'cause we're twins," Ella said nonchalantly. "Why is it bothering you now?"

Stella seethed. "I don't want to dress alike anymore."

Ella stopped. She just stood on the edge of the road and stared at her sister's back. "What? We like dressing alike."

Finally, Stella stopped too, spun around, and glared at Ella, her face filled with fury. "No. I don't. Not anymore. I don't want to dress like you. I don't want to be like you." Images of the C minus burned in her head.

"I don't even want our names to be alike anymore. Our names are stupid. You need to find another name," Stella snapped.

"That's crazy. My name is Ella. Why should I have to find a new one?"

"Because I said so."

"And why should I listen to you? What would I call myself anyway?"

Stella's hands went to her hips, taking the stance that had everyone in their family saying that Stella was the bossy one, even though Ella was more aggressive. But today, Stella didn't care about her sister getting mad. She wanted things to change and she wanted it now.

"I don't know. Change your name to whatever you want it to be. Be Star or something, because you're a star student," Stella said, using her fingers to make air quotes around Star.

Ella began walking again, her eyes straight ahead and focused on the horizon, like she was thinking. "Hmmm," she hummed, as if she suddenly thought her sister's suggestion was a good idea. "Star? I like that. Okay," she said, once again chipper. "I'm changing my name to Star."

Stella frowned, dropped her hands from her hips, and said, "Uh, I was kidding."

A wide smile spread across Ella's face. "No. Too late. And really, that is a good idea, Twinsie," she said, using the name they called each other during happier times. "Our names will still be similar because they both begin with S, but from now on, I'm Star."

"I'm not calling you Star," Stella said, mad at herself for even suggesting this. This wasn't going the way she wanted. Did she really want to have a twin with the name Star?

"You're the one that gave me the name." Ella looked offended.

"I don't care. It's stupid. You're stupid and I'm not calling you that," Stella scoffed as she speed walked past her sister.

Stella clutched her books to her chest and left Ella in the dust that swirled behind her as she stomped down the street. She was burning mad. Ella wasn't supposed to like the idea. She was supposed to run home crying.

Then . . . "Arggh!" Stella screamed at the piercing pain, and *her hand flew to her head. It felt as if something had just struck her.*

She spun around, and her eyes went to the rock still skipping on the ground. Her eyes were wide with shock. "Why did you hit me, Ella?" she screamed at her sister. Stella looked at her hand and saw the blood. "Oh my God, I'm bleeding."

Stella made a move, planning to lunge at Ella. She was ready to fight her right there. Fight her until one of them was on the ground. But then, Stella paused as Ella moved toward her.

Ella walked slowly, her eyes narrow and dark, her teeth clenched. Her fingers were balled into fists as her chest heaved. "I told you, my name is Star now!" Her voice was low and her tone was forceful as she spoke through gritted teeth. "And another thing. Don't you ever call me stupid again," she said, as if she'd been holding her own emotions inside. "I'm not the one taking a C minus home to Mama, and because of that, you're no longer the one in charge."

She hadn't said the words, but Stella heard the threat in Ella's tone. It was the way she sounded, and the sinister look in her sister's eyes, that made Stella tremble. Ella was always quick to anger, but this was different. This was . . . rage in her eyes. She couldn't believe it—she was afraid of her sister.

That was the first time she remembered Ella, who she'd called Star ever since, had scared her. But it would hardly be the last.

Now, Stella tried to shake away the thoughts of that time, but still, memories remained. She remembered how the next day, Ella had announced to everyone in class that she would now be known as Star. Stella chuckled bitterly as she recalled the way Mrs. Glover thought it was a fantastic idea.

"Star is the perfect name for you," she said. "Because you're a star already."

When Ella changed her name, she changed her attitude too. She'd been right; Stella was no longer in charge, so Stella had fallen in line with everyone else. Since then, Star was the only name anyone ever called her.

That had been the beginning of the end of their close relationship.

Chapter 10
Leslie

Silence felt like it was echoing inside the waiting room as they sat. Leslie glanced at Maxine and Walter, who sat across from her and Nona. Star and Ty sat in the corner. A young couple sat teary-eyed at the back of the room as CNN blared news no one cared about right now.

Leslie was grateful that everyone was distracted. Their introduction to Nona had been brief, and no one questioned their friendship. Leslie was glad for that—and the fact that Nona was here. Because right now, with Nona stepping out to reschedule her caseload, Leslie felt lonely among her own family. She knew she should probably try to engage her sisters in conversation. But there really wasn't a lot for her to say.

Finally, Star looked her way. "My beautician is reading your book," she said. "She looked at your picture and didn't believe you were my sister."

Leslie cringed. She knew Star didn't mean anything by her words. If anything, Star had been her protector growing up, ready to fight anyone who blatantly disrespected Leslie. Only Star—like everyone else—didn't realize her you're-pretty-for-a-dark-girl mentality did just as much harm.

"Oh," Leslie said, then added, "thanks for telling me," because she couldn't think of anything else to say.

Star nodded and grinned, then turned back to Ty.

At least she tried, Leslie thought.

Leslie tapped her foot, checked her watch, and glanced toward the waiting room entrance. Little particles of dust floated around in the sunlight as she slouched in the uncomfortable plastic chair.

Leslie exhaled her frustration as her gaze went to the clock on the wall, then the window. It was obviously broken because only the long hand was visible and it was pointing to the eight. They probably did that on purpose so hospital visitors wouldn't know how long they'd been waiting.

"This is ridiculous," Leslie mumbled, though she didn't know if anyone even heard her because no one replied. They'd been here for over an hour and they'd yet to see their mother. The doctors had been running tests on Mama Pearly when they arrived at the hospital, so they'd had to wait.

Suddenly, Star turned back to her. "She especially didn't believe me," Star continued, as if she and Leslie were really having a conversation about this, "when she Googled you. Your bio, all those articles about you never mention where you're from or anything about your family."

Leslie simply stared at her sister before she said, "I just try to keep my personal life private."

"Hmph," Star said, the corner of her lips turning up in a sly grin. "You don't be writing about us up in those books, do you?"

She chuckled, although she didn't find her sister's words funny; she found them pathetic because her question meant she'd never read her books. "I write romance. So no," Leslie replied.

"I'm romantic." Star's grin widened as she turned to her husband. "Aren't I, Ty?"

"You sure are, baby. But she doesn't need to write about our romance because she doesn't write freaky-deaky stuff."

Star broke into a fit of giggles. "You are so nasty."

"And you like it," Ty said, squeezing her thigh.

Maxine glared at both of them. "Really? Mama's down the hall fighting for her life and y'all out here carrying on like teenagers in heat?"

The admonishment caused both Star and Ty to lean back into their seats and the smiles to disappear from their faces. Though Ty did take his wife's hand.

The silence returned and Leslie, who just wanted to get up and run out of the room, run out of the hospital, and run out of Smackover, sank into her seat. If this wasn't her mother . . .

"Hey, everybody."

They all looked up as Stella walked into the waiting room. Surely she hadn't been traveling in a silk sleeveless shirt, ankle slacks, and heels. She looked like she was going to a business event, not a hospital.

Leslie waited to make a move. That was a habit she had, being the youngest. People always greeted them in chronological order. But when neither Maxine nor Star made a move, Leslie stood up.

"Hey, Stella." Leslie sniffed as she reached for her sister and they embraced.

Walter stood and hugged Stella too. "Glad to see you, sis."

That was it; everyone else stayed seated, didn't part their lips.

Stella turned to her oldest sister first. "Maxine," Stella said with a curt nod.

"Stella," Maxine replied.

"I told you it was going to take you forever," Star said.

Now Stella turned to her twin. "Hello to you, too, Star." She looked at her brother-in-law. "Hey, Ty."

Ty nodded his greeting, but kept his seat next to his wife.

Stella set down her purse on the empty chair next to Leslie. "How's Mama?"

"We haven't seen her yet," Leslie replied.

"What?" Stella glanced around the waiting room. "So, you guys are just going to sit up in here wondering? I don't think so. What's her room number?" She spun toward the door.

Maxine jumped up and grabbed her arm.

"What you're not going to do is roll up in here, the last one to arrive, and begin tossing around demands to the people who are taking care of Mama, and who will be here long after you're gone."

Stella's eyes went to her sister's grip on her arm. "And what you *are* going to do is take your grubby hands off me."

Star jumped between them—something she'd done countless times. "Really? This is what you guys are about to do? In here? With Mama . . . sick?"

Walter stood as well. "I agree with Star. Tensions are high and this isn't helping. The doctors say we'll be able to see your mother in a little bit, Stella. So please just wait patiently. That's what we've been doing."

Stella and Maxine glared at each other before Stella snatched her arm from her sister's grasp and retreated to the other side of the waiting room.

The tension greeted Nona as she returned with a sweet tea and handed it to Leslie.

"Don't ask," Leslie whispered. Nona didn't say a word as she slipped in the seat next to her. Leslie figured an introduction to Stella would have to wait.

An angry silence now filled the space between the Bell sisters. Stella stood glaring out the hospital window. Maxine had her head buried in her Bible, her foot tapping anxiously. Star, in an unusual turn of events, was the only one unbothered, seeming to take solace in the soft stroke of Ty's hand on her hair as she lay with her head in his lap.

Leslie's thoughts were interrupted when a portly white man in a lab coat entered the waiting room.

Maxine bounced from her seat, the first to rush to his side. "Dr. Woods, how is she?"

The doctor's eyes scanned around the room.

"You remember my sisters?" Maxine said.

The doctor nodded. "Yes." He peered at each of them over his glasses. "My, how you ladies have grown."

When their replies were only a stare back, he cleared his throat. "We finished all of our testing and you can see your mother now. She's weak, so I really can't let everybody go in there at once," he said, looking from one sister to another.

"Oh, I'm going to see my mama," Star said, standing and preparing to go back to see her mother. Ty instantly stood with her.

"Me too," Stella added. "Maxine can stay out here because she's already seen Mama," she said, not mentioning Leslie at all.

Before Maxine could interject, Walter stepped up and stepped in. "I have a suggestion. Why don't the four of you go in? I'm sure the doctors will make an exception so that Mama Pearly can see all four of her daughters." He looked like he was pleading with Dr. Woods with his eyes. "Isn't that right, Doctor?"

The doctor hesitated, then nodded.

"Fine," Maxine said.

"Okay," Star said.

"I'm right here, baby," Ty said, kissing her cheek.

Nona squeezed Leslie's arm, but said nothing.

Leslie followed behind her sisters, voiceless as always. The sisters trudged down the hall, all eyes focused on the door at the end, their destination. As soon as Maxine pushed open the door to their mother's room, Star released a moan. Leslie glanced at the antics of her sister, but this time she couldn't blame Star. It was all Leslie could do to stand upright at the sight of their mother, hooked up to a half a dozen tubes, each one a color of the rainbow. Star gripped the wall like she was about to pass out.

"Star, you're going to have to hold it together. Mama can't see you acting a fool," Maxine whispered.

"I got you," Leslie said, taking Star by the arm as they made their way over to the hospital bed.

As she held up her sister, Leslie wondered, for a moment, who was going to help her? The sight of their mother surrounded by all these contraptions made Leslie feel like a deflated balloon, with all the air slowly draining out.

"I thought you said she was doing okay," Stella whispered, her eyes on their mother.

"I said she was stable," Maxine replied as the four surrounded the bed, Maxine and Stella on one side while Leslie, still holding Star, stood on the other.

"What's wrong with her?" Leslie whispered, shaking as she wondered how much longer she could be the beacon of strength for Star. "What kind of cancer again?"

Maxine brushed her mother's hair from her face. "Doctors are saying stomach cancer."

"Why didn't we know this?" Stella exclaimed.

"Will you keep your voice down?" Maxine ordered. When Stella lowered her eyes, Maxine continued, "She kept it from everybody. I didn't even know."

"You lived with her every day and you—"

"Don't start with me, Stella," Maxine warned, cutting her off. "You don't know what it's been—"

"St—-stop it!" The whispered demand rose up between them.

All four of their heads spun toward Mama Pearly as her eyes, still shut, began to flutter open.

"Mama!" Leslie released Star, leaned down, and hugged her mother.

Then, the others did the same.

"Oh my God, Mama. You had us so scared," Star said, her voice trembling with emotion.

It seemed like it took a moment for it to register that her four daughters were with her. "Leslie, Stella, Star, Maxine." She breathed out the names as if she was taking roll call.

"Yes, Mama," they said together, their voices combined in harmony.

Her lips twitched into a smile. "My g-girls," she mumbled. "You . . . came."

"Of course we did," Leslie said as tears rolled down her cheeks.

"I . . ."

"Mama, don't try to talk. You're too weak." Maxine fluffed her mother's pillow, to make her more comfortable.

"I kn—know." She took a deep breath, like inhaling gave her strength. "I stayed around much longer than I . . . than I thought I would." She exhaled her exhaustion.

Star took her mother's hand. "How long have you known you were sick?"

"Oh, don't . . . don't you w—worry about all that," she said, squeezing Star's hand. She closed her eyes, as if that moment of rest had given her enough energy to carry on. She opened her eyes and continued. "I was just holding on long enough to see all my . . . to see all my girls together."

"Don't say that, Mama," Leslie cried.

"Mama, why didn't you tell me?" Maxine's voice quivered as she spoke. "I've asked you multiple times if something was wrong. Every time I saw you moving a little slower, or clutching your stomach. You told me it was just old age. I'm so sorry I didn't know."

"I didn't tell you because you ain't no doctor . . . and you ain't God." Mama Pearly paused, took another deep breath, and continued. "So, there's nothing you could've done but worry me."

Her breathing was shallow, as if just speaking winded her.

"Mama, why don't you just close your eyes and rest a little more?" Star said.

Leslie glanced up and watched Maxine step away from the bed, and when she saw Stella follow her, Leslie knew things were about to get heated.

"I just don't understand. How did you not know this was going on with Mama? You were living up in her house?" Stella asked her older sister. "Weren't you watching her? Taking care of her?"

Maxine glared at Stella. "Are you serious right now?" Maxine didn't give her time to answer. "When's the last time you've been here to check on her? Better yet, we don't even have to talk about all of that. When was the last time you picked up your cell phone and even called to check on her?"

"No, no, no," Pearly replied, her brow furrowing as she tried to push herself up.

"Mama, no!" Leslie helped her mother lean back onto her pillow. "Don't get worked up." Then she cut her eyes at her sisters. "Y'all are ridiculous."

Mama Pearly's eyes filled with tears. "Th—there's just so much hate in this family. I don't want my last days filled with hate."

"Mama, stop saying that," Star said. "Stop talking about your last days."

"I'm just t—telling the truth." Her chest rose, then fell as she spoke. "And I can't rest in peace until y'all find some peace." She sighed. "I need you to heal the hurt."

"What hurt? I'm not hurt," Maxine said defiantly.

"Me either," Stella said, folding her arms.

Leslie turned her eyes away from her mother.

"Yes, you are."

Mama Pearly's eyes went to each woman. "All of you are hurt. You're hurt because of the secrets. The secrets that have festered inside." Her eyes rested on Leslie for a moment before Mama Pearly turned her head.

Leslie frowned a little. What was her mother talking about?

"Mama?" Leslie called her, but her mother kept her head turned away.

"Mama?" Mama Pearly turned her head toward Star, and that made Leslie frown. Star asked, "What are you talking about? What secrets?"

"We all need to . . ." Mama Pearly took another deep breath and kept her eyes on Star. "Just . . . come . . . clean."

"Come clean about what?" Star said.

Maxine looked at the machine, adjusting the IV bag. "It's probably all the drugs they have her on," Maxine said. "Got her talking crazy." Then Maxine glanced up and looked straight at her mother. "We don't need to be listening to nothing she's saying."

"Not facing it doesn't make it go away," Mama Pearly muttered. She gave a long stare at Maxine, which caused raised eyebrows from all three Bell sisters.

But before anyone could comment, Mama Pearly's eyes closed and she went silent.

Chapter 11
Stella

A passerby might think the Bell family was enjoying Thanksgiving dinner. Maxine had warmed up the food Mama Pearly had cooked on Sunday and now it was spread out across the dining room table that had been in their family since Mama Pearly was a little girl. The full spread looked like it was ready for a holiday soiree: collard greens with smoked turkey, fried chicken, macaroni and cheese, black-eyed peas, mashed potatoes, candied yams, and hot water cornbread. Plus an assortments of pies that would put Patti to shame.

"Wow, Maxine, when in the world did you have time to cook all this?" Star asked, passing plates to her children.

Jordun and Jabari took their plates, then sat at the card table Maxine had set up off to the side.

"This is what Mama was cooking before . . ." Maxine's voice trailed off.

"Cooking for who? The church?" Stella asked.

That made Maxine chuckle. "This is how Mama cooked every week."

Walter joined in her laughter as Maxine set another bowl on the table. "We had to get a deep freezer last year just to store all the food Mama Pearly cooked."

Stella was glad they were having a decent conversation. After Mama Pearly went silent on them, they'd gone into a state of panic. But the nurse had quickly appeared and assured them that Maxine had been right. The drugs had taken their toll, and their mother was out for the night. Though all four of them had wanted to stay at the hospital, Walter had convinced them to come back to the house to eat and rest.

"Ewww, what is this?" Cheyenne said, leaning over and peering into a glass bowl in the center of the table that Maxine had just set down.

"It's pickled pigs' feet," Walter said with a smile.

Cheyenne gagged. "Who in their right mind would eat pigs' feet, let alone pickled?"

"Cheyenne, don't be rude," Ty said as Star handed him a plate piled high with food.

"We want some pickles on pig feets," Jordun exclaimed.

Cheyenne grabbed a chicken leg and said, "Y'all are disgusting."

Stella surveyed the spread. "I haven't eaten like this . . . in years."

"I can tell," Maxine replied, taking her seat. "You're looking a little thin."

Stella was about to say something smart when the smile on Maxine's face stopped her. "I can only wish I'd be that size again. But the way we eat around here . . ."

Walter rubbed his hand on his wife's stomach. "No, ma'am. I like all my fluffiness." Maxine playfully popped his hand. He blew her a kiss before looking up at Stella. "No offense, Stella. You look great."

Stella managed a chuckle as she started fixing her plate. She was always on edge when it came to Maxine, so this playful side was definitely welcome. "None taken," she said.

Watching Walter with Maxine and Ty with Star left Stella with a longing to enjoy that kind of playful banter with someone she loved. But since she'd given up on love . . .

"Do you have any salad to go with my protein?" Cheyenne said, sliding into a chair at the end of the table. She studied the chicken leg on her plate, then picked it up and peeled off the skin.

Maxine took a deep breath. "We don't have salad here. And you need to sit at the children's table while you're up here desecrating the best part of the chicken."

Cheyenne glanced over at the card table where her twin brothers sat, then she looked to Star in protest. Star just waved her off.

"Ugh," Cheyenne said, standing and marching over to the kids' table.

Leslie's plate was the sparsest, covered by only a small helping of greens and two scoops of macaroni. But even with that, she just picked at her food. Nona, who sat to the left of her, had taken tiny portions of every dish, almost like she just wanted to sample everything to see what she liked.

Stella piled her plate high, fighting off images of her personal trainer chastising her. She paid good money for a trainer to keep her size-six frame intact, but it had been so long since she had her mother's home cooking.

"You know what I was just thinking about?" Star said as she started eating. "You remember that time Mama said she caught Daddy out back smoking cigarettes?"

Stella and Leslie slid back into their chairs just as Maxine laughed and picked up the story.

"One of my favorites," Maxine said. "Y'all were too young to remember. Stella and Star were only about three years old, but Daddy was holding Stella and sneaking a smoke. But then, Daddy heard Mama coming out and he stuffed that whole cigarette into his mouth. Mama asked him what was he doing, and all he did was shake his head. She asked him a whole bunch of questions and he couldn't say a word; he just kept shaking his head. Finally, she asked him if he had been out back smoking and Stella snitched, getting Daddy in trouble."

"What?" Stella grinned and pressed her hand to her chest as if she couldn't believe what her sister was saying. "No way. I would never have snitched on Daddy."

"Oh yes, you did." Maxine chuckled. "Before Daddy could even shake his head, you said, 'Yeah, Mama, Daddy's smoking. He has a new trick 'cause the cigarette is in his mouth," Maxine said, imitating Stella's baby voice.

As the laughter continued, Stella protested. "I do not remember that, even though that's exactly the way Mama used to tell it," Stella said with a nostalgic smile. "But I hadn't heard that story in years."

"Do you remember that crazy dance Daddy used to do?" Star asked.

Maxine chuckled. "The Boogaloo Shakedown?"

That did make Leslie smile, because it was one of the few videotapes they had of their father. In that video, the joy was on his face as he did that dance right here in the living room, and he tried to get Mama Pearly to "shakedown" with him.

"Mama said Daddy made that dance up, but he swore James Brown personally taught it to him," Maxine said.

"Because I'm so sure Smackover was on his tour stop," Ty joked.

"Maybe that's where Leslie got her active imagination." Stella laughed.

Stella's laughter was interrupted when her phone vibrated. She picked it up from the table and glanced at the screen. It was her assistant, Cass.

Hey, Stella. Don't know if you heard. Jacob Malone had an altercation last night.

Stella set her fork down. Jacob was a tight end with the Falcons and her newest client, who had just signed an endorsement deal.

What kind of altercation? she typed.

Fight at a bar. He hit someone in the face with a Bud Light bottle. Guy went to the hospital. Heard he got 14 stitches.

Stella sighed. This was not what she needed to be dealing with now.

As the chatting continued, Maxine glanced at Stella, who had not put down her phone. Maxine cleared her throat, but Stella stayed focused on her phone.

Finally, Maxine said, "Stella, do you think you could put your phone down long enough to enjoy dinner?"

"I have business that I'm trying to take care of." Stella continued typing without looking up.

"But this is dinnertime," Maxine said.

Stella inhaled sharply but set the phone down. She glanced at Maxine, then her gaze slowly moved around the table. The laughter from just moments ago was gone. Leslie's eyes were down as she continued picking at her food. Star and Ty were preoccupied with Lil Ty, who was sitting on her lap, fussing. Walter sat and ate his food in silence. This was the Bell family Stella remembered. The only joy in the room came from the sound of the twins, who giggled and played with their dinner.

Suddenly, Stella couldn't help it, and the words rushed out of her mouth. "Why are we pretending that we're some big, happy family?" Stella paused and looked at each of her siblings. "We're here for Mama only, so why are we sitting here in this house with one another trying to play nice? We all know that none of us want to be here breaking bread and catching up."

"We were all doing just fine, so why did you have to say anything? Why did you have to mess this up? You always do this." Star spat out her words like rapid fire as she handed the baby to Ty. "You're right, we're no longer close, but we're family, and maybe it's time we try to act like we love one another."

"Says the girl who spent her whole childhood mad at the world," Stella scoffed.

Unfazed, Star smiled as she said, "Well, I know you wouldn't have noticed because you haven't taken the time, but I'm a different person now."

With Lil Ty settled on his lap, Ty turned his attention to the conversation. He rubbed his wife's back, a proud grin across his face. "She sure is. My baby is the poster child for pleasantry."

They giggled and kissed, then giggled some more. Stella just rolled her eyes, though she felt a pinch inside her. It was something. After all these years, they still acted like they were madly in love.

"We are not pretending to be one big happy family," Maxine said, not allowing the pleasantry from Star and Ty to sit in the air long. "We are honoring our mother's wish and we're . . . together." It was almost as if it pained her to say the word *together*. "I know that each of you have gone on about your lives and you could care less about what our mother wants, but can you at least try to honor her wish? Can we just sit here and be civil . . . together?"

"That is not fair," Star said, losing her smile. "I care about Mama Pearly." She looked genuinely hurt.

Maxine shrugged. "I didn't say you didn't care about Mama. I said you don't care about her wishes. And that's the truth."

"It's your truth." Leslie glanced up, speaking her first words. "Nobody told you to stay here in Smackover. You could've left. You could've gone on with your own life. Mama would've been just fine."

Maxine took the napkin from her lap and placed it on the table. "Mama's laid up in the hospital on the brink of death," she said through clenched teeth. "Does she look just fine to you?"

"I'm not talking about what happened to her now. You keep throwing it in our faces that we went on with our lives and you didn't. I'm saying that you could've left when we did."

"Really?" The sarcasm was thick in her tone as Maxine's eyebrows rose. "So suppose I'd done what each of you have done." She paused and looked at her sisters. "Suppose I'd left. Can you imagine what would have happened to Mama if I hadn't been here?"

"My point is," Leslie said, slowing down her cadence. Now she looked back and forth between her sisters like she was hoping for some reinforcement. "Maxine chose to stay here, and every chance she gets, she holds it against us because we didn't."

"Yeah, because we wanted something more than—" Stella paused and glanced around the dining room with its weathered, yellow-flowered wallpaper, creaky floors, and the ceiling that looked like it was about to cave in at any moment. "—Than this."

"And what's wrong with this?" Maxine said, motioning around the room. "*This* is who you are. No matter how hard you try to pretend that you're someone else, no matter how hard you try to run from your birthplace. You're a country girl from Smackover, Arkansas, and no matter what you say, how you dress, or how much money you make—none of that will ever change who you are."

Stella glared at Maxine and slowly rose from her seat. Walter jumped up and held up his hands. "Ladies," he said. Now it was his turn to set his eyes on each of the Bell sisters. "We started out so well. Let's get back to that and just enjoy this dinner. I'm sure none of you want all of this good food to go to waste?"

Her eyes were still on Maxine as Stella returned to her seat. When Walter sat back down, Maxine looked around the table as if she'd been the one to settle them all down. Then, with a nod, she picked up her fork and continued eating.

Now the house was quiet except for the scraping of forks against the porcelain plates. Even the giggles and the chatter from the twins were gone.

"Maxine, do you mind if I use your restroom?" Nona asked, standing from the table.

"Of course," Maxine replied. "It's at the back of the house. Through the kitchen."

As Nona excused herself, Leslie pushed back from the table.

"Well, it's been a long . . . day. And I'm tired. We're just gonna head back to the hotel."

"Hotel?" Maxine frowned, her tone filled with incredulity. "Why are you staying at a hotel?" she asked Leslie.

"Where else would we stay?" Stella replied for her sister. "I'm planning to get a room too."

Star laughed. "You're going to stay at the Super 8?" she asked her twin. "I thought you only stayed at the best five-star hotels. I can't even imagine you there." Star glanced at her husband, and he laughed with her.

"I don't know why where I'm staying is a joke to you, or any of your business, for that matter."

"I'm just saying, it must be bad if you're willing to stay at the Super 8 rather than here in Mama's house." Star's laughter faded. "You don't even want to stay with your own sisters."

Stella pressed her lips together to stop herself from lashing out and telling Star to shut up.

"No matter what you think of me," Maxine said, "or of each other, you're supposed to stay here—in your home," she stated, as if that was one of the Ten Commandments.

"No, this is *your* home," Stella said, "as you've already made clear," she paused and glanced at her watch, "how many times in the last hour?"

Standing behind her chair, Leslie nodded, then reached for her plate and turned to the kitchen, as if the issue now was left to be debated by her sisters because she was out.

"That's insane," Maxine said. "It just doesn't make any sense."

"Well, I'm going to stay here tonight," Star said, standing and making her way to the kids' table. She gathered their plates. "Me and Ty and the kids are staying because we ain't got no hotel money."

"Ladies," Walter said, his tone sounding weary, "didn't your mother ask you all to find peace? This is not at all peaceful," he said. When no one replied, he continued. "It was her wish that you all stay here and begin healing," Walter said.

At first, no one spoke, and Stella glanced around the room. "Well . . . if I were to stay," she held up her hands, "and I'm not saying that I will, but if I *were* to stay, where am I supposed to sleep?" Her tone was filled with disgust. "Have you counted how many people would be staying in this house?"

Walter spoke fast, as if he thought an immediate solution would satisfy Stella. "You and Leslie can take Mama's bed. Leslie's friend can sleep on the sofa. And then, Star, you and your family can sleep in the front guest room. Cheyenne already dropped her stuff in there. The kids can make pallets on the floor in there or in the living room."

"Ooooh, yay!" Jabari exclaimed. "I want to sleep in the living room."

Walter and Maxine kept their eyes on Stella.

"Fine," Stella huffed. "Let me check in and make sure everything is all set for this event that I'm missing tomorrow." Stella picked up her phone again. "Doggone it. My phone just died." She glanced at the iPhone on the table next to her. "Whose phone is this? Can I use it?"

Leslie strolled from the kitchen and, seeing Stella holding her phone, shouted, "No!" and reached across the table.

Stella shifted, though Leslie was too far away to touch her. "Girl, why are you trippin'? I just want to make a call, and it's not like the phone companies charge for minutes anymore." Stella chuckled as she tapped the screen to wake up the phone.

Again, Leslie lunged forward, but she couldn't reach her sister across the wide table. "Give it to me," she said, her tone filled with panic.

Now Stella frowned. "What is your problem? You can't even let your sister use your phone?"

"No," Leslie repeated, rushing around the table now. "Give me my phone, Stella."

Stella's eyes made their way to Leslie's home screen. She stared at it for a moment before her glance slowly returned to Leslie.

"M—my battery's dead too," Leslie mumbled as she snatched the phone from Stella's hand. Then she noticed everyone staring at her. "I'm going to go to the car and charge it," she said.

"You can use my charger," Star said, but Leslie had already dashed out the front door.

The legs on the chair scraped against the wood floor as Stella pushed back her chair and rushed out to follow Leslie, leaving Maxine and Star frowning.

Chapter 12
Leslie

The sounds of country living filled the air—crickets chirping, frogs croaking, and a distant mooing. And then the evening's sounds were pierced by Stella's demand.

"What the hell is that on your lock screen?"

"What are you talking about?" Leslie said as she stood in front of her car.

She jabbed a finger toward the phone. "What. Is. That?"

Leslie pulled the phone to her chest. "I have no idea what you're talking about."

"Don't play stupid with me, Leslie." Stella squinted, her hands planted on her hips. "Why does that look like a wedding picture? Of you and Nona?"

"Because . . . I was . . . I was in her wedding." Her eyes shifted. She never had been good at lying.

"No, ma'am. Not the way y'all looking at each other." Stella studied her. "Are you married? Nobody else may have noticed, but both of you have bands on your fingers. Is Nona your wife?"

Leslie folded her arms in defiance but remained quiet.

"Leslie! I don't care who you love," Stella said. "I'm just shocked that you would get married without us knowing."

Leslie began pacing in the gravel driveway. "What am I sup-posed to say? 'Hey everybody. This is my wife, Nona?'"

"Wow. So you *are* married." Stella paused, reflecting on the news. "When did this happen?"

Leslie stopped moving, then released a defeated sigh. "Yester-day. Maxine called about Mama during our wedding."

"*Yesterday?* Oh my God. You got married and you didn't tell us?" Stella took her sister into her arms and hugged her tightly. Leslie wanted to remind her that they hadn't spoken in months, but she remained quiet. "Does Maxine know?"

"Of course not." Leslie wriggled away from her sister's grasp, then turned her back to Stella.

"Does Mama know?" Stella asked.

"No one knows."

"Why wouldn't you tell any of us?" Stella grabbed her sister's shoulders and turned her around so they could be face-to-face.

A haze of mist covered Leslie's eyes. "Um, in case you haven't noticed, you guys aren't the most progressive family on earth." Leslie feigned a laugh as she dabbed at her eyes.

"Leslie, we love you. We just want you to be happy."

"Yeah, right."

Though she and Leslie hadn't been particularly close, it was as if Stella could hardly process how her sister could do something so monumental and not say anything.

"I'm seriously hurt behind this. How could you do something so important and not let us know?" Stella said.

"Because I don't feel like being judged." Even though she couldn't look Stella in the eyes, there was an edge to her voice.

"Who's going to judge you?" Stella paused. "Well, okay, Max-ine. But she judges everybody." Stella eased the phone from her sister's hand. Leslie resisted at first, but then let it go. Stella tapped the screen, and the photo popped back up.

"Wow. My baby sister's married." Stella handed the phone back to Leslie. "How did you and Nona meet?"

That made a small smile pop up at the corner of Leslie's face.

"I had boyfriends throughout college, even thought I was going to get married once, but it didn't feel right. Only I didn't know why. It wasn't like I was looking for a woman. But I believe love is love. And I happened to fall in love with Nona."

That made Stella smile.

"As long as you're happy, baby girl, I'm happy. There really is no need to lie."

Leslie released an exasperated breath. "Nona's family is so loving and tolerant and mine . . . isn't. And I just don't want her to see my family."

That hurt, but Stella understood. "I can't imagine that she's okay with you lying about your relationship. I know we have our flaws and we probably put the *dys* in *dysfunction*, but we love you, lil sis. You need to go in there and tell everyone the truth," Stella said, like the situation wasn't open for discussion.

When Leslie didn't respond, she continued, "Leslie . . . didn't Mama just tell us about coming clean? Come to think of it, you're probably who she was talking about. So she must've known."

Did her mother know? She'd been so consumed with her work when Leslie was little, she hadn't been attuned to Leslie's childhood pain. Leslie thought back to a conversation she'd had with her mother a few weeks back. Mama Pearly had commented that Leslie sounded *happy*. Leslie had slipped up and called Nona her girlfriend, but she'd cleaned it up and thought her mother hadn't noticed.

That conversation had ended with Mama Pearly saying, *"Seize your happiness."*

Had she known when she uttered those words?

"Maybe," Leslie finally continued. "Though I don't know how. She never said anything about it. I tried to tell her about my sexuality in a roundabout way, but it seemed like every time I got ready to tell her, she'd start talking about something else. Almost like she didn't want to know. You know we've always been a don't-ask, don't-tell type of family."

Stella nodded. "Right. Mama always said, 'What happens in the house . . .'"

"'. . . Stays in the house,'" Leslie said, finishing their mother's mantra.

Stella took her sister's hands. "Well, Mama wants you to come clean now. So introduce your wife to your family."

Leslie shook her head. "I can't take the judgment. I just want to be here for Mama. See her leave the hospital and then get the hell out of this town."

Stella tossed up her hands in defeat. "You know I don't agree with that, but whatever you want . . . though I do agree with the getting-out-of-this-town part."

Leslie hugged her. "Thank you."

"Now let's get back inside before someone else realizes your phone is fully charged."

They laughed as they walked back inside.

Thankfully, when Leslie and Stella returned to the table, Maxine was sharing another memory about their father.

Leslie smiled, even though that was a memory she had no part of. There had been too many of those kinds of moments when she was growing up. Discussions and laughter over past times from which she was excluded.

It was during those times that she hated being the baby, and while her sisters laughed, she wondered again, for what had to be beyond the millionth time, was this why Maxine hated her?

She and her sisters agreed on very little, but there was one thing that was a family consensus: Leslie's birth had created a shift into darkness for the Bell family. It wasn't her birth per se; it was more as if Leslie's birth was a marker for the worst time in their lives. Not only was their father, a long haul truck driver, gone, but his death was so tragic, so senseless. And then, the next day, Leslie had been born.

Leslie was grateful when the conversation shifted, until Maxine started asking Nona questions.

"So, Nona. Continue telling us about yourself," Maxine said, cutting her a slice of sweet potato pie.

"I'm a psychologist with my own practice." Nona took the saucer. "Thank you."

"A psychologist. How nice."

Nona dug into her pie and moaned at the first bite. That instantly endeared her to Maxine.

"Oh my God. This is so amazing," Nona said.

Maxine's face filled with pride. "It's my mama's recipe. I'm the only one who bothered to learn it."

Stella and Star simultaneously rolled their eyes.

Nona continued talking, filling them in on her family between bites. She fit in naturally. That didn't surprise Leslie. Nona was a natural everywhere. And as long as Maxine thought she was just a friend, all would be well. However, Leslie still didn't feel at ease, especially because Stella kept giving her the side-eye.

"Such a sweet girl," Maxine said after Nona had filled her in on some charity work she'd done at the Children's Hospital. "Do you have children?"

"No, but I'd like them one day," Nona replied.

"Oh, I'm sure you'll make a great mother. Find you a nice young man and have a house full of kids." Maxine chuckled.

Leslie dropped her glass, spilling tea onto the table.

"Oh, this is ridiculous," Stella said as everyone scrambled to clean up the mess. "Stop this charade right now."

"No, Stella," Leslie said, panic spreading across her face as she stared at her sister.

"What are you talking about?" Maxine said.

Nona stopped just as she was about to put the last piece of pie in her mouth. Her eyes grew wide.

"Stella . . ." Leslie said through gritted teeth.

Stella was unfazed as she leaned up on the dining room table, placing her forearms on the table. "Maxine, Nona is Leslie's *wife*."

All movement at the table stopped. Leslie's hand went to her forehead, and in that moment, she wished she could simply disappear. Leslie wanted to grab Nona's hand and take off running, not stopping until she was back in Houston.

"Her. What?" Maxine said.

"Her wife," Stella repeated. "Leslie is thirty-six years old and it is ridiculous that she doesn't feel comfortable enough to tell her family that she is married to a woman."

Maxine stared at Leslie, then at Nona, then back at Stella, as a momentary silence filled the room.

"Oh. My. God," Maxine said, clutching her chest. "You . . . you're a . . . you're one of *those*?"

"Maxine!" Star admonished.

Leslie slowly raised her head out of her hands. She felt her blood rising, but she kept her tone even. "If by *those* you mean a successful Black woman who has finally found true love, then yeah, I'm one of *those*."

"This will shonuff kill Mama," Maxine muttered, shaking her head like she'd received devastating news.

"How do you know Mama doesn't already know?" Leslie replied, her eyes tingling with fury.

It was Maxine's turn to fume. "No way Mama condoned this," she said.

Leslie glared at Maxine. Nona's hand had grabbed hers under the table, probably trying to keep her from losing it. "You don't know what Mama knows. It's obvious because you didn't know that she had cancer that she doesn't tell you everything."

Maxine's nostrils flared, then she stood and went to the dining room china cabinet. She flung the drawers open like she was frantically searching for something.

"See, this is why you should have stayed right here in Arkansas. You go to the big city and start picking up all their wayward ways," she muttered as she snatched another drawer open.

"Now, honey . . ." Walter said.

"No, I'm saying what everyone is thinking. It ain't right. And I'm not going to accept it." She continued digging through the drawer.

"No one is thinking anything but you and your antiquated religious self," Stella said.

"Auntie Maxine. It's a new age. People love who they love," Cheyenne interjected.

Maxine whipped her head in the girl's direction. "Did anybody ask you anything? There's a reason you are at the kiddie table! Stay in a child's place and out of grown folks' business."

"So my voice and opinion don't matter?" Cheyenne asked with an attitude.

"They do not," Maxine replied.

Cheyenne rolled her eyes and put her earphones back on.

"You need to get your children in check," Maxine snapped at Star.

"Don't worry about what I do with my child. You worry about Walter Jr. Why he ain't here. Why he ain't never *here*," Star said.

"He isn't here because he doesn't want to have anything to do with Maxine. She ran his life so hard, he ran off the first chance he got," Stella said.

Maxine was indignant as she opened another drawer. "My son is a distinguished doctor. He's busy saving lives."

"That he is. A distinguished doctor who hasn't been home since the day he left," Star said.

"That's not even what we're talking about," Maxine snapped,

finding whatever it was she was looking for. She turned back to face Leslie. "I cannot believe you. But it shouldn't surprise me. Sin is in your DNA."

Leslie had no idea what Maxine meant by that, but she didn't even care anymore. This was just another dump in Maxine's bucket of hate.

"Walter, you need to remind your wife that none of us are without sin," Stella said, not taking her eyes off Maxine.

Walter sighed and just rubbed his forehead.

Maxine continued spewing her rage. "And then you would bring this, this sin into my house."

"It's not your house," Stella said. "It's our mama's house."

"No, it's *my* house," Maxine yelled.

"Okay, everybody, let's settle down," Walter finally said, holding up his hands as if he was a referee. In the span of three hours, he'd broken up three fights with the Bell sisters.

"No, you need to check your wife," Stella said.

"Would you all stop it?" Leslie shouted. "See, this is why I don't ever want to come home. Why none of us do. This is insane. I can't do this anymore." Her eyes filled with tears as she turned to Nona. "Let's go."

"Go where?" Star said. "You can't leave. Mama needs you."

Leslie took a deep breath as she gathered her things. "We're staying at the motel. I'm going to see about my mother in the morning, then I'm leaving."

"And now you're about to have this idolatry at the motel. Sister Jennings' daughter works at the front desk there. The whole world is gonna know about you and be talking," Maxine moaned.

"I don't care what this funky town talks about," Leslie said.

"Look, Maxine, you're overreacting," Star said. "Let the girl live her life. She's—"

Maxine cut her off. "I'm not having it. And I don't have to in my house."

"Don't worry. I don't want to be here." Leslie took her anger out on the wood floor as she stomped toward the door. "You can go to hell, Maxine."

"You and your sinful life will beat me there," Maxine called out after her.

Nona stood awkwardly. Maxine glared at her in disgust.

"Nice to meet everyone," Nona said, before scurrying out the door after her wife.

Chapter 13
Stella

Maxine huffed as she cleared the table. She stacked the empty plates on top of one another, gathering them like a skilled waiter. She took the plates into the kitchen and returned to the dining room. A blanket of silence had filled the room.

"Well, I guess we know what Mama was talking about when she said come clean," Maxine said, wrapping some foil around the bowl of macaroni and cheese.

"I guess so," Star replied as she patted Lil Ty's back and bounced him on her lap while he dozed off. "You still didn't have to act like such a jerk."

"Humph," Maxine said. "Leslie didn't have to bring that sin up in my house either." She shook her head. "I just don't understand it." She reached for Stella's dessert plate. "Are you done?"

Stella studied Maxine for a moment before sliding the plate in her direction. "Why do you act the way you do with Leslie?"

Maxine didn't stop clearing the table as she said, "What way?"

"You're bossy as it is, but you're on a whole other level with Leslie."

Maxine didn't miss a beat as she replied, "Because she's the baby of the family. And if I don't look out for her, it's not like you're going to do it. You're too busy with your lavish life down there in Atlanta."

"Don't turn this around on me," Stella said.

"Whatever. I'm going to do the dishes. Make yourself at home because I know you're not going to bother helping. Visiting hours are at ten in the morning. We can go see Mama then."

She left without waiting on a reply.

Star slid back from the table, bracing Lil Ty on her shoulder. "Well, I was going to offer to help, but she's in jerk overload, so she's got it. I'm tired. We're calling it a night."

On cue, her family followed her out.

Stella contemplated going to the motel to check on Leslie, but if she didn't know anything else, she knew that she needed to give Leslie some space right now. She hadn't intended to just blurt out Leslie's news, and though she didn't usually have regrets, if she could rewind time, she would've kept her mouth shut.

Stella plugged her phone in, waited for her phone to recharge, then checked more emails. Before she knew it, the house was eerily quiet. She sat taking in the silence and the memories. Try as she may, she couldn't mentally connect to this place. She'd been gone so long, she felt detached. Maybe because she'd been so anxious to leave in the first place.

The uneasiness building in Stella's stomach continued to grow. Something wasn't right with Maxine. She was more than her usual judgmental self. Why would her sister's choice of a spouse invoke such rage? Something told Stella this was deeper than religious conviction.

The thought accompanied Stella out to the car to retrieve her suitcase. After pulling it out and closing the trunk, she stood in the driveway for a moment. She strained, trying to make out the sounds of the night creatures that penetrated the air.

When they were little, they used to see how many sounds they could identify. Now, she wouldn't know a cricket from a cicada.

Stella's thoughts returned to Maxine as she headed back inside. The light in Maxine's room was off, so Maxine and Walter must've already gone to sleep.

Stella headed to her mother's room, where she undressed and slipped on a tank top and pajama pants. But instead of getting into bed, she glanced at her mother's antique mahogany dresser. A memory of sitting there while her mother brushed her hair flashed through Stella's mind.

Have I ever told you how lucky I am to have you as a daughter?

A pang fluttered through her heart as she thought about those special times with her mother. Those times that made Stella feel like she was really her mother's favorite. It wasn't until she was a teen that she realized her mother made them all feel that way.

Those words meant the world then and now. Stella only wished her mother's love had been enough for her back then, when she so desperately wanted something different.

Stella ran her fingers along the top of the dresser, then opened the drawers. She lifted some of the clothes and held them close, inhaling her mother's lavender-infused laundry. She'd been using wool dryer balls sprinkled with lavender for as long as Stella could remember.

Stella placed the clothing back and was just about to close the drawer when she noticed a manila envelope peeking from the back. Stella pulled out the envelope, opened it, and started going through the paperwork inside.

Stella sifted through a bunch of legal documents. The deed to the house. A burial policy. Some church-related papers. She stopped at her father's obituary and fingered his photo as she tried to summon up the few memories she had of him.

She released a long sigh, slid the papers back into the envelope, then returned the envelope to the drawer. She then turned her attention to a large box that sat in the corner near her mother's antique chest. Stella closed the drawer and moved over to pick up the box.

She opened it and smiled at the stack of photos. Stella took a seat on her mother's bed and began removing the photos one by one. A picture of her mother brought an even bigger smile to her face. She marveled at her mother's beauty. Mama Pearly could've easily passed for Creole with her pearl-colored skin and natural curls. She was slender, with intoxicating eyes that smiled even when she didn't.

Her mother was smoking one of those long cigarettes while sitting in a booth at what looked like a nightclub.

Stella fingered the photo, suddenly stopping at the date. July 1984. Stella paused, confused lines creasing her forehead. Leslie was born in September 1984. Their mother smoked cigarettes while she was pregnant? *No way,* Stella thought as she stared at the picture.

Mama Pearly looked exceptionally thin, and though she'd never weighed more than 150 pounds, nothing about this picture said *pregnant.*

"Okay, that's strange," Stella mumbled as she dug through more photos.

She found another picture from the same time frame. In that one, also dated September 1984, her mother held a glass of what looked like whiskey. No way her mother drank *and* smoked while she was pregnant with Leslie. She wouldn't have taken the chance on harming her child.

Stella's mind raced back, but no matter how much she tried, she couldn't remember the details of Leslie's birth; she was just too young when her sister was born. Still, it seemed like she should at least recall rubbing her mother's belly or some type of memory of her mother being pregnant. But her memory bank came up blank.

Slowly, Stella sifted through the pictures, stopping at a few with her, Star, and Maxine. But then, as she shuffled through more, she frowned. Something didn't make sense. Going back over the dates, her eyes began to widen. She stood, then lined up the pictures in chronological order. As she stared at the photos, a thousand explanations circled in her head and one of those thoughts started roaring louder than the others and caused Stella to sprint across the room. She opened the door slowly, hoping that it wouldn't creak; then she tiptoed past Maxine's bedroom, through the living room and to the guest room, where Star and her family were sleeping.

Stella eased open the bedroom door, careful not to disturb Lil Ty in his portable crib, then tiptoed to the left side of the bed. She stared down at her sister and Ty before she crouched down and whispered, "Star, you up?"

When Star didn't move, Stella gently shook her. Ty, who had his arm wrapped tightly around Star's waist moaned, then turned over, his back now to his wife. Star slowly opened her eyes.

"Stella? What's up?" She bolted up. "Is it Mama?"

"No," Stella whispered, putting her finger to her lips to keep Star quiet.

"Then why are you waking me?"

"Come here. I have something to show you." Stella didn't wait for a reply as she tiptoed out.

The sounds of Star's feet hitting the hardwood floor filled the room as she followed Stella through the house to their mother's bedroom.

"What are you doing?" Star asked, rubbing her eyes. "This better be good. I just got the baby to sleep."

"Let me ask you a question," Stella said, easing her mother's bedroom door closed. "Do you remember anything about Mama being pregnant with Leslie?"

"What kind of question is that at two o'clock in the morning?" Star asked, yawning her disinterest. "We were three. Why would we remember?"

"Don't you think it's strange, as many pictures as Mama took, there were never pictures of her while she was pregnant with Leslie?"

"Well, for one, I don't think it's strange because I didn't know that until this moment. But I get it 'cause the novelty of having children usually wears off by the fourth child."

"No, this is more than that." Stella sat on the edge of the bed and showed Star the photos she had laid out. "Look at this." She picked up the first photo she'd questioned. "This is when Mama was pregnant with Maxine." She put another Polaroid photo in front of Star. "This is me and you." She jabbed the last row of pictures spread on the bed. "And then look at this. Mama is smoking and drinking in these pictures."

"Okay. And? You know she liked to occasionally drink and smoke; she did that socially. She and Daddy agreed to stop smoking, which is where the cigarette story came from."

"Yeah, but she wouldn't have done any of that while she was pregnant." Stella sat back and let her words sink in.

Star frowned, studied the picture herself. "What are you trying to say?"

Stella fanned out the family photos. She'd made three rows of pictures. "These are all when we were babies." She pointed to the last row. "Where's Maxine in these pictures? They were all taken around the time Leslie was born."

"I don't know." Star cocked her head like she was trying to make sense of her sister's picture display.

"When Mama said come clean, she said for *all* of us to come clean."

"There's nothing for me to come clean about," Star said, her eyebrows raising.

Stella hesitated, looked away from Star, then said, "I mean, me neither, but when she said that, I just noticed Maxine's demeanor."

"So, again, I don't understand. What are you trying to say?"

Stella paused, contemplating her next words, the ones she'd spent the past hour analyzing in her head. "I think Maxine acts like Leslie's mother because she *is* Leslie's mother."

A beat.

"You know you sound ridiculous right now?" Star finally said.

Stella bucked her eyes as she used her hands to emphasize her point. "That would explain so much."

Star sat at the foot of the bed, adjusted the loose braid that had fallen out of her bonnet, then looked at Stella to see if she was serious. "So you want to believe that Maxine had a secret baby and Mama took it and raised it as her own? And they've been lying to everybody all these years?"

When Stella nodded, Star added, "Leslie isn't the only one with an active imagination in the family."

"I'm serious, Star. I always knew it was something," Stella said. "You know she was meaner to Leslie when we were growing up."

"Exactly. If Leslie was really her kid, she would've treated her nicer." Star stood. "You're really reaching. I'm going back to sleep."

Stella shook her head. "I don't know. I think that's what Mama Pearly was talking about."

"I think you and Maxine just can't stand each other and you're looking for something scandalous to throw in her face."

"Why don't we just ask her?" Stella said.

"Yeah, sure. Let's just go say, 'Hey sis, did you really give birth to Leslie and lie to everybody all these years?'"

"We can start there."

"I think you just need to let it go. Find something else to fight with Maxine about. Something plausible."

Stella gathered up the photos as she stood. "No, we're going to get some answers."

Star stopped her twin as she headed to the door. "It's late and there's no coming back from an accusation like this, Stella. At least sleep on it."

Stella weighed her sister's words. "Okay, fine. But in the morning, we're getting answers."

Star flashed a leave-me-out-of-it expression as she turned and headed back to bed.

Chapter 14
Leslie

The sun peeked through the tattered, stained curtain at the Super 8. Leslie yawned, stretched, then slowly opened her eyes. Nona was on her side, propped up on one arm, looking down at her.

"Good morning," Nona said.

"Hey, babe," Leslie said, giving her a quick peck on the lips. "Are you staring at me in my sleep?"

"I've been worried about you. You tossed and turned all night."

Leslie pulled herself up against the headboard, memories of last night's dream dancing vividly in her head.

"I had a dream that . . ." she paused and looked around the dingy motel room, ". . . that . . . this was all a dream. But the fact that we're here, I guess it's not."

Nona gently ran her fingers down Leslie's arm.

"No. Unfortunately, it's not."

"Well, let's get comfortable, because I don't plan on leaving this room until they let us back in to see Mama."

"Sweetheart, you can't hide out here all day."

"Why not? You don't think Super 8 has room service? We could order in and just chill."

Nona chuckled as she threw back the covers and stood. "They didn't even want to give me a spare towel, so I doubt it."

"I know, you're right." Leslie sighed, though she made no move from her spot in the full-size bed. "Maybe we can just sneak over to the hospital, see Mama, and then go home."

"Leaving is not the answer, Leslie," Nona said, walking into the bathroom. The sound of running water filled the room. A minute later, Nona returned with a wet hand towel, which she was rubbing in a circular motion on her face—her morning ritual to keep her skin youthful. "I've been telling you, you have to accept who you are in every aspect." She pointed out the dingy window. "And this place made you who you are."

"Okay, don't start analyzing me. I'm not one of your patients."

Nona eased back down on the bed. "You know that's not what I'm trying to do." She set the towel on the nightstand and took Leslie's hands. "I'm just saying, the only way forward is to face the past. Whatever this heaviness of hate your family is carrying needs to be addressed. And the only way you can do that is to talk to them. Ask them questions about how they feel, and enable them to ask questions about you and your life so that you can all get a better understanding of what the tension actually is and how it might be eased."

Leslie snatched her hands away. "You know, if I want a professional diagnosis, I'll call your office and make an appointment."

Nona's shoulders slumped. Leslie inhaled, exhaled, then slid closer to her. "I'm sorry, babe. I don't mean to snap at you. I know you're just trying to help." She buried her face in her hands. "You just don't understand, though. All my life my sister has judged me and made my life miserable, and I just don't want to deal with it, especially now that I don't have to."

Nona scooted so that their thighs touched. She took Leslie's hand. "You can't change the way people are. You have to accept them just like you want them to accept you."

"Why can't I just leave and never talk to them again?"

"That's what you've been doing all this time. But you still carry it—whatever *it* is—inside there." She tapped Leslie's heart.

Leslie wanted to protest, just as she'd done every other time Nona had tried to discuss her broken relationship with her family. When she didn't say anything, Nona took that as a cue to continue.

"You try to tell yourself you don't care. But you do. And so you need to face it, head on. Homophobia is typically based on lack of knowledge on the topic, and Maxine is only repeating stereotypes and opinions she has been exposed to in her environment. Some family members really aren't homophobic, they just don't know what to say or how to say it, and comments may come out awkwardly."

Leslie raised an eyebrow. "Oh, trust me, Maxine is homophobic."

"Well, allow her time to be shocked and time to take the news in. You have to be sensitive to her feelings too. Remember, what did that author say in her amazing book that made me get up the nerve to ask her out on a date?" Nona snapped her fingers like she was just remembering. "Oh yeah, 'coming out may be more of a process than an event.'"

Leslie finally managed a smile. "I see you throwing my words back on me."

"You aren't a *New York Times* best-selling author for nothing." Nona pulled the covers off Leslie. "So let's get moving. You go talk to your sister, get some answers."

"You don't want to come?"

"You know I do, but I think I'll be a distraction. This is something you have to face on your own," she continued.

"You're right, babe. But you're wrong about being a distraction." Leslie stared into Nona's eyes. It was amazing all that Nona had put up with in Leslie's journey to self-discovery. Nona had been gay all her life, coming out to her parents in high school. But she never forced her views on Leslie. In fact, she'd given Leslie a safe space to just *be*.

"I was wrong to ask you to stay here," Leslie continued. "I want you by my side. I need you by my side. And I don't care what Maxine or anyone else thinks. I will proudly tell my sister, my family, and anyone else that they need to accept me. Us. Or they can write me out of their lives."

"Let's not go to such an extreme." Nona smiled. "But that's the Warrior Queen I fell in love with. Now, let's go face your family."

Leslie stared at her wife. "Have I told you how much I love you?"

"Not today."

Leslie pulled Nona close, choosing her embrace to show Nona just how much she was loved.

Chapter 15
Stella

It had been years since Stella was awakened by the sound of a rooster crowing. Growing up, Rex, their prized rooster, had been her daily alarm clock. Rex was long gone, probably Sunday dinner years ago, but there had been a steady stream of roosters in his place. And the one cock-a-doodle-dooing this morning was among the loudest she'd ever heard.

Stella yawned, pulled back the covers, then swung her feet over the bed, grimacing as the cold from the hardwood floor shot up through the bottoms of her feet.

The heaviness of what she'd discovered last night had only grown. And now it felt like a boulder sitting on her back as she made her way out of the bedroom and into the kitchen where the smell of coffee permeated the air.

Stella poured herself a cup from the glass carafe, which sat right next to the unused deluxe Keurig Stella had sent her mother last Christmas. She scooped two spoonfuls of brown sugar into her coffee and brought the piping-hot liquid up to her lips. As she savored the taste of the coffee, she noticed Maxine sitting on the back porch, a cup of coffee in her hand, gazing out at the pasture across the street.

"Morning," Stella said, pushing open the screen door and

heading out onto the porch. She took a seat in the rocking chair next to Maxine.

"Morning," Maxine replied.

"You checked on Mama this morning?"

"Of course. She's still sedated. They will be running tests all day, so they said we shouldn't come until after two." She turned and studied her sister. "How'd you sleep?"

Like I was suffocating under the weight of your secret, Stella wanted to say. Instead, she simply said, "Surprisingly, like ol' times." At home, she slept on a $3,000 memory foam mattress and 1,200 count sheets. But last night, on her mother's worn mattress and lint ball–covered sheets, once she was finally able to drift off, Stella had one of the soundest slumbers she'd had in years.

"Umph," Maxine said, her gaze still ahead.

Stella wrestled back the words she really wanted to say. "I see Mr. Calhoun still has all those cows," she said.

"Yep."

Stella sighed, took another sip, then said, "So, I guess you still have an attitude about Leslie and her wife?"

Maxine cringed. "Wife." She spat out the word like it burned her tongue. "Just shameful."

Stella shook her head "It's bad enough you act twenty years older than you actually are, but you have an old folks' mindset too. Why do you care who Leslie is sleeping with?"

That seemed to pierce Maxine even more as her body grew rigid. "The world is hard enough for us. She already has to work harder because she's a woman, a dark-skinned one at that. Now she done gone and made it even harder."

Stella fought the urge to dive into a colorism discussion with Maxine. It hadn't worked when they were young; she was sure it wouldn't work now. Maxine always had given Leslie a hard time about her skin color.

"She's happy. Shouldn't that be all that matters?" Stella said.

Maxine shook her head. "It's just wrong," Maxine said.

"Says who?"

"Says the Lord."

"The Lord also says a whole bunch of other things that all of us still do in some form or another." Stella leaned back in the chair and slowly started rocking. "What is it you say, 'Let he who is without sin cast the first stone.'?"

"You can make light of this all you want, but I'll never accept it." The finality in Maxine's voice let Stella know anything she said would be a waste of energy.

Stella sighed, took another sip of her coffee. "Must be hard being so perfect," she mumbled.

"I never claim to be perfect, but I do try to live my life in a way that would be pleasing to the Lord."

Stella studied her sister. The conviction in her voice matched the expression on her face. She truly believed what she was saying.

"You're even more self-righteous now than when we were growing up," Stella said, anxious to blurt out her theory. But Star was right. This was heavy. If Stella thought things were bad before, they would be even worse if she was wrong in her accusation.

"I'm not self-righteous. I'm right."

The self-assured expression on Maxine's face made Stella dismiss her apprehension. She leaned up, her gaze burrowing into Maxine.

"Everyone can't have a perfect life, meet the perfect man, and live happily ever after."

Maxine balked. "You don't know my life. You think you do, but you don't." She sipped her coffee.

"Au contraire," Stella said. "I know it very well, and because everybody else's doesn't align up as perfectly as yours, you judge them, look down on them."

Maxine looked like she was about to say something, then changed her mind and just resumed her rocking.

When Stella didn't take her eyes off her, Maxine said, "How do you expect me to act with this news about Leslie? And then, to think you knew about it."

"Not that it matters," Stella said, "but I just found out. I hadn't talked to Leslie in months outside of a few texts, but as long as she's happy, what difference does it make?"

Maxine's silence signaled the end of the conversation.

Stella set down her coffee cup on the wicker end table that sat in between the two of them.

"So, I have a question I need to ask you," Stella said.

"What?" Maxine didn't look at her, just kept gazing at the pasture across the street.

"It's about your relationship with Leslie. It just seemed to be different from ours. You were bossy to all of us. But for me and Star, it was kind of in a protective way. You dealt with Star's insane meltdowns and my attitude. We argued, but it was like regular sibling stuff . . . maybe a bit extreme, but regular, you know? However, when it came to Leslie, you were just . . . mean. I don't know how else to describe it."

"I have no idea what you're talking about," Maxine said, speeding up her rocking.

"Just trying to understand why you've always had such disdain for Leslie," Stella said.

The chair moved faster. Faster. Maxine gripped the handles like she was trying to get the strength to propel herself off the porch.

Finally, Maxine said, "Now you're just digging for stuff."

"No I'm not."

She abruptly stopped rocking and stood. "Look, I'm not having this conversation . . ."

Stella stood as well and jabbed a finger in Maxine's direction. "And see, it's that right there . . . Anytime somebody tries to have a conversation with you about Leslie, you up and run, as if you think we are going to discover your secret."

Maxine's hands went to her hips. "What secret would that be?"

Stella was quiet, careful, before releasing words that she could never take back.

"I think Leslie is not our sister. She's your daughter."

"You sound crazy." The strangled laugh that escaped Maxine was confirmation this wasn't Stella's overactive imagination, as Star had said.

And now, the way Maxine's body had tensed up, her shoulders erect, her hands trembling until she balled them in fists, confessed nonverbally.

"No, no. And, in fact, I'm more convinced now than ever," Stella said, the reality of this lie piercing her heart. "You're supposed to be so holier-than-thou and you deny your own child? What kind of woman are you?"

"Shut up," Maxine barked, her nostrils flaring. "You don't know what you're talking about."

"I know you got knocked up and then tried to hide it." Stella hadn't intended on being so crass, but she was convinced she'd uncovered the truth, and the fact that they'd lived a lie for more than three decades infuriated her.

"You probably were all loose and promiscuous, and then you had the audacity to judge everybody else," Stella continued.

"Shut up!" Maxine screamed.

Stella stared at her sister. The strong, impenetrable façade Maxine wore on a constant basis was replaced by a scared woman whose secret had finally been revealed. Her housecoat trembled as she stood trying to catch her breath.

Stella was about to say something, but the way Maxine fell back into the rocking chair and began sobbing made Stella's anger pause. She wasn't used to this . . . this human side of her sister.

"You don't understand," Maxine sobbed.

Until that very moment, Stella had been focused on gloating over her sister's fall from grace. But Maxine's tears—and now confirmation—hammered home the reality of this situation.

"My God." Stella's hand went to her mouth in shock as the reality of everything set in. "Leslie is your daughter. She is going to die when she finds this out."

Maxine vehemently shook her head as she locked eyes with Stella. "She can never know. You cannot tell her. You cannot say anything. It would crush her. And Mama." Maxine jumped up and clutched Stella's arms. "Mama and I swore to take this to our graves. Promise me you won't say anything. Yes, I gave birth to her, but Leslie is Mama's daughter. I can't . . ."

Maxine's words trailed off and her gaze went directly over Stella's shoulder. Stella turned around to see Leslie and Nona standing on the other side of the screen door, looking at them in shock.

Chapter 16
Leslie

Leslie heard the words—all of them—but she couldn't process the reality of what they meant. And then her eyes locked with Maxine's.

"Yes, I gave birth to her . . ."

"Leslie," Maxine said in horror.

Leslie shook herself out of the daze she'd been in for the past few minutes. She pushed open the screen door and stepped out onto the porch. Nona stood behind her.

"You . . . you're . . . my mother?"

"Leslie, I'm so sorry," Stella said, taking a step toward her. "I . . . I . . . never meant for you to hear it like this."

Leslie kept her gaze fixed on Maxine. "Is what Stella said true? Is what you just said true? Did you give birth to me?" She didn't give Maxine time to reply. "You said you did. Why would you say that?" Leslie pushed out the words, her voice filled with panic.

Maxine shook her head, wringing her hands as she spoke. "It's not like that."

"That's not an answer," Leslie said.

Maxine stuttered as she glanced around, as if she was searching for an escape route. "I . . . I . . ."

"Answer me!" Leslie yelled, the bass in her voice causing everyone to jump.

"I can explain . . ." And then Maxine stopped talking.

"Jesus." Leslie began pacing the width of the porch. "Is that why you were mean and hateful to me my whole life?"

"I wasn't mean and hateful." Maxine's voice was soft, her tone low, as if keeping her voice down would take some of the sting away.

"Yes, you were! All my life."

Leslie's chest heaved as a thousand memories flooded her mind. All of the name-calling. All of the disdain. Maxine made Leslie regularly question what she'd done to invoke so much hate. And it was the mere fact that she was born?

"Baby . . ." Nona said, her arms going around Leslie's waist to stop her from pacing.

The way Maxine flinched as she watched Nona touch Leslie enraged Leslie even more.

"You have the audacity to stand in judgment on me and you're out here having babies and giving them away." Leslie knew she was scaring Nona as her wife had never seen her enraged like this, but she couldn't stop.

Maxine turned her attention back to Leslie. "It's not like that at all," she said.

"What is it like, then?" Leslie screamed.

"Leslie, calm down," Maxine said. "Please . . . please let me explain."

"Explain! Because right now, you're saying a whole bunch of nothing."

Maxine stood speechless.

"You had thirty-six years to come up with an excuse. Don't go silent now."

"I—I was just so young." The way Maxine trembled was a sight none of them had ever witnessed. "You've got to understand."

"Oh my God. Oh. My. God." Leslie shook as well. "You are my mother." This time it wasn't a question.

Nona rubbed Leslie's arm, no doubt trying to calm her down. "Sweetheart . . ."

"So Mama isn't my mama." Another statement. This time it was followed by a pained cry.

Maxine nodded as tears streamed down her face. "Yes. Yes, she is. She loves you. She nurtured you. She raised you."

"Did she give birth to me?" Leslie screamed.

Again, Maxine cowered.

The screen door swung open and Star appeared in her pajamas and bonnet. "What in the world is all this noise? My kids are still slee . . ." Her words trailed off as she looked at Maxine, then Leslie. Then Stella.

"You didn't?" she said to Stella. Her eyes took in the horror on Leslie's face. "Wait. So it's true?"

Before anyone could reply, Leslie started fanning herself. She was on the verge of hyperventilating. "Who all knew? Am I the only idiot who had no idea?"

"I didn't know," Star quickly interjected.

"N—nobody knew," Maxine said. "I—I . . . I didn't tell a soul."

Suddenly, everything made sense. It was so obvious. Why she was so different from her sisters. All of the lies about her getting her dark color from her grandfather.

"I'm so sorry, Leslie," Maxine said.

Now the tears streaming down Leslie's face matched the ones drenching Maxine's. "My whole life has been a lie. Mama lied. You lied."

"You have to understand, we did what we thought was best," Maxine said, taking a step toward Leslie.

"Is my daddy black?" Spittle flew from her mouth as she spoke.

"What?" Maxine asked.

"Is. My. Daddy. Black?" Leslie repeated.

"Yes, wh—why would you ask that?"

"No. Midnight black. Blue black. Is that where I get my color from? The color you despise."

Thoughts of Maxine's only intimate moments with her filled Leslie's head. The diligent care as she dipped her hand into the thick, pasty Eucerin lotion tub, then slowly working it into Leslie's skin as it melted down and made her skin smooth and shiny.

"This is gonna lighten your skin," Maxine would tell her.

And when that didn't work, she went to cocoa butter. And when that didn't work, it was some homemade concoction.

Leslie would look at the tub of lotion sitting on Maxine's all-white dresser and shiver. She hated it and loved it. Loved it because it was the only iota of affection Maxine showed her. Hated it because it didn't work.

The smell of it to this day reminded her of how she was the dark-skinned daughter of a light-enough-to-pass black woman.

Star would make jokes and Stella would come to her defense, saying, "Jokes are supposed to be funny, and that isn't funny."

That had been her life—all her life. And all that time, Maxine and Mama Pearly knew she got it from her father. Leslie didn't know what a panic attack felt like, but if she had to guess, it would be exactly how she was feeling now.

"Answer me!" Leslie bellowed.

Maxine's eyes shifted downward. "Y—yes . . . he was a very dark-skinned man."

"Who is he?" The thought that she could be walking down the street and bump into her father and never know it both distressed and angered her.

"It . . . It's no one you know," Maxine stammered.

"So he was good enough for you to lay down with, but when the two of you procreated his spawn, it was too much for you both?"

Stella reached for her sister. "Leslie . . ."

Leslie held up her arms and backed away. Stella gently touched her sister's arm. "Leslie, calm down."

Leslie jerked away from her. "No, get away from me. Both of you. You two and this need to battle each other." She spun in Stella's direction. "You don't care who you destroy as long as you can one-up one another."

Stella looked shocked. "I . . . I was just trying to prove that she isn't as great as she thinks she is."

"All of y'all make me sick," Leslie said.

Nona eased up to Leslie and wrapped her arms around Leslie's waist. "Let's just go back to the motel," Nona said.

"No, I'm going home."

"Leslie . . ." All three of her sisters spoke her name at the same time.

"Stop," Leslie screamed. She took deep breaths as she beat the air with her fists like a jackhammer. "None of you ever talk to me again! I gotta get out of here." She bolted down the steps of the back porch.

She heard Nona say, "I'll talk to her." But Leslie wanted to tell Nona to save her breath. This was the final straw to sever her ties to this family forever.

Chapter 17
Maxine

The cold compress on Maxine's head was doing little to ease the throbbing. Walter kept rubbing her hair as Star stroked her hand. She was laid out on the sofa, wondering how in the world everything had gone so wrong.

"It's okay, sis. Leslie's just mad right now. She'll get over it," Star said.

"She's never going to forgive me," Maxine cried. "Nobody understands."

"We don't, but things will calm down and you'll have a chance to explain," Star said.

Maxine closed her eyes, praying the cold towel could ease the throbbing as her memory raced back thirty-six years.

Maxine put the chain on the door to the bathroom, then took off her clothes and stared at herself in the full-length bathroom mirror. The sight of her swollen belly disgusted her. Her body disfigured through no doing of her own. His seed growing inside her. It all was so repulsive. She swallowed the bile that tried to force its way up every time she looked at herself naked, and climbed into the stand-alone tub. It had been a hard and exhausting week and she wanted nothing more than for Calgon to take her away. As the bubbles from the bubble bath surrounded her, Maxine had just closed her eyes when she heard the door jiggle.

"Maxine, open this bathroom door. Why do you have the chain on the door?" Her mother's voice was stern. Mama Pearly didn't believe in locked doors in her house.

"Hold on, Mama."

Maxine jumped out of the water and reached to grab a towel, but as soon as she stood, the door was kicked open.

Mama Pearly's eyes immediately went to Maxine's swollen belly.

"Sweet Jesus," she muttered.

Maxine's hands tried to cover her stomach, which at six and a half months sat firmly protruding. She'd hidden her pregnancy from her mother with baggy clothes and excuses of round-the-clock studying. Of course, she knew her secret would be revealed in twelve more weeks, but Maxine hadn't figured out that far ahead.

"Let me explain, Mama."

"I knew it. I knew it. I knew it. I knew it," Mama Pearly said, her expression a mixture of pain and sadness. "I can't believe you're with child. I can't believe you're out here having sex."

"It's not like that, Mama," Maxine said, snatching the towel from the sink and covering her naked body.

"I'm looking at your belly. It's about to burst any day. If it's not like that, what is it like? You let some boy climb on you and take your virginity. And you couldn't even respect yourself enough to make him use protection?" Tears were streaming down her face. That caused Maxine to cry as well.

"I didn't let anybody do anything!" Maxine finally said. "I swear."

Mama Pearly's anger tempered. Maxine was her truthful, dependable daughter, so for her to swear meant she was telling the truth. Mama Pearly lowered her voice, bracing for the truth. *"Then what happened?"*

"I . . . I can't tell you," Maxine whimpered.

"Why not? . . . You better tell me something," Mama Pearly added when Maxine didn't speak.

"Maxine?"

Maxine was snapped back to the present by her husband's voice. "Sweetie, are you okay?"

She looked around at her family, staring at her. Stella had slithered into a corner, but she kept her eyes glued to Maxine, probably eating this all up.

"No. I don't know if I'll ever be okay again." Maxine sniffed. "There's just so much you all don't understand."

Star continued soothing her. "It's not up to us to understand, Maxine. Nobody is judging you."

Maxine and Stella's eyes met. "Oh, she's judging me, all right," Maxine said.

"You know, you are foul," Star replied, looking up at her twin.

Everyone shifted their gaze to Stella, including Cheyenne, who was sitting in the corner, trying to act like she was uninterested but probably covering everything for Snapchat.

"How am I foul? You don't think Leslie needed to know the truth?" Stella's tone was defensive.

"Not like that, Stella," Star said.

"Well, it's not like I told her. It's not my fault she overheard-"

"I don't even want to hear it." Star waved her off. "But I hope you're happy. I'm sure this is exactly what Mama wanted for her girls on her deathbed," Star added, her voice dripping with sarcasm.

She cut her eyes at Stella and told Maxine, "Come on, why don't you sit up and let me make you some tea. We can't see Mama till this afternoon, so you just go get some rest."

As both Star and Walter helped Maxine sit up and get comfortable on the sofa, Ty scooped up the baby, glanced at Stella,
shook his head, and went back into their bedroom.

"What?" Stella said when she saw Cheyenne looking at her.

"This family makes me want to never have kids so the blood-
line can end with us." She put her earphones back on, blocking
out their dysfunction, as she headed into the room with her father.

Chapter 18
Stella

Stella had hoped a drive through town would give everyone time to calm down. She'd been dialing Leslie's number to no avail, and had even driven by the motel in hopes of finding her. But Leslie's car wasn't there, and Stella prayed her little sister hadn't made good on her threat to go back to Houston.

She released a long breath, picked up her cell, and called the hospital. Maybe she'd go see her mother. Maybe if they got some good news about Mama Pearly, everything else wouldn't matter.

"El Dorado Memorial, how may I direct your call?" the cheery operator asked after answering the phone.

"Pearly Bell's room, please?"

"Please hold."

Stella didn't know what she expected. Did she think her mother was just going to pick up the phone and start chatting?

A few seconds later, the operator returned. "I'm sorry, Ms. Bell is under a Do Not Disturb order."

"This is her daughter."

"I understand that, but unfortunately, the orders apply to everyone."

"So, I won't be able to see her today?"

"I'm sorry. You won't. But the order lifts tomorrow."

Stella considered protesting but figured it would get her no-where, so she thanked the operator, hung up, and just continued driving aimlessly.

Once she reached the highway, Stella thought about turning right to go toward Little Rock, but instead, she made a left and followed the dirt road into town. She passed the elementary/mid-dle/high school, and nostalgia filled her. Nothing about it had changed. The long building that witnessed children enter in kindergarten and exit in the twelfth grade, was still antiquated, with windows permanently fogged from years of humidity. The dirty bricks looked like they would crumble at any moment. And though fresh rosebushes lined the front of the school, everything else remained the same.

Stella left the school, heading toward the park where the teenagers used to hang out—where she'd gotten her first kiss, where she spent time talking to her friends about life outside of Smackover. After a few minutes there, Stella made her way down to Main Street. Smackover was a town where many things were "the." As in, "*the* post office," "*the* grocery store," and "*the* traf-fic light." About half the roads in the county didn't show up on Google Maps. And about half of the ones that did show up were private roads: driveways or roads through private property. The place had left a lot to be desired, and Stella desired more than this place could ever deliver.

Stella's heart constricted as she saw Murphy's Gas Station to her right. It was abandoned, weathered boards covering broken windows. Still, she put the car in Park and turned off the engine. This used to be the sole stop for the Greyhound bus. Being here sent her mind racing back.

Stella had been nervous on the whole bus ride to Atlanta. She'd expected at any moment that Star, her mother, Maxine, someone, would come and expose her lie.

It wasn't until they pulled into the Greyhound station and the driver said, "Welcome to Atlanta," that she began to relax. When she stepped off the bus, the August heat blanketed her, as if welcoming her to her new life. Only then did she smile.

She'd hailed a taxi, given them the address to Spelman's campus, sat back, and took in the sights of the city. She'd been to Little Rock a few times, but other than that, she'd never left Arkansas, so she was in awe of the tall buildings, bustling freeways, and tree-lined highways.

Stella leaned her head against the glass as she peered at a billboard announcing Michael Jackson in concert. Another billboard was promoting Planned Parenthood. Stella's heart thudded against her chest. There was so much to see. So much to discover, and she was ready for it all.

A tear trickled down her face as the taxi pulled between the columns with the words Spelman College. As the driver eased onto the campus, Stella was amazed at how massive it was. All of the buildings and the people moving in, and the sprawling green lawn. She'd seen the Spelman brochures, but in her wildest dreams she never imagined this place would make her forget all about Smackover.

The thought of home made her remember Star, and she pushed the image of her sister standing on the porch waving goodbye from her mind.

"I'm doing the right thing," she whispered.

She really believed that. Her twin was committed to Ty. She wouldn't have been happy all the way in Atlanta without him. This was best for both of them.

"Is this the building you want?" the driver asked.

"Sure," she said, not able to tell one building from another.

She grabbed her suitcase from beside her, paid the driver out of the one hundred dollars her mother had given her, then stood on the curb for a moment. She took out the paper from her purse and checked the name of the place she was supposed to report to. Yes, this was the building.

With a deep breath, she lifted her suitcase and lugged it into the registrar's office.

Inside, she paused at the door, overwhelmed by all the people. There were four long lines of girls dressed in frayed, hemmed denim shorts and tank tops and guys in jeans and polos. There was an array of hairstyles she'd only seen in Right On! *Magazine, including a girl who passed right in front of her with the asymmetrical haircut she'd begged her mother for just last month. Everyone was with someone, chatting among themselves, some of the groups mixing as if the guys and girls already knew each other.*

She got in the first line with the heading A–D.

Finally, Stella reached the front of the line. "Hi," a perky young woman greeted Stella. "How may I help you?"

"I need to pick up my room key and get registered for my classes."

"Yes, ma'am. What's your name?"

That was the part of the memory when Stella always felt bile rise in her stomach and threaten to spew out.

She pushed that thought aside, and her mind returned to everything that had transpired today. This was not how she saw everything playing out. But then, that had been an issue she'd had her whole life.

Baby girl, you've got to think before you speak.

Mama Pearly's words swirled in her head. She'd said them so many times over the years. When she'd demanded Star change her name. When she'd asked her sixth-grade teacher why she didn't get her missing tooth replaced. When she'd cried because Randy Watkins uninvited her to the prom because she told him she was only going with him because Bruce Cooper had asked someone else.

Everything you're thinking doesn't need to come out, Mama Pearly had told her on several occasions.

Stella had gotten better about that over the years, keeping a lot of her thoughts about Lincoln to herself. But obviously, she hadn't mastered it enough, she thought, as she second-guessed her decision to confront Maxine.

Stella jumped at someone tapping on her window.

"May I help you?" An elderly man with pale skin that looked like it had battled a lifetime of acne peered into her window. "You sho' been sitting out here a mighty long time."

"Oh, I'm sorry. Just reminiscing. Is this still a bus stop?"

"Nah. You got to go to El Dorado now to catch the bus. It stopped coming here 'bout eight years ago." The man cocked his head. "You Miss Pearly's daughter?"

Stella nodded. "I am."

"One of the twins, right?"

"Yes, sir."

"Yo Mama sho was proud of you." He smiled, showing off a mouthful of missing and decaying teeth. "She was proud of all you girls."

That brought a nostalgic smile to Stella's face. Their mother had bragged on each of them, no matter what they'd done.

The man tapped her hood.

"Well, I just wanted to make sure you weren't somebody up to no good over here. Old Man Murphy closed this gas station down last year, and the drug addicts sometimes try to break in to sleep here. I wish they'd go on and tear it down."

"Well, I didn't mean to worry you. I'll be on my way now."

"Heard Miss Pearly was in the hospital. Tell her the whole town is praying for her. She's one sweet woman."

"Thank you, sir. I'll let her know."

Stella pulled off and back onto the roadway. Left with nowhere to go, Stella returned to her mother's. Maybe this time away had given everyone a chance to calm down.

Ten minutes later, she was walking into the living room, where she was met by her twin's wrath.

"I really hope you are happy now," Star said, shaking her head as Stella set down her purse.

"Me? Why are you acting like this is on me?"

"Because it wasn't your place to reveal that. But you always gotta one-up Maxine. I swear, I don't understand why the two of you always go at it so."

Stella stood like a child who had just been chastised. Was Star right? Did she do that only to get back at Maxine? Even though the two of them had their issues, it pained her when Star took Maxine's side over hers. They were bound from the womb. No, the two of them weren't close, but they were still twins. Star should always have her back. They were supposed to be connected for life. But they'd stopped being that way a long time ago, and Stella had no one to blame but herself.

"Why is everyone so mad at me? I didn't know Leslie would overhear. But don't you think Leslie deserved the truth?"

"It's not your truth to tell," Star repeated.

Maxine reappeared in the doorway. "She never has cared about anything but what she wants."

"Maxine, you're supposed to be lying down," Star said.

"I came to fix me some tea."

"Walter would've done that."

"He got a call." Maxine paused, dabbed her neck with the wet towel she'd been holding, then said, "You're just evil, Stella."

"I'm the one who's evil?" Stella replied, appalled.

"Yeah," Maxine said. "You always want to condemn me for standing in judgment of others, but you're just as dirty. In fact, I would say you're worse than me. At least Mama and I had a reason for our deception. We were thinking about Leslie. Your lie was purely selfish."

Stella felt a stab in her heart. No way Maxine knew what she'd done. "I have no idea what you are talking about," Stella said.

Maxine glared at her sister.

"I'm not the only one with secrets, Stella."

Stella's eyes widened as her heart rate quickened, but no words would form.

Maxine seized the moment. "Oh, it doesn't feel good when the shoe is on the other foot, does it?" Maxine spat. "While we're spilling secrets, why don't we spill them all?"

Stella found her voice. She had to, in case Maxine was about to do what Stella thought.

"You're angry, so I'm not about to do this with you," Stella said as she grabbed her purse to leave.

"Nah," Maxine said, stepping to block Stella's path. "You want to come clean. Let's come clean."

Stella refused to let her fear show. "So now you're about to make up some lie to try to get back at me? Really?"

"We both know it's not a lie," Maxine replied, her mouth spreading into a wicked grin. Stella was aghast at the look in her eyes. "Did you enjoy your time at Spelman?" Maxine asked. "Is that where you made all the connections for that posh job you have? Did it lead to a good life for you? All that money you make." Her tone was patronizing and obviously confusing to Star, whose eyes danced back and forth between her sisters.

"Wh—what are you talking about?" Stella stammered.

"Oh, we got amnesia now, huh?"

"Maxine, don't," Walter pleaded, suddenly appearing in the living room.

Stella wanted to turn and run, but she was paralyzed with fear that Maxine was threatening her as payback.

"No, I'm sick and tired of her," Maxine said. "She went off and built this life that makes her think she's too good for everybody else. That we're some country bumpkins who are beneath her. And she thinks no one knows that it was built on a lie."

Stella just stared at her sister, speechless. She knew.

"What is Maxine talking about?" Star asked, her gaze now resting on Stella.

"Answer your twin sister; tell her what you did," Maxine said, never taking her eyes off Stella.

After all these years . . . Stella really thought no one would ever know. Her heart raced; her vision blurred. This couldn't be coming out. Not like this. She would resort to pleading if she thought it would shut Maxine up.

"Don't do this," Stella said, her tone low, her voice shaky. "I'm sorry, okay? I'll fix things with Leslie."

"Oh, now you want me to have some sympathy for you?" Maxine replied. She seemed like she'd gotten a burst of energy. Walter stood off to the side, defeated, like he knew there was no stopping Maxine now.

"Would somebody tell me what's going on? Stella, what secret is she talking about?" Star demanded.

"Stella, you don't want to tell her?" When Stella didn't reply, Maxine turned to Star, her adrenaline pushing her for payback. "I guess I'll do the honors. You know how you were always the smarter one in school? You had some issues, but academically, you were a beast."

"Maxine . . ." Stella said, her voice trembling.

Maxine ignored her as she continued. "Do you remember when that college recruiter came, and he had you and Stella apply for Spelman?"

"Yeah, and?" Star said, looking back and forth between the two of them again.

"Maxine, stop," Stella said.

Maxine smiled. Walter just lowered his head as he continued to shake it.

"Why are you bringing that up?" Star said. "Stella got in. I didn't. I made peace with that a long time ago."

"But I remember how devastated you were."

"It's just because I really thought I had it. I wanted it so bad, because everything was jacked up in my life, and I thought it would give me a fresh start."

"Oh, I know. I was there while you cried yourself to sleep every night, especially after Stella left." Maxine didn't take her eyes off Stella as she spoke.

"Stop beating around the bush," Star said, "and tell me what you're talking about."

"You were accepted to Spelman," Maxine said matter-of-factly.

"No, I wasn't. I got a rejection letter." Confusion covered her face.

Maxine never took her eyes off Stella. "No. What you saw was *Stella's* rejection letter. *She* was rejected. You were accepted. But your lovely twin sister forged the denial letter for you and then went to Spelman in your place."

"What?" Star was stunned. Her brows furrowed as she unpacked Maxine's declaration.

"Star, I can explain," Stella said.

"Yeah. Let's hear you explain." Maxine sat on the sofa, tapping the armrest with her fingers like she'd gotten to the good part of a movie.

Star spoke before Stella could. "So . . . I was the one who was supposed to be at Spelman?" Her words were measured. She turned to Maxine. "And you didn't say anything? As hysterical as I was, and you never said a word?"

Maxine wagged a finger. "No, ma'am. I didn't find out until years later. When the alumni office called here looking for Ella Bell. Mama and I did some digging and discovered the truth. By then, Stella had graduated and it was too late."

Ty eased up behind his wife. Stella hadn't even seen him come into the room.

"Babe, breathe," he whispered as Star repeatedly balled and unballed her fists.

"She stole my life." Star took slow, deep breaths. "This family . . . wow . . . this family is full of secrets and lies."

This was a day that Stella had hoped she would never have to face. So she had no words prepared in her defense.

"Say something," Star yelled, causing Stella to jump.

"You . . . you didn't even want to go to college," Stella cried. "You were up and down, all over the place. Then you were all in love with Ty and you said you were just gonna stay here."

"I would've gone with her to Atlanta," Ty said. He was angry as well, but Stella could tell he was trying to stay calm for Star's sake.

Stella wanted to tell him to shut up and stay out of it, but she kept her attention on Star.

"It was just . . . I mean, it was a great opportunity, and you know how you were. You would've just messed it up," Stella said.

Star released a pained laugh. "How I was? Wow." She stepped closer to Stella, but Ty pulled her back.

"Have you ever considered that maybe if I had another opportunity, I would've taken it. How dare you take that away from me?" Star cried.

"I'm so sorry." Stella genuinely meant that. Though judging by her twin's furrowed eyebrows, flaring nostrils, and rage-filled eyes, it didn't even matter.

Star backed up and started pacing, still balling and unballing her fists. "All these years. All these years, I thought I wasn't good enough. I thought I'd failed. I was happy for you, but I thought I'd failed. And it was all a lie." Star was shaking.

"Star . . ." Stella said.

"It was all a lie!"

Ty stepped in front of her. "Babe. Remember what the therapist said. You can't control someone else's actions. You can only control your reactions."

Therapist? Stella had no idea her sister was seeing a therapist.

Was that person responsible for this kinder, gentler Star? Hopefully, that therapist had also taught Star the art of forgiveness.

"Breathe, baby," Ty said. His words calmed her as she took more small, deep breaths.

"Star, you have no idea how sorry I am," Stella said.

The coldness in Star's eyes caused Stella to swallow her apology and purse her lips.

The daggers she threw with just her eyes pierced Stella's heart. She knew that expression would haunt her forever.

"I'm with Leslie. Don't ever, ever talk to me again," Star said as she let Ty lead her out of the room.

Stella glared at Maxine. Though she no longer looked smug, she didn't carry one ounce of regret either.

Maxine gave a slight shrug. "Doesn't feel good, does it?"

Stella didn't reply as she bolted into her mother's room, threw herself across the bed, and cried as the memories came racing back . . .

"What's your name?"

Stella hesitated, took a deep breath, then spoke the words she'd practiced on the bus ride to Atlanta, "It's . . . Stella." She handed the woman her driver's license. "But everybody calls me Ella. It's probably listed as Ella Bell in your system."

It felt like Dominique Dawes was doing somersaults in her stomach. Would this work?

"Yes, Miss Bell, I see you right here. So, should we leave it as Ella in the system?" the clerk asked. "It can easily be corrected if you want."

"You know what, that's a good idea, just to avoid any future problems, because my license says Stella. You can go ahead and change it."

"Of course." The woman smiled, happy to help.

"Here you go," she said, handing Stella a piece of paper. "That will tell you where to pick up your room key. I see

you're a presidential scholar, so your balance is paid in full. Welcome to Spelman."

And just like that, Stella's new life began.

In this moment, Stella wished she had just gotten on the highway and gone home to Atlanta. But not only did she not want to leave her mother, she couldn't leave behind the secret that had been revealed. The past had come back with a vengeance, and it was time to face it, no matter the consequences.

Chapter 19
Maxine

Usually, knitting brought Maxine peace, but she'd constructed a whole scarf in the past hour and still her nerves were frayed. She'd practically begged the shift nurse to let her sit in here with her mother. And the woman must've taken pity on Maxine, with her swollen and puffy eyes, because she'd agreed, with the caveat that Maxine not disturb her mother.

She'd hoped being in her mother's presence would ease the pain that was ripping through her heart. It hadn't. Nothing was able to help her forget the fiasco that had just upended her world.

Three quick taps on the hospital room door made her glance up. Walter stood at the threshold and she sighed.

"I knew I'd find you here," he said.

Walter had left her sleeping while he had run to the church and handled some business. As soon as he'd left, Maxine had felt like her own home was suffocating her. She'd jumped right in her car and made her way to the hospital.

"Thought they said you couldn't see Mama Pearly till later," Walter said.

"I had to come."

Walter nodded his understanding. "How is she?"

"Same. She hasn't moved since I got here about two hours ago."

They both glanced at her, the slow hum of the machine filling the room. Mama Pearly looked like she was in a deep sleep, her body showing no sign of the cancer ravaging her insides.

"We're staying prayerful," Walter said. He turned his attention back to Maxine. His eyes were filled with questions. Like everyone else, he was in search of answers.

He said, "You want some coffee?"

She really didn't, but she knew her husband deserved some clarity. Maxine inhaled, set the yarn and knitting needle in her purse, then folded her hands in her lap as she looked up at her husband.

"Yes. Coffee would be good."

She stood, kissed her mother on the forehead, and then walked through the door her husband was holding open.

Silence accompanied Maxine and Walter down the hall, on the elevator, into the cafeteria, and as they ordered their coffee. It only lifted when they sat across the table from each other.

"I'm sorry for keeping something so huge from you," Maxine finally said. He'd asked her for an explanation right when it happened. But Maxine had been too distraught, and he'd respected that.

Walter nodded slowly before he reached out across the table and squeezed her hand.

"Forgiven. This is big. But I also know you. And I know for you to keep something this huge from me, there had to be a valid explanation."

She bit down on her lip, sighing her dejection. "Tell that to Leslie."

"Why don't you tell it to me first?"

Maxine lowered her eyes, her attention suddenly on her cup of coffee. "I don't even know where to start."

"The beginning is always the best place."

Tears were already burning behind Maxine's eyelids as she

nodded, then she closed her eyes. In her mind, she grasped Walter's hand and took him with her, back to that time. . . .

"Hey there, pretty woman."

Maxine hated when he called her that, and she had a feeling that he knew how she felt about it. He was family, so he'd known her since she was born, yet for the past month, and only when they were alone, he'd call her "pretty woman." He emphasized the woman, *and on more than one occasion, she'd reminded him that she was only fourteen years old.*

The way he'd started looking at her—his beady eyes bugging out and staying on her whenever she walked into the room. And the way he stared and licked his lips like he'd just eaten some greasy fried chicken—it all creeped her out. And right now, it was especially creepy in this dark kitchen, with only the moonlight shining through the small window over the sink.

"I—I was just getting something to drink. Good night." *Maxine set her glass down and scurried by him, still feeling his stare. She hurried back to the guest bedroom, where she slept whenever she spent the night here.*

She shut the door behind her, and then closed her eyes, grateful that she'd gotten away. But just moments after she'd crawled into the bed and tucked herself under the covers, the door of the bedroom creaked open.

Her eyes popped open at the same time, and the beat of her heart sped up as he crept into the room, easing himself inside. He tiptoed in as if he was being careful. As if he wanted to make sure that no one heard him sneaking into the room where he didn't belong.

"Whatchu rush out for?" he said.

"I . . . I'm sleepy," she said, peeking from under the covers and hoping that would be enough for him to leave her be.

"I got something to help you sleep."

"I don't need nothin'," she said.

But it was as if she hadn't spoken as he ran his hand down his bare chest, unzipped his pants, then stepped out of them, leaving them in a ball on the floor.

Maxine's eyes widened in horror as she watched him stroke himself through his boxers, and she felt the bile rising up to the edge of her throat.

He moved toward her, slowly, like a panther about to attack its prey. In her mind, she was ready to jump up and run, but her body wouldn't move.

Then he dropped his boxers, exposing himself. His protruding belly and his flabby chest covered in little beads of hair made her want to gag. "Wh—what are you doing?" *she asked.*

"What you want me to do," *he said, as if she'd given him some kind of invitation.* "What that little body of yours is calling out, begging me to do," *he continued as he inched closer to her.*

"No!" *She pushed herself back in the bed until she was up against the headboard, and when he still moved toward her, she parted her lips to scream, but before her horror could escape through her mouth, his long, pudgy fingers clasped around her throat. The hands that once tossed frisbees her way were seconds away from choking the life from her body.*

"If you make a sound, I swear I'll kill you," *he muttered.* "Then I'll kill your mama, and your sisters."

Kill Mama Pearly? No! And the thought that he might hurt Stella and Ella too made more than tears come to her eyes, it made her heartbeat skip in fear.

She would rather die than cause something to happen to everyone she loved, so Maxine swallowed back her angst. She tried to reconcile the hands pushing down her shorts, wrapping around her throat, holding her still, with the hands that had affectionately bounced her on his lap as a little girl. She couldn't believe they were one in the same. Her skin burned with revulsion.

When his fingertips crept down the inseam of her sleep

shorts, Maxine braced herself for what she knew was about to happen. In that moment, she felt the fear rise from her stomach into the back of her throat.

When he spread her legs, she squeezed her eyes shut, and she prayed for God, or someone, anyone, to save her. Then he entered her.

"Yessss," he moaned as he broke the sanctity of what she had sworn only her husband would have the pleasure of doing.

As the bed thudded, she cried inside and out. He moaned. Then pounded. Groaned. Then pounded some more.

Her life felt startling and horrible and inescapable. As beads of his sweat dripped onto her, a whimper escaped her lips.

"Shut up," he hissed as he humped. "You know you want this."

She bit her lip to fight back the scream, but inside she shouted. As he took her virginity, she tried to control her mind, transporting herself somewhere else. But no matter how she tried, she couldn't remove herself from this bedroom, she couldn't run away from this moment that she'd never forget.

All she could do was wait for him to finish so she could die.

He made a horrible gurgling sound as his back arched and his body quivered. Then he released another muffled groan before his body went limp.

The hand around her throat fell away, and she peeked at him through moistened lashes.

"Umph, umph, umph," he said as he crawled off her. "Just as good as I knew it would be."

He stood, pulled up his boxers, stepped back into his pants, and said, "Told you you were gonna enjoy it." He dressed, then headed to the door as she trembled in the dark. "And not that anyone would ever believe you, but if you speak a word of this to anyone, everybody you know and love is gonna die."

In that moment, she had a flash—the day at the park, where a bunch of men were playing dominoes. And then one of them ended up on the ground, bloodied.

Looking at the man who'd been responsible for that attack back then, she knew he spoke the truth right now. She had no doubt that he was capable of killing.

"Sleep tight, pretty woman. I'll make hotcakes for you in the morning. Just the way you like them."

Then he slipped out of the room.

"I promised myself I would never, ever speak about that night out loud again," Maxine said as she angrily swiped away a tear from her cheek. Not only had she told herself she would never speak of it again, but she had long ago promised herself that she wouldn't cry over it either. "The only time I told that story was to Mama." She paused, looking up at her husband through eyes that were still glassy with her tears. "And I didn't give her all the details that I just gave to you."

"You said it was a family member. Who?" The way Walter's fists were balled at his side, Maxine knew her husband wanted to put his religion on the shelf and go beat her rapist to a bloody pulp.

Maxine shook her head. Answering him was the last thing she wanted to do.

"Maxine . . ." Walter continued when she didn't answer.

"It was a relative, but Walter . . . I really don't want to talk about that anymore."

His shoulders slumped, and Maxine could tell he wanted to push the issue, but thankfully, he just said, "Why didn't you go to the police? He raped you."

"Oh, trust me, Mama wanted to. But then I begged her not to because I felt like it didn't really count as rape."

"Didn't count?"

"You know. Because I knew him, I didn't think it would count in the same way as if I had been attacked by someone I didn't know. Someone who was walking down the street. I figured once everybody found out, everybody would have an opinion and they would have taken sides. It would've been horrible for Mama. She would've had to endure the humiliation of everybody in town knowing our business."

"Sweetheart, I am so sorry," Walter said, moving to her side and wrapping his arm around her shoulders. He paused as she lay her head on his shoulder. "So, is that . . . that's what happened?" He stopped again, as if he didn't want to ask, but he wanted to know. "Leslie?"

Maxine nodded, and fresh tears shone in her eyes. "I didn't know I was pregnant at first. I didn't get my cycle, but I had just started menstruating, so I thought periods came and went. I didn't know. Then as my belly started to grow and I realized what was happening, I had daily visions of going to the top of the highest building and diving off."

Walter gasped. "Sweetheart, no," he whispered.

She nodded. "But then Mama caught me in the bathtub one night. And when I told her what happened, she went into action and planned it all out. She decided I would go away to stay with Aunt Grace, my daddy's sister in Detroit, and once the baby was born, she would take the baby and raise her as her own. I told her I didn't want to do that. I just wanted to put the baby up for adoption, leave her in Detroit. But she insisted, and I was just too numb to argue."

"What about your father? Did he know?"

"No. Daddy would've killed him with his bare hands if he ever found out."

The crush of this revelation pushed Walter back in his seat. "Wow. How did she explain to people when she showed up with this baby?"

"Honestly, I don't even remember. I spent the months from when Mama found out to giving birth in a daze. I didn't look at my body and see a body, I saw a crime scene. The feeling of being violated never went away."

Maxine remembered the first time she'd laid eyes on Leslie. Every time she saw Leslie's dark chocolate skin that matched his . . . light brown eyes ripped from his genetic pool, and course, rough hair that reminded her of the hair on his chest, she grew enraged all over again.

Shame filled Maxine's face. "Mama and I agreed that it would end badly for Daddy if he knew who the baby's father was." The tears she'd been pushing back escaped. "My daddy's last few months on earth were spent believing I'd gotten pregnant by some random boy at school," she softly cried. "I don't know what Mama said to get him to agree to raising Leslie. He . . . he died before we ever had a chance to talk."

Walter pulled Maxine to him, hugging her tightly, as if he were trying to absorb her pain.

Maxine welcomed his embrace. It brought comfort—for the moment. She knew the real issues were just beginning.

Chapter 20
Leslie

Leslie eased into the hospital room, closing the door to the sounds of the nurses' shoes squeaking on the pristine tiles. She didn't know how long she'd have here before she was thrown out.

The sight of the wires glued to her mother's chest, coming up through the neck of her hospital gown, made Leslie's heart constrict.

Leslie stood, staring down at the slow rise and fall of her mother's chest. She had so many questions. *How could her mother carry such a lie? How could she not know how doing so would breed such hate in Maxine?*

Yet in this moment, with her mother fighting for her life, should any of these questions really matter?

Leslie sighed as she took her mother's hand, grateful that Nona had talked her into staying in Smackover. Being here in this moment hadn't been her plan. When she'd first left Maxine's she'd driven through the streets of Smackover like she was on a NASCAR speedway and sped right back to the motel.

Without saying a word to Nona, she jumped out of the car and ran inside. She hadn't even taken the elevator, choosing instead to run up the three flights of stairs before she busted into the room.

There was no way for her to process all that was going on in her mind as she tore her clothes from the wire hangers, stuffing everything that she'd unpacked back into her suitcase.

Just a few minutes later, Nona had come into the room and stood at the door, watching Leslie dash about as she tossed everything they had into their two bags.

When she zipped up the luggage, she turned to Nona with both suitcases in her hands. "I'm ready to go," she'd told her wife.

Nona had looked at her for a moment. "No," she'd said. "Not like this. You have some issues to face."

"No, I don't. I don't care what any of them have to say," Leslie had shouted. "You heard what I told them. I never want to see any of them again. Damn them all!"

Nona had let her rant for a few more minutes before she took the suitcases from Leslie, sat her down on the bed . . . and that was when Leslie broke down.

Nona held her as she cried out, all of her pain so evident. Leslie had cried and cried until she realized that no matter what she was feeling, there was no way she could leave Mama Pearly. Not right now and not like this.

Leslie sighed again as she replayed that scene. Mama. That was a lie. Her mother was really her grandmother.

"I know you were just trying to protect me, Mama," Leslie whispered, "but how could you lie to me all these years? Was it because you knew that Maxine didn't love me and you were trying to protect me from that? Or was it just that Maxine didn't want to have any children and you couldn't bear the thought of her giving me away?"

Leslie stopped that thought. That wasn't possible. There was Walter Jr., and Maxine certainly loved her nephew . . . or rather, her brother.

"Wow," she whispered. Knowing now that her nephew was her brother brought a whole new set of pain. So Maxine had been good with giving birth to Junior but not her?

"Whoa, what are you doing in here?"

Leslie turned slowly to face the nurse. When she and Nona had arrived thirty minutes before, the nurse had told them there was no change with her mother, and the doctor had advised the nurses to keep visitors away. But she had to see Mama Pearly. So Nona had distracted the nurse while she'd snuck into the room.

"I didn't see you come in," the nurse said with a frown.

"There was nobody at the desk," Leslie said.

The nurse nodded, but then she shook her head as her expression softened. "Sweetie, you really shouldn't be in here. Your mother needs her rest." She walked over and opened the mini-blinds covering the small window in the corner. Though Leslie didn't know why, since the view was only of an adjoining building.

"I know, and I'm sorry, but I have to be near her right now," Leslie said.

"I understand," the nurse said as she started checking Mama Pearly's vitals.

Leslie wanted to tell her no, she didn't understand anything. But before she could say a word, the door swung open and Maxine appeared in the doorway.

The two of them stared in silence—hurt in Leslie's eyes, regret in Maxine's.

Leslie took a deep breath, turned to the nurse. "My apologies. I'll leave now."

She hurried out of the room, brushing past Maxine and heading toward the elevator, ignoring her sister/mother as she called out her name.

Chapter 21
Stella

The ringing just wouldn't stop and finally, without opening her eyes, Stella patted around on the nightstand until she found her phone.

"Hello," she said, her voice thick with sleep.

"Hello, beautiful."

"Lincoln?" She yawned and stretched. "What time is it?"

"It's almost ten. Are you in bed already? Maybe this is why I've been so worried about you."

Stella pushed herself up and leaned against the headboard. She knew she'd been exhausted, but today must've truly been draining because she'd checked into the motel shortly after six. Her plan was to check on Leslie and spend a little time with her before going to the hospital to check on her mother. One good thing about these small-town motels: There wasn't such a thing as privacy. She'd simply asked the girl at the front desk which room her sister, Leslie Bell was in, and without hesitation, the woman had said 316. But when she'd knocked on her room, there'd been no answer. Her plan B was to come back to her room and lay down for just a half hour or so to process all that had happened today.

But, clearly, plan B had its own ideas.

"You still there?" Lincoln said.

"Yeah."

"I was worried about you. I just have a feeling that this is taking a toll on you more than you're letting on."

"No need, I'm okay. Just a lot going on. You can't even imagine."

"I knew it," Lincoln said. "I felt it inside. Do you need me to come there?"

For the first time, Stella's immediate reaction wasn't *absolutely not*. She thought about all that had gone down and how even though they'd all been hurt, Maxine had Walter, Star had Ty, and Leslie had Nona. She was the only one who was going through this alone. Even still, she said, "Thank you, Lincoln. That's sweet, But I'll be fine."

"How's your mother?"

"Same. Praying for some good news. We couldn't see her this morning. I'd planned to go up there this evening, but I fell asleep."

"Well, I'll be praying for some good news too."

Stella eased out of the bed. "Thank you. But listen, let me call you later. I need to go check on my sister."

"Oh . . . kay." Lincoln stretched out the word, sounding like he didn't want to let her get off the phone. "But remember, I'm here for you."

She closed her eyes, savoring words she didn't realize she needed to hear.

"I'll let you know if I need anything," she said.

She hung up, then pulled herself out of bed and went into the bathroom, rinsed her face, then grabbed her room key.

She took the stairs up one floor to the third floor and knocked on her sister's door again. Nona opened the door within seconds.

"Hi, Stella," she said, barely cracking the door.

"Hi, Nona. I need to speak to Leslie," Stella said and took a step forward, expecting Nona to step aside and let her in.

That didn't happen. Nona eased the door closed until Stella could hardly see her. "She really doesn't want to see anyone," Nona said.

Stella shrugged, as if that was no big deal. "Well, I'm just going to sit outside here in the hallway until she sees me," Stella said, raising her voice to make sure Leslie heard her.

Stella heard rumbling, then the door opened wide and Leslie appeared.

"What, Stella?" she said, moving in front of Nona and folding her arms.

"I wanted to check on you. I'm so sorry you found out like this," Stella said, getting right to the point. "I would've said something to you, but I just found out last night. Actually, I didn't even know for sure. I stumbled on some pictures, began asking some questions, and what you heard this morning was me trying to find out if what I'd discovered was true. I promise you, I didn't know."

Leslie didn't say a word. She just stood, folding her arms tighter, as if that would keep Stella away.

"I know you're hurting, sis," Stella continued.

"I don't think you should call me that, *Auntie*."

At first, Stella frowned, and then it was as if it hit her. All day, her focus had been on Maxine being Leslie's mother. This was the first time that she was considering that Leslie was her niece. Still, she said, "I just want to make sure you're okay."

"I'm not." Leslie swallowed, like she was determined not to cry.

"Okay." Stella nodded. "I completely understand that. Can I come in and talk?"

Leslie lowered her eyes, then bit down on her bottom lip.

Stella said, "If you're not ready, that's okay. I'll just sit right here until you are."

Stella leaned against the wall and began to slide down like she planned to sit when Leslie said, "All right."

Stella smiled. That was one thing all her sisters . . . and her niece . . . knew about her. She was persistent. She was sure Leslie knew that she'd never leave.

Leslie stepped aside and motioned for Leslie to come in.

"I'll go and get you something to drink," Nona said, excusing herself. She flashed a sympathetic smile at Stella as she exited.

Once they were alone, Stella said, "I know this is hard," as she took a seat at the desk.

Leslie plopped down on the bed. "That's an understatement." She tilted her head as she glanced at Stella. "So you really didn't know?"

Stella held up one hand as if she were about to take an oath on a Bible. "I swear I didn't. We were just toddlers when you were born."

Leslie leaned back against the headboard and massaged her temples. "So, what happened? How did I end up Maxine's daughter with Mama not being my mama?"

Stella shook her head. "That part I really don't know. Maxine is distraught and won't talk about it. I can only assume she got knocked up and didn't want anybody to know."

"Do you have any idea who my father is?"

"I don't know that either. Only Maxine and Mama can answer these questions. I know what you know. So you're going to have to ask Maxine."

She shook her head so hard Stella was sure Leslie would have whiplash in the morning. "I'm never talking to her again." Leslie's tone was adamant.

"I know you say that right now, but Maxine loves you," Stella paused when Leslie gave her a long side-eye, "even if she has a warped way of showing it."

Now, Leslie rolled her eyes. Stella stood and walked over to the bed, pausing only for a moment before she wiped the tear that streamed down Leslie's cheek.

Stella lowered herself onto the bed. "We're going to get through this."

"No," Leslie said before Stella could respond. "It's too much. I mean, how could she dote on Junior but throw me away?"

Stella had wondered that herself. But she knew no amount of

speculating would yield answers. "The only thing I can assume is that she was a lot older *and* married with Walter Jr. And she didn't throw you away. She gave you to Mama Pearly, one of the most loving people on the planet. Maybe doting on Junior was her way of loving both of you."

"Really, Stella? You know I'm not that little six-year-old who adored those stories you used to make up for me. I'm a grown woman who makes up my own stories now, and even though I write fiction, I know facts. And the fact is that Maxine hated me, you know that."

Stella stayed silent; she didn't have any words to combat the truth that Leslie spoke.

"I bet she wanted to abort me," Leslie said, making up the story, needing to have something she could believe. "Yes, that's it. She wanted to abort me and Mama wouldn't let her. That's what it was."

"I don't know, baby girl. But I do know this," Stella replied, "the only way you're going to get any answers is to talk to her yourself. And before you say, *hell no*, you need to get answers, or this will haunt you for the rest of your life."

Leslie sighed deeply, as if she knew Stella was right. "Fine," she finally said, "I'll talk to her, but only if you come with me."

"Right now, if I saw Maxine, I probably would hurt her."

Leslie looked confused. "What happened?"

Stella sighed. She'd come to check on her sister, not rehash her own transgressions. "Long story, and I don't want to get into it right now, but I do think you need to talk. I got a room here at the motel too. Let's get some rest, then, in the morning, I'll go with you back down to the house, but I can't stay."

Leslie looked like she didn't have the energy to unpack her sister's drama. So she simply said, "Okay."

Chapter 22
Maxine

"*P*ush, Maxine, push."

"Argggh!" Maxine screamed from the depths of her soul. It felt like someone was using their bare hands to tear her insides out.

"I see the baby's head," the doctor said.

"Come on, Maxine. It's almost over," Mama Pearly encouraged. She squeezed Maxine's hand, and her mother's touch was the only thing that was familiar in this strange town, with this strange man looking all up in her private parts.

Maxine took a deep breath and inhaled every iota of strength she could muster. She wanted this thing out and she wanted it out now.

"Arggggh," she exhaled, screaming as she pushed. Then, suddenly, she felt a sliver of relief as the baby slipped out of her.

She heard a wail, then, "It's a girl," the doctor said.

While the nurses moved about, Maxine fell back against the pillow, spent.

"She's a beautiful little chocolate thang," the nurse said as she tried to hand the milky- covered baby to Maxine.

Maxine turned her head, her eyes only focused on the ecru-colored wall. "No," was all she said.

"I'll take her," Mama Pearly stepped up and said.

Tears ran down Maxine's cheeks as she kept her focus. From the moment she'd realized she was pregnant, she'd had a dozen prayers: for God to make her trip and fall and lose the baby. Or for a stillbirth. Or for her to wake up from this nine-month-long nightmare. Or even for Aunt Grace—despite being seventy years old—to offer to raise the baby. Each one of her prayers added up to one thing: that this day, when she'd give birth and hear her baby cry, would never come.

And yet here she was. Facing an ecru wall.

"What do you want to call her?" Mama Pearly asked.

"I . . . I don't care," Maxine muttered, the tears still coming.

While her body felt exhaustion from the pain of childbirth, her heart was numb.

Mama Pearly held the baby with one hand and stroked Maxine's hair with the other.

"I know this is hard, sweetie. But we will get through this. God is pleased at this precious baby. And it doesn't matter how she got here."

Maxine wished that she could share her mother's optimistic outlook, but as the baby wailed in her mother's arms, all she could think was how in the world she was supposed to live with the worst memory of her life.

Maxine was shaken from her thoughts.

"Sweetheart, did you hear me?" Walter asked.

"I'm sorry." She'd been sitting on the back porch, the slow, steady rocking helping her to dissect everything that had happened in the last twenty-four hours. They'd made it thirty-six years with this secret, but Maxine should've known every day would have its reckoning.

"I said, Stella is here," Walter said.

Maxine sighed. While she regretted spilling Stella's secret, she didn't have the energy to deal with anything other than Leslie and her mother.

"She's with Leslie," he added when she didn't move.

Maxine paused rocking, and her thoughts stopped with the motion too.

"You owe her answers," Walter said.

Maxine nodded as she stood; then she followed her husband into the living room. At the entryway, he stepped aside and let Maxine pass him.

"Hi," Maxine said, her gaze set on Leslie. "I'm glad you came back."

"Trust me," Leslie said, disdain in her tone, "I didn't want to come. My first thought was just to leave this family of lies and return home."

"This is your home."

Leslie opened her mouth to protest, but before she could do that, she said instead, "So what I really want to know is why." Leslie swallowed hard and pushed out her next words. "Why Walter Jr. and not me?"

"It wasn't like I was trying to decide between you and Walter Jr."

"Is it because you were ashamed to have gotten pregnant with me?" Leslie continued.

"Or is it that you didn't want people to know you were having sex?" Stella asked.

Leslie spun toward her. "Stella, I asked you here for support, but please stay out of this. This is between me and Maxine." She turned back to Maxine. "Or should I call you Mama?"

Maxine jutted out her chin. "Pearly is your mother," she said somberly.

"Oh, trust me, I know that. That's who was my mother all my life. So that's who will be my mother till the day I die."

"As she should be."

Leslie's stance softened. "Maxine, I need to understand this because I'm struggling." Her voice shook like she was struggling not to cry. "I was alone on my wedding day because I didn't want my perfect sister there judging me," Leslie continued. "I was too ashamed of what you'd say about me, but as it turns out, you are just as scandalous as everybody else."

A tear slipped from the corner of Maxine's eye.

Walter stepped to his wife's side. "Leslie, I understand you're hurt, but you need to watch your tone."

"Walter, no disrespect, but this isn't about you either," Leslie said.

"Just hear her out," he said, his arm protectively going around Maxine.

"So you've known, too?" Leslie replied, her glare turning to Walter. "All this time. You've known that I'm her daughter and not her sister."

"Actually, I didn't. Maxine has carried this burden alone. And you have no idea how it has torn at her." He turned to Stella. "How about we step out and let the two of them talk?"

Maxine's heart raced. She wanted to grab Walter and make him stay. She couldn't be alone with Leslie.

Stella gently touched Leslie's arm. "Are you going to be okay?" she whispered.

Leslie glared at Maxine, but nodded at Stella.

Walter nodded, and Stella followed him out of the room.

Maxine's gaze shifted to the floor. Leslie had so many questions, it didn't seem as if she had enough time to answer them all.

"Why did you hate me, Maxine?"

"I never hated you." Maxine sighed, walked over to the living room window, and gazed outside. "I hated how you got here," she finally confessed.

"You hated that you were promiscuous? That it shattered your good-girl image?" Leslie said.

Maxine sighed as she turned to face Leslie. The pain on Leslie's face broke Maxine's heart. Shortly after Walter Jr. was born, Maxine used to have nightmares that Leslie had found out the truth and never forgave her. This was the face in those nightmares.

"You weren't born because I was promiscuous. I really was a good girl. I tried so hard to be a daughter Mama could be proud of." She inhaled deeply, swallowed the truth that had been buried inside her for years, then released it once again. "Someone that I knew and trusted raped me."

Leslie paused, shock filling her face. "Rape . . . ? I . . . I'm the product of a rape?"

Maxine took a deep breath, then relayed a watered-down version of what had happened to her. Leslie didn't need to know all the horrible details.

Leslie quivered in horror as Maxine finished her story. Maxine couldn't make out whether it was fear, despair, rage, or all three that danced across Leslie's face.

"You said it was someone you knew. Who?" Leslie said. The tone of Leslie's voice let Maxine know that she wasn't going to let this drop. Her first thought was to lie, just to protect Leslie. But that's why they were here. "His name was Kenny. And Mama . . ."

"When did Mama find out?" Leslie said, cutting her off.

Maxine was glad that Leslie hadn't asked more questions about Kenny, because if she had to go down that road again . . .

"Over these last twenty-four hours, I've had a lot of time to think about this, and I believe Mama started suspecting early on," Maxine replied. "I remember, she would watch me at the dinner table and study my face. Whenever she asked me something about how big I was or what clothes I was wearing, I'd just tell her that I was gaining weight, but she knew. When she found out for sure, she sent me to live with Aunt Grace until I gave birth. She was there with me when you were born, and we came back together. From that day, she raised you as her own."

Before Leslie could reply, the door swung open.

"Maxine," Walter cried out, "the hospital just called. We have to get there immediately. Stella is trying to find Star."

Maxine's eyes widened in panic.

"She went into town with the kids."

"Okay, I'll track her down. You three need to get to the hospital—*now*." Walter handed Maxine her purse and the keys to their car.

Neither Maxine nor Leslie asked any questions as they raced to the car. All of their own issues were momentarily tossed to the side as they united in trepidation over what had happened to Mama Pearly.

Chapter 23
Stella

This had been the most agonizing two hours of her life.

"Your mother's blood pressure has spiked," Dr. Woods told them when they'd all rushed through the doors together. "She's in dangerous territory and at risk of a stroke."

"Oh my God, what does that mean?" Leslie cried, and Stella watched as Nona held her up. Nona had arrived with Walter, Star, and Ty shortly after the three of them did.

As the doctor explained some more, Stella watched as Walter held his arm around Maxine and Star and Ty held hands like they were teenagers. Stella leaned against the counter, once again wishing she had someone to support her. She pulled out her phone, but before she could text him, she saw a text message from Lincoln.

Babe, you should be with your mom by now. Please text and let me know everything's okay.

A flash of longing passed through her. Right now, she not only needed Lincoln by her side, she wanted him there. She hadn't expected him to be so concerned about someone he'd heard little about, let alone never met.

I'm OK, Stella typed back. **At the hospital, waiting to see her.**

In just a few moments, a reply. **I want to call but I don't want to**

disturb you. Just know that I'm here praying for her and you. I'm here if you need me. I love you.

She paused, her fingers resting on the keys of her phone. Finally, she slowly typed . . . **I lov** . . . .Then she hit the backspace key, deleting her declaration, and simply typed, **Thank you.**

His concern had momentarily brought her comfort. But now, two hours later, Stella's heart felt like it was trying to escape from her chest as she envisioned life without her mother.

"When will we be able to go back?" Star asked the question they'd been taking turns asking for the last one hundred and twenty minutes.

"I know just as much as you know," Maxine said as she paced the full length of the waiting room.

"I just really needed to talk to Mama," Leslie said, rocking back and forth in her seat as Nona rubbed her back. "She can't die. She can't die."

"No. We're not going to talk like that," Stella said. "Y'all know Mama is a fighter."

They knew it, but the looks on their faces said they were no longer so sure.

No one said a word as they all retreated to their corners.

Daylight had turned to night, and now they shifted. Star lay with her head in Ty's lap, Nona and Leslie's eyes were closed as they held hands and rested their heads against the wall, and Maxine and Walter sat quietly reading their Bibles.

Stella sat in the corner, her legs raised in the chair and pulled in close to her chest. Talking to Lincoln had helped, but she still felt so alone. She had prayed through the night that God would see fit to give her more time with her mother. And when the morning's sun finally peeked its way over the horizon, Stella carried those prayers into the day.

As each of the sisters came to life, they took turns, going to get coffee and taking restroom trips. And every few seconds, one of the Bell sisters checked her watch.

It was about ten a.m. when Dr. Woods walked in. Every one of them jumped up and surrounded the doctor like they planned to keep him hostage until he gave them the news they wanted to hear.

"It's still touch and go," he said.

"When can we see her?" Maxine asked.

"I have given strict orders that none of you can go in the room."

"Doctor, please. You can't do that," Star cried. "I have to see my mama."

"We all have to see her," Stella said.

The doctor shook his head. "I understand, but I'm sorry. We've got to let her rest."

Before any of Mama Pearly's girls could respond, a boisterous voice filled the room.

"Well, *I* need to be able to see her."

Everyone turned toward a woman who looked to be somewhere in her midseventies. She was dressed in a suit that looked like she was about to lead the ushers in Sunday school. But that was not what stood out for all of them.

The woman bore an eerie resemblance to Mama Pearly: the same butterscotch skin, the same hazel eyes, the same curly gray hair, only hers was tucked under a pin hat like she'd just come from a Sunday tea.

Maxine gasped, while the sisters looked at the woman in confusion.

"And who are you?" Stella asked what they all wanted to know.

The woman's eyes met Maxine's, and the slight smile she gave her made the others turn to their sister.

The eldest Bell girl stood there, the little color she had drained from her face. Her eyes were wide, her mouth open. It was as if she was staring at a ghost.

Overhead, a voice boomed for Dr. Woods to return to surgery. "Ladies, just hang tight. I'll let you know when Miss Pearly," he paused as his eyes met the strange woman, "when she can have limited visitors."

Stella's eyes shifted from Maxine back to the woman. Now she stood with a haughty smirk.

"Do you know her, Maxine?" Star said when no one spoke up.

"Of course, she knows me," the woman said. "I'm Paula, your aunt."

"Aunt?" Stella said. "Since when?"

The woman stood erect and finally turned to look at Stella. "All your life."

Maxine still didn't say a word.

"Mama doesn't have any living sisters," Leslie said.

"Yes, she does." The woman fixed her gaze on Maxine. "Doesn't she, Maxine?"

Stella, Star, and Leslie stared at Maxine as she trembled.

"Maxine, what's going on?" Star demanded to know when Maxine didn't say anything. Stella strained the banks of her memory, recalling hushed chatter about someone named Paula. Once, when Stella was a teenager, she'd heard some people at church talking about a missing relative named Paula. But Mama Pearly had dismissed the talk as small-town gossip.

It still took seconds for Maxine to find her voice. Maxine said, "Yes. Th—that's Mama's sister, Paula."

"What?" Star said. "I thought Mama's two sisters died when she was young."

"Oh, I suppose I was dead to Pearly, but I'm here now," Paula said.

"Why are you here?" Maxine asked.

"Because my sister is dying, and I need to be here."

"Who even told you?" Maxine said.

Paula was indignant. "This is my hometown too, you know."

"No, we don't know," Stella said, looking on in confusion.

"It's a shame I had to find this out secondhand," Paula said.

"If you're Mama's sister, where have you been?" Leslie said. She'd been standing toward the back of the waiting room and stepped forward.

Paula turned to her and was about to say something, but then her eyes locked on Leslie. She stared at her, her mouth agape.

"Oh my Lord," she muttered. Paula shook off her temporary shock, then turned her attention away from Leslie. "Your mother and I fell out a very long time ago, but I put all of that aside in my sister's time of need and rushed here."

Maxine turned away, and Walter followed her to the back of the room. Stella didn't know whether to be more in shock at the fear in Maxine's eyes or the shock of this surprise.

"So I'm here now and I need to see my sister," Paula announced before turning to head toward the hallway. "What room is she in?"

It was as if those words gave Maxine energy. She dashed to the front of the room, reaching the exit before Paula. "No, ma'am. No. Ma'am."

"Little girl, if you don't get out of my way," Paula sneered, her lips pursed.

"I am long from a little girl," Maxine said. She raised her chest and pushed back her shoulders. "And the last thing you're about to do is go see my mama."

Star stepped next to Maxine. "No disrespect, *Miss* Paula, but we don't know you like that."

Stella stepped next to Star and added, "And because we don't know you like that, that means our mama didn't want us to. So we appreciate you coming in from wherever you came from. But now we'd appreciate it if you'd go on back."

Leslie was silent but stepped on the other side of Maxine, her effort, in this moment, to stand with her sisters. Nona stood behind Leslie, ready to back up her wife.

"Leave," Maxine said, stepping in front of Leslie. Her voice was firm.

Paula appeared to assess the barrier the women had made to block her from going down the hall.

"My, my, my," Paula finally said. "Pearly's girls are coming together to lock me out. How rich."

When Walter and Ty joined the Bell sisters, she finally took a couple of steps back. "It was a long drive from Jackson, and I could really use some coffee." She pulled the hem of her jacket. "I'm going to go to the cafeteria and the ladies' room. Then I'll be back." She sneered at Walter and Ty. "You might want to call in an army because that's the only way you'll stop me from seeing my sister when I return."

She took another long glance at Leslie before she sashayed out of the room.

Chapter 24
Maxine

The moment Paula was out of their sight, six sets of eyes shifted to Maxine. Without hearing any questions, Maxine knew they were demanding answers. How would she ever be able to escape their probing?

Maxine willed Dr. Woods to walk in with the news that they could see their mother.

Star was the first to speak. "Okay. So what gives, Maxine?" she said.

"What are you talking about?" Maxine said, thinking that playing dumb would give her the time she needed. Dr. Woods would surely walk by and she would be able to call him back in to talk to them. Then they'd forget all about Paula.

Leslie shook her head with disgust. "Mama was right about this family harboring so many secrets."

"But apparently we came by it honestly," Stella said.

"Maxine," Star turned to her again, "what is going on? You knew she had a sister?"

Maxine glanced around. There was no doctor coming to rescue her. Walter's expression urged her to be truthful. Maxine nodded. "Yes," she said.

"Wow! And nobody felt like we should know?" Star asked.

"Why would Mama keep that a secret?" Stella asked.

"You don't understand." Maxine sighed. "It's complicated."

"Then make us understand," Leslie demanded. "For once, stop with the lies and tell us the truth."

Maxine looked into Star's eyes, then Stella's, and, finally, her gaze rested on Leslie. It was the sight of her daughter that carried the most weight in this moment. And Maxine fell into one of the waiting room chairs, feeling the burden of the decades of secrets and lies.

"Mama and Aunt Paula fell out a long time ago," Maxine confessed.

"What kind of falling out could they have that would have Mama saying that she was dead?" Star asked.

"Not only that," Leslie said, her voice sounding like she was in shock again. "Mama was the one always preaching about forgiving family and how all that matters is family and all that you have is family. Do you know how many times I heard that lecture when I would call?"

"Me too," Stella and Star said together, and then shared a glance.

"So how could she even fix her lips to say that when she had an estranged sister over some little fight?" Leslie asked.

"It's a little more complicated than a little fight," Maxine said. "Or even a big fight, for that matter."

"So you know why they fell out?" Star asked.

"You know what I think?" Maxine said. "I think we should just focus on Mama right now. Anything else takes our attention away from where it should be . . . on Mama. We can talk about everything else later."

"No, we need to do this now," Leslie said. "I'm tired of living in a cloud of lies. Just once, could somebody in this family be honest?"

Paula stepped into the waiting room, as if that was her cue, slowly sipping her coffee.

"Yes, Maxine. Why don't you tell them why my sister and I fell out?"

Maxine wasn't sure what it was—maybe it was the way she stood, or tilted her head, or acted like her teenage niece had done something wrong, but for a moment, Maxine was taken back. To the days when Aunt Paula was one of her favorite people. When, before the twins were born, she'd spent summers at her house, where Aunt Paula showed her how to make tea cakes and they had tea parties where she taught her proper etiquette.

"The cat got your tongue?" Paula said, bringing Maxine back to the present.

"No disrespect," Star said, "but I don't like the way you're coming for my sister, so you need to fall back."

"What does that even mean?" Paula huffed.

"It means, please don't make me come out of character. I worked really hard to leave my aggressive ways behind me," Star said. "But I don't mind bringing them out of the closet when I have to."

Paula's shoulders rose all the way to her ears. "How dare you talk to me like that. I'm your aunt."

"So you keep saying," Star quipped.

"Guys, just stop," Maxine said, exasperated. "She is Mom's sister." Maxine knew her voice was weary. But she knew there was only one way this could end: badly.

"Why are you here?" Leslie said.

"It's time we let bygones be bygones." She stood erect again. "And I'm also ready for my apology, which has been years in the making." She glared at Maxine. "Are you going to give it to me?"

She stood, and before she could step to Paula, Walter grabbed his wife's arm.

"Sweetheart," he said.

Maxine snatched her arm away and spat at her aunt. "An apology for what?"

"Your lies."

Maxine's eyes watered as she swayed, like she was struggling to keep her balance. "My lies. Wow. Where is Uncle Kenny, by the way?"

With her peripheral vision, Maxine saw Walter tense, no doubt recognizing the name. Leslie must've been too engrossed in the drama because she didn't react.

"My husband is at the Holiday Inn, resting. He is not well, never has been the same since you ruined our lives."

"This isn't the time," Walter said to no one in particular.

"Somebody better start telling me what's going on," Star demanded.

Paula faced Star like she was happy to share the news. "Your sister seduced my husband."

"Seduced?" Maxine yelled and lurched forward, making Paula take two giant steps back. "Is that how you describe rape?" Walter grabbed her arm again to pull her back.

"Stop it," Paula spat. "You know my Kenny didn't do any such thing."

"I know exactly what your Kenny did." Maxine fought back tears as she continued. "He took my virginity, while you were sleeping in the other room, and he left me with a child. And when my mama tried to ask you about it, you took his side."

"Because I know how little, fast-tailed girls like you operate."

"Wait a minute," Stella said. "You were raped by her husband? Our uncle?"

"Oh my God," Star said.

Leslie was frozen, a look of horror across her face as reality registered.

Paula jutted her chin as she spoke. "If my Kenny had done something so horrible, why didn't you scream? Why didn't you say something? If something did happen, it's only because you seduced my husband."

"Do you hear yourself? I was fourteen!"

Maxine caught a glimpse of Leslie and wished she could retract these last ten minutes. She did not want Leslie to find out who her father was like this.

"This fracture in our family is your fault. That and the fact that your mother tried to shoot my Kenny," Paula said.

"Mama tried to kill him?" Stella said in shock.

"Tell them why Mama took a shotgun after your husband." Maxine was in full-fledged crying mode now.

They stared each other down. "Because you're a liar," Paula said. "Pearly shot my husband because she believed your lies, even though she knew the truth," Paula continued when Maxine didn't respond.

"Get out . . . get out," Maxine trembled.

Walter stepped to her side. "I agree, Ms. Paula. You should leave."

"Gladly. I'm too old for this stress," Paula said, spinning and exiting the waiting room.

Star rushed over to her sister. "Maxine. Are you okay?"

Maxine's legs gave out. Walter caught her just before she hit the floor.

Leslie moved in front of Maxine as Walter helped her into her seat. Her body shook.

"Is . . . is her husband my father?" Leslie said, standing over her. "You said Kenny . . ."

Nona took Leslie's hand to steady her as she let out a painful groan.

"Mama's brother-in-law raped you?" Star said, her hand over her mouth.

Stella took a seat next to Maxine. She hesitated before she reached for Maxine's hand and breathed with relief when Maxine didn't pull away. "Maxine, I'm so sorry," Stella said.

"When . . . where?" Star asked.

For the second time in twenty-four hours, she recounted the rape, only this time her eyes weren't closed. This time, she stared at Leslie the whole time she spoke, as if it was just the two of them. As if this was Leslie's story to hear.

"So Mama really tried to kill him?" Star said when Maxine finished.

Maxine inhaled, then exhaled, hoping she'd be sharing this story for the first and last time.

Maxine hadn't understood why Mama Pearly commanded her to take the twins and go down the street to Mother Channing's house for a while. The lack of answers and the strange way Mama Pearly was acting caused Maxine to drop off the twins and hurry back home. And now, as she tiptoed into Mama Pearly's room, she was glad she did. The hushed tone of her mother's voice mumbling to herself sent fear throughout her body.

"He messed with the wrong one . . ." she muttered.

"Mama . . ." Maxine's heart raced as she watched her mother slide a shell into the chamber of the long gun. The eerie calm that had swept over her had Maxine terrified. Mama Pearly slowly put another shell in. Then another.

"Mama . . . why do you have that?" Maxine whispered. She almost felt like if she talked too loud it would set the gun off.

"Paula and that slimeball husband of hers have lost their minds," Mama Pearly mumbled, though she didn't look at Maxine, and she wasn't sure if her mother was even talking to her.

"Mama, what are you doing?" Maxine asked. To this moment, she'd never known that her mother even owned a gun, let alone knew how to use one.

"Touch my baby, I'm gonna let this steel touch you," she muttered as she put another shell in the chamber.

At the mention of baby, *Maxine's hand went to her stomach. It had been two days since she told her mother who the father of her child was. She'd purposely waited until her daddy had gone on a long-haul run to Alabama. In those two days, her mother hadn't said a word to her, and Maxine had hidden in her room, ashamed.*

But her shame was gone, and now it had been replaced with fear—for her mother. She could tell the fury inside Mama Pearly was building.

Today, it looked like it had boiled over.

"Oh, it's about to be some consequences and repercussions," Mama Pearly muttered.

"Mama, don't," Maxine said, feeling the magnitude of what her mother was preparing to do. "It's okay. I'm okay."

Pearly cocked the shotgun and stood. "No, it's not okay. But it will be soon."

The look on her mother's face had Maxine scared to utter another word.

Mama Pearly pushed past Maxine, the shotgun at her side as she stomped down the dirt road. Maxine had no doubt where her mother was going. To Aunt Paula and Uncle Kenny's house on the corner.

She followed her mother, and inside she was pleading for Mama Pearly to turn back, but it was like her mother was in a different body. Mama Pearly walked on the side of Aunt Paula's wood-frame house, heading over to the towering oak tree where Uncle Kenny was sitting with some of the other menfolk. They were gathered around a scuffed card table, a spread of dominoes in front of them. Each of the five men at the table had a bottle of beer in front of them. They were all in their after-work clothes, just there to enjoy their weekly dominoes game.

Aunt Paula stepped on the porch with a tray of fried chicken when she spotted Mama Pearly.

"Hey, Pearly, whatchu . . ."

Mama Pearly didn't stop as she stomped toward the men like she was on a mission.

"What's wrong with you, Pearly?" Paula asked, scurrying down the steps.

One of the men flashed his toothless grin. "Hey there,

Pear . . . Oh, shit!" he said, scrambling away from the table as Mama Pearly stopped, raised the gun, cocked it, and pointed it straight at Kenny.

Kenny's chair screeched as he pushed it back and threw up his hands in the air. "Now look here, Pearly. Whatchu doin'? Don't come here starting no mess."

"Pearly!" Paula screamed, dropping her tray and racing over to the table. All of the men were staring like they were too scared to move. "What in the world are you doing?"

Mama Pearly kept the gun pointed at Kenny's head as she replied to her sister. "'Bout to blast your no-good husband to Kingdom Come." She never took her eyes off Kenny. This was a rage Maxine had never seen before. "I suggest anybody who don't want to have brain matter on them get to moving."

She didn't have to repeat herself as the other two men still seated around the domino table scurried away.

"Have you lost your mind?" Paula yelled. She stood just feet from Pearly, her arms outstretched like she was trying to make sense of the unfolding scene.

"I hope you got a black dress," Mama Pearly said.

"Mama, no," Maxine cried as she cowered behind her mother. She wanted to grab her mother's arm, but the way she was gripping that shotgun immobilized her.

"Pearly, listen to your girl," Kenny pleaded.

She jabbed the shotgun at him, placing the barrel of the shotgun squarely in the middle of his forehead. "Don't you say a word about my daughter!"

"Pearly, you gotta tell me what's going on," Paula pleaded.

"Ask your husband. Ask him 'bout that baby inside my baby!"

Paula's eyebrows scrunched as she looked at Maxine, then Maxine's stomach, then her husband.

"N—now, y'all know that gal fast tail. Anything she said about me's a lie," Kenny said.

"Maxine doesn't lie!" Mama Pearly pushed the barrel closer, denting his skin and causing him to recoil in fear.

"Whoa, whoa, whoa!" Kenny said, falling out of the chair and onto the ground.

Mama Pearly stood over him, the gun touching his temple.

"Come on, come on, come on," he pleaded. "Think about what you doing. You don't want to shoot me."

"Oh, you have no idea how much I want to shoot you," Mama Pearly said. Though her grip on the shotgun was steady, her voice shook as she spoke. "This family trusted you and you violated my child."

"I—I told you. That girl lyin'," Kenny stammered.

Maxine wanted to scream to defend herself, but the words wouldn't come out.

The pause that momentarily filled the air seemed to give Kenny confidence, almost as if he knew Mama Pearly wasn't really going to shoot him.

His shoulders relaxed. He smiled as he sat up. "You ain't gonna shoot me." He dusted himself off, pulled his dingy white T-shirt back down over his protruding belly. "Don't put that baby on me," he continued. "You keep calling her a child, but she all filled out." His eyes actually went over Mama Pearly's shoulder to Maxine. "Look at her grown-woman body. Ain't nothing childish about her. Plus, word around town is that she like a good time. So that baby daddy could be anybody."

Maxine finally found her voice. "I am not like that!" She struggled to keep the tears at bay.

"Baby girl, Mama got this," her mother said, cocking the gun again.

Paula stepped closer. "Sister, you heard my husband. He wouldn't do anything like that."

"Paula, shut the hell up before I shoot you too," Mama Pearly said.

"*Whatever.*" *Kenny slowly stood, putting his chair back upright. He gently slid into his seat.* "*Like I said, she ain't gonna shoot—*"

Before he could finish his sentence, the blast of the shotgun pierced the evening air, mixing with the howl of Kenny's pain.

"*She shot me! Oh my God, she shot me!*" *He fell back onto the ground, gripping his thigh where blood gushed out.*

"*Next time, I'm moving over an inch, teach you where to put that nasty thing,*" *Mama Pearly growled.*

"*Johnny Lee,*" *Mama Pearly spun toward the man who looked like he was contemplating tackling her.* "*I shot him in the thigh on purpose. The one for you will be in your chest.*"

Johnny Lee held up his hands and backed up.

Paula dropped to Kenny's side. "*Oh, Lord Jesus. Hang on, honey.*"

"*She shot me. That bitch shot me!*" *Kenny howled.*

"*You will live,*" *Mama Pearly hissed.* "*But if you ever come near me or mine again, I'll make sure you don't.*"

She turned and stomped off, with Maxine wobbling behind her.

When Maxine finished her story, all three of her sisters sat in silence. Star was the first to hug her. Then Stella. Maxine looked up at Leslie, praying that she would hug her too.

Instead, Leslie buried her face in her hands and cried.

Chapter 25
Leslie

Leslie stared at the cross hanging on the chapel wall, nestled in between two oversize royal-blue mosaic windows. There was an organ in the corner that seemed too big for this small room, and a communion table covered with a white lace runner with two dying plants on each side. She'd come here seeking peace . . . or comfort . . . or answers, but her mind drifted, and she wondered who was taking communion at a hospital, how'd they get the organ in this room, and when was the last time those plants had been watered.

When she was little, going to church had been the only time Leslie felt like she was wanted by anyone other than her mother. She took comfort in the way the preacher roared about how God loved us in spite of our flaws. And she was obviously flawed, yet she still found some peace.

Peace was completely evading her now.

Leslie had drifted away from her religious background as an adult—now she was more spiritual than religious—but here in the small hospital chapel, maybe God would appear and help her make sense of her upheaved life. Maybe He could help her understand why not only was Mama Pearly not her mother but her father was a rapist.

Leslie's mind went back to one of Nona's speeches about deviant behavior being genetic. Was evil embedded in Leslie's genes? If she had a son, would he be a rapist too? Could people tell, somehow, that she'd been created from violence? Was that why she'd been treated so badly all these years?

She stared at her reflection in the mirror above the altar and wondered aloud, "Which are the rapist's parts?"

Leslie studied her face. Well, at least now she understood the hatred. She was an unbearable reminder of a violent attack. How could she be loved?

"The girls told me you'd left the waiting room. God told me you'd be here."

Leslie looked back at the voice that had intruded on her thoughts. She smiled at the sight of Mama Pearly's best friend.

"Mother Channing," Leslie cried, turning and running into the old woman's arms. The warmth of her embrace made Leslie remember and sent her into tears.

Growing up, next to her mother, Mother Channing did her best to make Leslie feel loved, and it was only in this moment that she remembered that. Why had she forgotten? Was it that negative memories always overpowered positive ones?

"Shhh," Mother Channing said, rocking her as she sobbed. "It's gonna be all right."

After a few minutes, Mother Channing motioned for her to take a seat in the pew.

"I got here about thirty minutes ago. Your sisters filled me in on everything." She shook her head in disgust. "The good Lord knew what He was doing when He made sure Paula was gone by the time I got here. We hadn't seen hide nor hair from her in years and she just show up like this."

"Is it true? What Maxine told us? Is it true?"

Mother Channing gave her a slow nod.

As if she needed clarification, she said, "So he . . ." She paused as if the word that defined her existence was too hard to say. Finally, it squeaked past her lips. "So, he raped Maxine?"

Mother Channing took her hand when she said, "He did."

"And my mother, I mean . . . she tried to kill him?"

Mother Channing nodded. "Yeah. Your mama knew how to work a shotgun. Though, if she wanted to kill Kenny, he would've been dead. But yes, she was livid about what he did to her baby."

"So, you've known all these years too?"

She began to nod again, but then she shook her head. "Yes, but wasn't my place to tell," Mother Channing said, as if she knew that was Leslie's unasked question. "As close as your mother and I were, she never talked to me about what happened to Maxine in detail. All I knew for sure was that Maxine had been violated and she was gonna send her to Detroit to have the baby. Maxine went away, and then a few weeks later Pearly followed. A few weeks after that, Pearly came back to Smackover. You were fresh from the hospital. They drove all the way back from Detroit, because . . . well, your daddy died."

Leslie tried to process Mother Channing's words. "Mama was such an advocate of the truth. How was it possible that she'd been comfortable living a lie? And then everyone just fell in line?"

"No. I was the only one who knew," Mother Channing said. "Your daddy knew Maxine was pregnant, but your mama never told him by who, because she knew Ernest would've killed Kenny, and he would've made Maxine get rid of the baby."

Leslie thought about her father, the story of his death. Now she questioned everything.

"Daddy. I've always been told he died coming to the hospital when I was born. Is that a lie too?"

Mother Channing's shoulders sank. She brushed lint from her skirt, then clasped her worn hands. "Not completely. Your daddy did die in a car accident on his way to Detroit to pick up you, your mama, and Maxine."

So her birth was still to blame for his death? The thought of her mother, coming back to Smackover, with a new baby, a traumatized daughter, and grieving a dead husband made fresh tears spring to Leslie's eyes.

"It's not your fault, suga," Mother Channing said, taking her hand. "You have to know that. You might not understand your mother's decisions, but she was never trying to hurt you. She's human, she's flawed. The most important thing was, she kept this secret because she loved not only Maxine but because she loved you. She told me that a baby shouldn't suffer because of how it was conceived. She believed that with everything inside of her. So she set out to not only protect you but to give you the best life possible."

Leslie dabbed at her eyes as a memory flashed of her mother pressing her hair and telling her, *Don't tell anyone, but you are the most beautiful of the Bell girls because you're different.*

"Honey, as parents, we do the best we can," Mother Channing continued. "We often don't get it right, but I can promise you, everything your mother did, she did in love."

Leslie pressed her back against the pew, digesting Mother Channing's words. "He raped a fourteen-year-old girl and his wife took his side. How could Paula believe him over her family?"

"Women do it every day, but the thing is, sometimes women do it because they really believe the man. That's not what happened with Paula. She knew Kenny wasn't no good from way back. Never has been much of anything." Mother Channing shook her head, disgust written across her face.

They sat in silence for a moment, and with her eyes focused on the cross, Leslie said, "My father is a rapist." When Mother Channing didn't say anything, Leslie added, "What am I supposed to do with that? How do I process knowing I'm a product of rape?"

"Pearly was right about one thing. Being conceived by rape

doesn't define you," Mother Channing said. "It's not just genes that make a person, it's how you choose to live your life. Nurture. Not nature."

They both looked up as Nona entered the chapel.

"Everything okay?" Nona asked, glancing between Leslie and Mother Channing. "I was trying to give you some time."

"Well, hello, young lady. I'm Mother Channing."

"Hi. I'm Leslie's . . ." Nona hesitated, and looked at Leslie.

"She's my wife, Mother Channing," Leslie said, looking straight at Nona with adoration.

Mother Channing cocked her head, studied Nona for a second, then looked back at Leslie, and said, "Your wife?"

Those two words made Leslie's smile fade away. "Mother Channing, please. Don't get all judgmental on me. I can't take it." Leslie sighed.

Mother Channing leaned back a little, like she was trying to get a better look at Leslie. "Judgmental? Now why would I do that?"

Leslie immediately became apologetic. "I'm sorry. I just assumed you would start judging."

"Well, what's that they say about assuming? Makes an ass out of you and me." She rubbed her hands against her lap as she stood. "I got my own sins to worry about, honey. No, I'm not for gay marriage, and that's why I'm not gonna marry a gay person." She leaned over and patted Nona's hand. "Quiet as it's kept, I'm not gonna marry a straight person either."

That brought a small smile to both Nona and Leslie's faces.

"Chile, what you two do is between you and God. Okay? You got bigger things to worry about." She tapped Leslie's chest. "Like healing that hole inside you. When Pearly wakes up, you can fuss her out all you want, then you hug her, thank God for keeping her alive, and we'll all go live as reasonably happily ever after as possible."

Mother Channing grinned like she'd just solved a quadratic equation.

"You make it sound so easy," Leslie said.

"It's only hard if we make it so. Now let me get on this altar and ask God for forgiveness for what I'm gonna do to Paula when I see her." Mother Channing winked as she headed to the altar.

Chapter 26
Stella

For the past hour, Stella had watched as Star doted over Maxine. Her twin sister truly was a different person from the girl she'd known growing up. The rage that consumed her—especially in their high school years—was gone. And though she was still overweight, she'd dropped at least two dress sizes since they'd graduated high school. She genuinely seemed happy. Prior to today, that would've assuaged some of Stella's guilt. Now, it just opened a vault of what ifs.

"I'm going to take Maxine down to the chapel," Walter said, extending his hand to help Maxine stand from her spot in the waiting room. "Call my cell if anything changes." Maxine somberly followed her husband out, moving in a zombielike state.

Moments after they left, Ty stood. "I'm gonna get us something to drink." He turned to Stella. "You want anything?"

"I'm good. Thank you," Stella said, grateful for Ty's acknowledgment.

Ty leaned in and kissed Star like he was leaving for war. "I'll be right back with some tea, baby."

"Can we talk, Star?" Stella asked after Ty was out of the waiting room. Leslie had been gone about thirty minutes and now that it was just the two of them, Stella wanted to seize the opportunity.

Star clucked her tongue, her reaction stoic as she said, "Talk about what?" She folded her arms.

"Come on, Star."

Star sighed, and Stella braced herself for her sister's wrath. Instead, Star leaned back in her seat, stared at Stella for a moment, then said, "I was going to ask you how you did it; you know, stole my identity."

The shame was instant.

"But Ty convinced me that it doesn't really matter. It's not going to change anything."

Stella opened her mouth to explain, but Star held up a hand to stop her. "Do you want to know why I love Ty so much?"

That was an odd question, given the direction of their conversation. "You always have," Stella answered.

Star nodded. "And I always will. But I'm asking, do you know the reason why I love him so much? And the answer is, Ty gets me. From the moment he met me, he got me. He loved me . . . every inch of me. And he taught me to love myself."

Her smile reached her eyes as she continued. "I know you look down on him and how he hustles for a living. But you don't take into account what makes him a good man. Not only is he hardworking, he's a wonderful father. I love that about him, but before all of that, Ty was there for me when no one else was."

Stella knew that. Ty had been the calm to Star's storm.

"Yeah, Ty put up with a lot." Stella laughed, trying to lighten the heaviness. "You were always mad."

Star didn't return the laughter. She looked straight at her sister when she said, "I was mad at the world, especially when we hit high school. You have no idea what it was like, being the *fat twin*, how bad my self-esteemed suffered as I wondered why I couldn't be the *fine* one that all the boys lusted after."

Stella knew what her sister was talking about. Fat and Fine . . . that was what they'd been nicknamed. It started in their eighth year of school. The summer before, Star had ballooned to over 230 pounds and was really self-conscious about her weight, espe-

cially when the boys on the football team called them Fat and
Fine whenever they passed. That didn't last long; it stopped after
Ty gave one of the boys a black eye.

"Do you remember choir practice with Mrs. LeBeurge?"

Turning her attention back to her sister, Stella stretched her
memories, and her mind raced back to the woman known around
town as the Diva of Central Arkansas.

*Mrs. Emily LeBeurge was as close to a celebrity as the
Smackover Public Schools had ever seen. A former Off Broad-
way actress and singer, she'd moved to Smackover with her oil
baron husband. But she'd become known after she hand-
picked a sixteen-year-old girl from her music class and coached
her all the way to the final round of* Star Search.

*For that reason, she was always on the lookout for her next
big star. So when Stella and Star had walked into her music
class on the first day of school their ninth grade year, Mrs.
LeBeurge had zeroed in on Star.*

*"Star Bell, please come to the front," she said shortly after
class started.*

*Star was used to the limelight, so she'd gladly gone to the
front of the class.*

*"I would like you to sing the first stanza of 'Amazing
Grace,'" Mrs. LeBeurge said.*

*"Excuse me?" Star said, her eyes bucking in astonishment.
She wore a new ruffle shirt that Mama Pearly had bought
them for back-to-school, and it wasn't until Star was standing
in front of the class that Stella noticed the buttons stretching
like they were hanging on for dear life.*

Mrs. LeBeurge repeated her request.

"I'm sorry, ma'am, I—I'm not a singer," Star said.

*For some reason, Stella thought it would be funny to give
her sister a hard time, so she'd proclaimed, "She's a really good
singer, Mrs. LeBeurge. She's just acting shy."*

"I knew it," Mrs. LeBeurge exclaimed, her eyes dancing with excitement.

"What?" Star didn't find anything amusing. *"Stella, why you lying?"*

"Stop using such language and do as you're told," Mrs. LeBeurge commanded.

"Yeah, Star. Do as you're told." Stella giggled.

Mrs. LeBeurge used her ruler and hit the table, causing Star to jump. *"Sing!"*

Tears welled in Star's eyes as she opened her mouth. Slowly, she released the words. *"'Aaaaaaaah-maazing gracccce, how sweet the soooound.'"*

The room erupted in laughter, including Stella, who found it hilarious because Star sounded like a wounded cat. Each syllable trembled as the words left Star's mouth. Miss LeBeurge frowned her confusion.

"Star, I can look at you and tell you can sing. Now do this correctly before I send you to the principal's office," she said.

Star fought back the tears as she continued, *"'... that savvvved a wretch liiiiikkkke me.'"*

Now, she sounded like two wounded cats, an injured house dog, and several students fell out of their seats, they were laughing so hard.

Mrs. LeBeurge's eyes grew wide. *"Oh my,"* she said, her hands clutching her pearls.

This boy named Ricky yelled from the back, *"What's wrong, Mrs. LeBeurge, you ain't never seen a fat girl who can't sing?"*

"I take it by your silence that you remember," Star said, snatching Stella from that day.

Stella had thought it was funny then. Even after Star refused to speak to her for a week.

"It was just a joke," Stella said. Now, decades later, that excuse sounded pathetic.

"Everything was a joke when it came to me."

"But you had stuff going for you too. You were the smart one, without even trying. You had Ty, who was crazy about you."

"I was also young and I couldn't understand why Ty wanted me. Why anyone would want me. None of you guys realized how much your fat jokes hurt. The 'she's pretty to be so fat,' and 'if you just lost weight, you'd get all the guys.' Remember our fifteenth birthday when Reverend Sams came for dinner. Everybody had cake but me. Reverend Sams told Mama I wasn't ever gonna get a decent husband if she let me eat that cake."

"Yeah, but she still gave it to you."

Star sighed away decades of hurt. "It's what Reverend Sams said. It's what everybody said . . . all of the talk and 'jokes' left scars that were etched on my heart. Yes, academically, everyone marveled over me . . . but it didn't take away the way I felt inside."

Stella thought back to how Star would fake sick on the days they were supposed to do height-weight testing, how she claimed to have twisted her ankle the day they had to run a track meet in PE, and countless other times Star would bail out of school activities. Stella had chalked it up to her sister heading down the wrong track, never to her avoiding having to face her weight issues.

"People looked at me with disgust, so I ate to cope. And I got angrier and angrier." The memories were obviously painful, but Stella didn't know what to say. Star continued. "Mama Pearly tried to make me feel better by constantly telling me I was beautiful, but that's what mothers are supposed to do, so I didn't believe her."

That crushed Stella. There were so many regrets Stella had, but she knew years from now, when she looked back, this would be one of her greatest regrets. If she had been more in tune, maybe she could have helped her twin.

Because since she'd been here in Smackover, she'd been blasting Maxine for not knowing their mother was sick. And she had been unable to tell how bad the woman she was connected to in the womb had been suffering inside.

"I'm sorry, Star," Stella said, her apology carrying more weight that she could ever explain.

Star nodded, and Stella hoped that was a sign of her accepting her apology. Star said, "I get why you did what you did."

Stella's heart skipped as she smiled. She hadn't been expecting that.

"It was foul," Star continued, snatching Stella's smile away. "Unbelievably foul. And there will always be a piece of me that will wonder what would have happened if I'd had that chance. If I'd had the same opportunities as you."

Stella lowered her eyes. That shame would stay with her the rest of her life.

She glanced up, a mist covering her eyes.

"I may not understand it, but I know God is faithful, and I have faith that He positioned me right where I was supposed to be," Star continued.

Now Stella had to blink to stop her tears from falling. It was amazing, she'd taken something so serious from her sister, and here Star was extending her grace.

They were twins, but for the first time, Stella really could see how different they were. Because if the tables were turned, Stella had no doubt she wouldn't be able to extend the same grace her twin had given her.

Chapter 27
Maxine

Maxine had just been wondering if she should suggest they all go home and rest when Dr. Woods entered the waiting room. Like the last time he'd entered, the Bell sisters bum-rushed him, eager for news about their mother.

"How is she?" Maxine was the first to speak.

He released a relieved sigh. "Your mother is a fighter. We've got her heart rate and blood pressure stabilized and she's awake and alert. I'm stunned at her turnaround, but I shouldn't be. Miss Pearly always has been a praying woman. I guess God answered her prayers. She pulled through a scary time."

"What?" Star exclaimed. "Does that mean she's going to be okay?"

"It means she's out of danger."

The sisters clapped and hugged and laughed their way through their embraces.

"Hold on, hold on," Dr. Woods said. "She's out of immediate danger, but the cancer is still there. Your mother still has a long road ahead. We've stopped the bleeding and got her stabilized, but the cancer has spread to other organs. We can do chemotherapy to prolong her life just a little bit more—" He paused, like the next words pained him, "—you have about six-to-nine months."

That sucked the joy out of the room.

"I'm so sorry," he told the solemn sisters. "I wish I had a better outlook." He took a deep breath and stepped out of his professional demeanor to gently reach out and squeeze Maxine's hand. "I know you're anxious to see your mother."

"Yes, can we go now?" Maxine asked. Though she wanted to fall into a puddle and cry, she couldn't help but be grateful that God had given her a little more time with their mother.

"Yes, give the nurse about twenty minutes," Dr. Woods said. "I've ordered some more tests. I'd like to get those wrapped up. Then you can go back. Now, please excuse me. I have to get to another patient."

They stood in shocked silence, even moments after he was gone. Again, Maxine was the first to speak, "Okay, God has given us more time with Mama. So, let's just do all we can to make these six months the best she has and pray that Mama is among those who beats this." Her gaze went from one of them to the other. Her words were genuine as she continued. "I know you all have to get back to your lives, but maybe we can work out some regular visitations, you know, where we all come spend time with Mama on a more consistent basis."

They exchanged glances, and one by one, they all nodded.

"Yeah, I'll come back more," Stella said.

"We all will," Star added.

Walter stepped up. "Look, I know this isn't the news we wanted to hear. But Mama Pearly has lived a good life, and you all are about to give her the best six-to-nine months or however much longer God sees fit. And the first step in this is what you've already given to her." His eyes went from one sister to the next, briefly resting on each sister as he continued, "You've given her what she's dreamed of, and that's for her girls to be unified as a family."

The thought brought a weak smile to each of their faces.

Finally, Star said, "Can we make that promise to Mama to stop the fighting and try to bring some joy into her life?"

Everyone nodded.

Maxine smiled her relief. "This is going to make Mama so happy. The day she collapsed, she was talking about how much she wanted her girls to reconcile."

While Maxine truly did want them to do this for Mama Pearly, she hoped it would propel Leslie to open her heart to forgiveness.

"Leslie, are you in?" Stella asked since she'd not said anything and was just standing there with a solemn look on her face.

She slowly nodded, but it was Nona who spoke. "Yes, we are a six-and-a-half-hour-drive away. We'll come back at least monthly."

She'd said *we* with conviction, causing Leslie's eyes to meet Maxine's. Maxine knew the way she responded would begin the healing process—if there was to be one.

Maxine pushed back her convictions, deciding to focus on the more important task of getting Leslie to forgive her.

"That's perfect," Maxine said with a warm smile.

Her response caused Leslie's shoulders to dip with relief.

"Has it been twenty minutes?" Leslie asked. "You think we can go back now?"

"Better to ask forgiveness than permission," Star said, pushing past Maxine and heading down the hallway. Everyone quickly followed, including Walter and Ty.

Star was the first to enter the hospital room, but her sisters pushed in right behind her. And they all cried tears of joy when they saw their mother sitting up in her bed.

"Hey," Mama Pearly said, her voice weak. Her lips were dry, but her smile was wide.

"Hey Mama," Maxine said, the last to hug her. "You look good."

Her hand went to her stringy curls. "Hush, you know I don't." Warm satisfaction filled her face as her gaze went to each daughter. "How y'all doing?"

They were silent, but it was the way they looked at one another that told Mama Pearly what she wanted to know.

"Did y'all do what I said?"

They exchanged glances.

"All secrets out?" she continued. She glanced at Maxine for confirmation, and her eldest child nodded.

Mama Pearly turned to Leslie first. Her eyes were filled with regret. "I'm s-sorry, baby girl. For not telling you . . . Don't be mad at Maxine. I just wanted . . ." She took a deep breath, as if she were summoning up strength to continue. "It wasn't the right . . ." She inhaled again. "Hate takes too much energy. Try love instead."

A tear slid down Leslie's face as she took her mother's hand. "It's okay, Mama . . ."

Mama Pearly's eyes went over Leslie's shoulder to Nona. "Is that . . . is that your girlfriend?"

Leslie's teary eyes widened in shock. "You—you know?"

She nodded, "Suspected; you just seemed happier lately. Figured you were in love. Then, when we talked a few weeks ago, you slipped up and talked about your girlfriend."

Leslie stood like she didn't know what to say.

"Come here." Mama Pearly motioned for Nona to come closer.

"Hi, Miss Pearly." Nona took Pearly's hand and squeezed it. "I'm Nona."

Mama Pearly gave a weak smile. "Nice to meet you, Nona."

Leslie bit down on her lip, took a deep breath, then said, "Nona is my wife."

Maxine drew a sharp breath. Her first instinct was that this didn't need to be done here, but she quickly dismissed that thought when Mama Pearly said to Leslie, "Does she make you happy?"

"She does."

"Then that makes me happy."

Mama Pearly closed her eyes for a moment, opened them, squeezed Leslie's hand, then pulled away and extended her hands to Stella and Star. As Leslie and Nona eased out of the way, the twins stepped up and locked fingers with her.

She looked at Stella first. "I know Star. She's going to forgive you, but you got to work on forgiving yourself." To Star, she said, "By the time we found out, I knew nothing good could come from the truth. That's what I thought at the time." She looked to all her girls. "Y'all carried secrets because that's what I taught you, but secrets . . . just . . . fester." She took a deep breath and turned back to Star. "I'm sorry I could never get you to believe the truth . . . that you're a beautiful, intelligent woman. Thank God for Ty," she added, smiling toward Ty as he eased up behind his wife.

"Always," he said.

"It's okay, Mama," Star said.

Mama Pearly turned back to Maxine. "And Maxine, I thank you and Walter for taking care of me. But it's time for you to enjoy life, get out of Smackover . . . at least visit other places. This is home, but there's a whole world out there to explore."

"Mama, hush your mouth, talking like you're going somewhere," Maxine said, waving away her mother's comments.

"I'm just saying things that needed to be said."

"Okay, so you've said it, so it's fine," Maxine said.

"I'm just glad everything's out now." She smiled as she sank into her pillow, exhausted from the verbal exertion. "I'm tired now . . . Gonna rest."

"I really want to stay with you a little longer," Leslie said.

"I know, but it will be better if you can come back tomorrow when I have a little more energy." She closed her eyes.

"Well, we'll be back in the morning, Mama," Stella said.

"I love each of you," she said without opening her eyes.

In unison, they replied, "We love you too, Mama."

Maxine stepped to the bed and kissed her mother's forehead. Stella, then Star, followed, and finally Leslie moved to her bedside. She stared at Mama Pearly for a few moments, and Maxine held her breath as she watched.

Finally, Leslie leaned over and kissed her forehead. "Good night, Mama. See you in the morning," she said.

And that let Maxine breathe.

Chapter 28
Leslie

The smell of fried fish greeted them the moment they stepped out of the car. Walter, Maxine, Star, and Ty had been in one car. Leslie, Nona, and Stella exited behind them.

"My goodness," Star said, peering toward the elderly man in a button-down beach shirt, khaki shorts, with black dress socks up to his knees, leaning over a cast-iron fish fryer. "What's going on here?"

Leslie released a small chuckle. "It looks like a man is frying fish in the front yard."

The man dropped a piece of fish into the grease and waved. "Hey y'all!" he said.

Walter closed his car door and chuckled. "I had Deacon Charlie come by and get us some fish going for dinner," Walter said. "Why are you in the front yard, though?" he asked him.

"Best fish is fried outside," Deacon Charlie said, waving his tongs in the air. "Had to park my deep fryer here because there's no plug outside, so I had to run an extension cord from inside." He picked up another piece of fish, shook the cornmeal off, and dropped it into the piping hot grease. He jumped back as specks of grease splattered in the air.

"Well, let's go in through the back," Walter said to everyone, "because the deacon is blocking the front door."

"Yep, I'll have the fish finished in about twenty minutes," Deacon Charlie said.

"I'll drop some French fries in the pot too," Maxine said.

They left the deacon and made their way around to the back.

"Good food, good meat, good golly, can't wait to eat," Stella sang as they ascended the steps on the back porch. The good news about their mother had put them all in a much better mood.

Leslie shook her head, thinking that her sister must've forgotten about fried foods and what that could do to her waistline.

Star laughed. "You remember Mama saying that all the time?"

"Yeah. She picked it up from Daddy. It was his favorite expression whenever there was food on the table," Maxine said as she walked in the house.

"That is like, so lame," Cheyenne said. She was sitting on the back porch, drawing on a large pad. Jordun and Jabari were running around the large sycamore tree and Lil Ty was asleep in a playpen next to Cheyenne.

"Thank you for watching your brothers," Star said, picking up Lil Ty and taking him inside.

"Don't mind me. I'm just the hired help," Cheyenne said.

Ty shook his head at his daughter and headed in behind his wife.

Leslie and Nona were the last to reach the back porch and just as Nona opened the screen door, Leslie said, "Nona, you can go on in. I'm going to sit out here and talk to my niece for a minute."

Just as quickly as the words left her mouth, Leslie reminded herself that Cheyenne was actually her cousin. How in the world would she ever be able to reconcile this new life?

As Cheyenne rocked in the chair, she lifted her pad once again, and as Leslie leaned against the post, together, they took in the sight across the way. They quietly watched Mr. Calhoun gather his dozens of cows together.

Cheyenne's glance moved between the field and her pad as she sketched away. "How did you guys ever live here?" she finally asked.

Leslie shrugged. "When it's all you know, it's all you know."

"I can't imagine growing up on a farm."

"This isn't a farm," Leslie said.

"Ummm, Mama said you guys had chickens. That sounds like a farm to me."

"Well," Leslie nodded, "I guess you have a point there. What you doing?" she asked, taking a seat in the chair next to Cheyenne and peering over at her drawing pad.

"Drawing." She stopped and looked at Leslie. "Can I ask you a question?"

"Of course."

"Why haven't we ever seen you?"

That made Leslie tense. She shifted uncomfortably as she thought about all the times she'd blown off Star's invites, when she'd made excuses. She'd lost valuable time holding on to the past. The bad part was Star hadn't really done anything to her. She'd just lumped Star into part of her past that she wanted to forget.

"You did see me when you were little," Leslie said.

"Yeah, but I'm sixteen now. There's been a long time between when I was little and now."

That stung. "I don't know," Leslie said, looking away from her. "I've just been kind of busy."

Cheyenne returned to drawing. "Like, I was looking at colleges in Houston, but I didn't know anybody. So, I mean, I was just thinking that, you know, if I had known you were there, I could have come visit you."

That made Leslie sad. She'd never thought about the value she could've added to Cheyenne's life just by being there.

Cheyenne continued. "We're not bad people. Well, Jabari and Jordun are." They enjoyed a moment of laughter. She paused, her pencil resting under her chin as she added, "Mama said you write books."

"I do."

"At home, she brags on you to all her friends like you're Beyoncé or something."

"Not hardly." Leslie paused, moved by Cheyenne's words. "But she brags on me, for real?"

Cheyenne nodded, without missing a stroke. "She's real proud of you, always talking about her famous sister. One of my teachers reads your books too. She asked me if I could get you to sign one. I told her we didn't know you like that."

Leslie flinched. "I'm sorry about that, Cheyenne."

She paused once again and looked straight at Leslie. "I know Auntie Maxine says I'm just a child and should just stay out of grown folks' business, but . . ."

When she paused, Leslie gave her a nod. "Go ahead. I value your opinion."

"Why everybody in this family, well, except for my mama, but I think it's because my daddy keeps her cool . . . but why are y'all so angry?"

Leslie weighed her question and thought back over all the interactions over the last two days. She'd cried more in these past forty-eight hours than she had in the last forty-eight months. She'd felt more than anger—she'd felt a rage that she didn't even know was inside her. But it wasn't just her, it was all of them, and Leslie realized that anger had become their fifth sibling. "We had extenuating circumstances. For me, my siblings," she paused for a moment, "especially Maxine, were just really mean to me growing up. And I guess I just never forgot that."

Cheyenne shrugged. "I'm mean to Jordun and Jabari because that's what I do. But can't nobody else be mean to them."

"Well, our relationships are a little more complicated than that."

Cheyenne resumed her drawing. "I don't get it, but maybe I'm not meant to get it. Grandma Pearly is always saying family should love one another. At home, I feel the love. Here, I don't. Being here makes me sad."

"Well, we've all promised to work on that," Leslie assured her, committed now more than ever to fulfilling that promise.

Cheyenne nodded like she didn't really believe it.

Leslie didn't know what else to say, so she simply said, "What is that you're drawing?"

"My portfolio. I like drawing fashion."

"Fashion? The way you were looking across the field, I thought you were drawing something in nature." Leslie leaned closer so she could get a peek. "Wow. These are awesome." Then, Leslie frowned. "That's interesting."

"What?" Cheyenne asked, glancing between her aunt and what she'd drawn.

"Your models. They all look the same." She pointed to their faces. "Why did you make all your models dark brown?"

"Huh?" Cheyenne asked.

"You don't want to have some variety?"

She frowned her confusion. "No. My models look like me."

Leslie summoned up the words that people had told her all her life. "Well, don't let the color of your skin hold you back. You still can accomplish whatever you set your mind out to."

Cheyenne leaned back, narrowed her eyes, and looked at Leslie like she was speaking a foreign language. "What are you talking about?"

"I'm just saying, you know, I'm dark-skinned. So I know sometimes it can be hard." Leslie found herself stumbling over her words.

"Hard? To do what?"

"Just . . . I don't know . . . shine in this family when we . . . look so different," Leslie said.

"But it's not hard."

Now, Leslie was the one to lean away to get a closer look at Cheyenne. "What do you mean? It's not?"

"Um, I wouldn't trade my skin color for anything in the world," Cheyenne said, cutting her off. "My boyfriend—don't tell my mama because she be trippin'—he said my smooth espresso complexion is what he likes. He said that's what attracted him to me. But even if he didn't tell me that, I already know that I'm beautiful."

"Wow." Leslie paused, shocked to hear those words from a brown-skinned teenage girl. "I love your confidence."

Cheyenne returned to her drawing. "If I don't think I'm pretty, how can I expect anyone else to think that about me?"

Leslie chuckled. "Who would've thought it."

"Thought what?" she said, looking up.

"That I could come to Smackover, the place where I'd learned so many not-too-good things, but I could sit with my sixteen-year-old niece and learn such a valuable lesson."

"That's not a lesson. That's common knowledge. Yeah. I mean I heard the whole light-skinned-is-pretty being a thing. But that beauty is in the eye of the beholder is a thing too. It's not just some cliché. So whether I have pink or black hair. No matter the hue of my melanin, I'm just me. Beautiful me."

Leslie stared at Cheyenne in awe. Yes, times were different; brown-skinned women like Lupita Nyong'o, Naomi Campbell, and Viola Davis graced the covers of magazine, showcasing the beauty of dark skin, but the scars of Leslie's childhood were not easily healed. She marveled at how Cheyenne wouldn't have to deal with that.

"I wish I had your confidence when I was your age," Leslie said.

"You could. Maybe you chose not to." She laid her drawing pad in her lap and leaned forward like she was about to school Leslie. "I look at it this way. I could be all sad about what I don't have and what I don't look like. Or I could just make the best of what I do have and who I am." She shrugged. "And I'm not just making the best of it, I'm living it because there's nothing wrong with the way I look."

Leslie wanted to give a standing ovation in appreciation of Cheyenne's words. "You are superamazing," she said.

"Thanks." She closed her pad. "I can't get inspired with the smell of cow poop in the air, though, so I'm done. You think Aunt Maxine has MTV here? It's time for *Wild N' Out*."

"*Wild N' Out?*" Leslie had never heard of that show, but still, she said, "I think I can use some of that right now." She stood and reached out her hand to Cheyenne. "Let's go see if Maxine has MTV." Cheyenne tucked her drawing pad under arm, took Leslie's hand, and they walked inside.

The Bell home was experiencing something it hadn't in a long time—joy.

They'd devoured every piece of Deacon Charlie's catfish and now everyone was sitting around the living and dining room watching Jordun and Jabari, who were doing a dance-off.

"Watch this," Jabari exclaimed as the sounds of Michael Jackson's "Wanna Be Startin' Somethin'" filled the small transistor radio that sat atop the TV. "Grandma Pearly said this was her favorite move." Jabari hunched over, did a robot move, then some kind of jiggle that caused Star to bury her face in her hands.

"Lord, help my rhythmless son."

"No. This is Grandma's favorite move," Jordun said, jumping in front of his brother and doing a James Brown split.

After a few seconds of more dancing, Ty stepped up, "Okay, boys. Y'all go outside and play while we still have a little sunlight."

He didn't have to tell the boys twice; they raced out the door like they loved every moment of country play.

"You know, Jabari dances just like you," Maxine said as the house phone rang.

Walter stood and walked into the kitchen to answer it.

"No, ma'am. I had rhythm at his age," Star protested.

"You really didn't," Stella said. "Remember when you tried to do that praise dance that Easter when we were thirteen."

Stella stood and mimicked an awkward move, outstretching

her arms, wiggling her fingers while curving her body in a snake motion.

"Oh my God, I did not look like that!" Star said.

"No, I remember that," Leslie said. "We were all so embarrassed."

"Except Mama." Maxine laughed. "She stood up talking about, 'Look at my little Debbie Allen.'"

Their laughter was interrupted at the sight of Walter in the doorway.

Maxine was the first to notice the somber expression on his face. "What's going on, sweetheart?" Maxine asked.

He moved in slow motion as he stepped toward her.

"Walter?" Maxine sat up in her seat. "Who was that on the phone?"

All eyes were on him, all laughter ceasing, a dreary silence hanging above them.

"Th—that was the hospital," he stammered.

"Is Mama okay?" Star asked, sitting upright in her seat.

His eyes filled with tears as they locked with his wife. "She . . . Mama Pearly is . . . she's dead."

Chapter 29
Maxine

Death was a part of life, but that didn't make it any easier.

Maxine stared at her reflection as she sat at the vanity in her bedroom. She'd put one pearl earring in her ear and sat with the other clutched in her hand. Once she put in that earring, her ensemble would be complete and it would be time to go. Maybe if she never put in the earring, she'd never have to go bury her mother.

This past week had been the longest of her life. One minute she was enjoying some rare quality time with her sisters, the next she was back at the hospital listening to Dr. Woods explain how their mother had another massive stroke and never woke up.

I'm sorry, she's gone.

Dr. Woods's words would forever haunt her. The connection she had with her mother was now permanently broken, and that reality left Maxine feeling like a boat without a rudder.

Maxine had been all prepared to dive right in and get to planning her mother's funeral. But Mother Channing had shown up the day after Mama Pearly's death with a folder where her mother had planned everything out, down to the type of flowers she wanted at her funeral.

"She didn't want to give you girls any reason to fight," Mother Channing had said.

The fact that as the prospect of death hung over her, Mama Pearly was concerned about her daughters' fighting, produced a twisting feeling in Maxine's heart.

But there literally had been nothing for them to do, and that left nothing but too much idle time for Maxine. That meant more time to mourn.

Maxine had expected all of her sisters to leave and show back up just in time for the processional in the funeral.

But none of them had left. Stella had set up an office at the motel, and she spent this past week burying herself in her work. Maxine couldn't be mad at her, though. She understood people grieved differently and for once, she tried to recognize her way—nonstop tears—shouldn't automatically be considered the right way.

She inhaled strength, dismissed the ridiculous notion that delaying would mean denying, and placed the pearl earring in her ear just as Walter peeked his head in their bedroom door.

"Are you ready?" he asked. "Everybody's out front."

"How am I supposed to ever be ready for this? How can anyone be ready for this?" Maxine said, continuing to stare in the mirror as she adjusted the collar on the black, knee-length dress, which felt like it was suffocating her.

He walked in the room and stood next to her. "You aren't. You just know that she's in a better place."

Maxine knew that her husband meant well, but she wanted to yell that the place for her mother was right here.

Walter hesitated, his expression shifting. "Um, so Paula is here." Another pause filled the space between them. ". . . With her husband."

Maxine's head whipped in his direction. "Are you kidding me?"

"I know I'm a good Christian man, but I needed an extra side helping of holy to keep from finishing the job your mama started." She could tell by his labored breathing, he was trying to be calm for her sake.

Maxine swallowed. She hadn't seen Kenny in thirty-six years.

When she'd come back from Detroit, Kenny and Aunt Paula had moved to his hometown of Jackson, Mississippi, and no one in Smackover had publicly talked about them since.

"He had the audacity to show up here?" she asked.

"I think Ty's out talking to them. We asked them to just go on to the church. Paula is indignant. She feels like she should be in the family procession," Walter said.

"No, absolutely not. Not with him."

"That's what I figured. I told Paula she could ride. But if she insisted on him going, they needed to go on."

"Thank you," Maxine said. It was times like these when she was so grateful for her husband. "Does Leslie know he's here?" The idea of Leslie having to face Kenny—on this of all days—made her stomach churn.

"No. She's in the bedroom going through some photos with Nona."

"Good. I'd like to keep it that way," Maxine said.

Star tapped on the door. "You okay?" she said, easing in. Maxine looked at her, thankful that through this all, Star had been the beacon of strength. Though Ty had returned to Hot Springs for the week with the kids, Star had stayed behind and done all the things Maxine knew she wouldn't be able to do.

"I'm going to go on out," Walter said, giving the sisters privacy.

"Mama would be so proud of you right now," Maxine said, swallowing the lump in her throat.

That brought a smile to Star's face. "I tried to make her proud."

A beat. Then Maxine said, "I'm sorry I revealed that about Stella and Spelman."

Star shrugged. "It's okay."

"I think Stella buries herself in her work to run from the guilt," Maxine said. She'd revealed that secret to get Stella back, but it hadn't made her feel vindicated. It made her feel guilty.

"I hear you. I have forgiven her," Star said. "Just like Leslie will forgive you for the way you treated her."

While Leslie had remained here, she'd been distant. No longer angry, but definitely distant.

"I doubt that very seriously," Maxine said, standing to her feet.

"In time she will," Star said.

Before they could say another word, they heard Paula's voice booming from the other side of the door.

"Maxine," she yelled, "this so-called religious husband of yours is being very un-Christianlike, telling me and my husband that we can't ride in the family car."

Maxine looked at Star. "You're in charge today. Go handle your aunt."

"You ain't said nothing but a word." Star spun around and burst into the dining room. "Aunt Paula, what you're not going to do is *this*," Star said, meeting her before she made it to Maxine's bedroom.

Stella and Leslie appeared in the doorway. No words were spoken as they stepped next to Leslie. Maxine eased up behind them.

"Here we go again, ganging up on the poor old woman," Paula said, her gaze going from one Bell sister to the next.

"Now's not the time. It's not the place," Star said.

Stella eased closer to her twin. "You hadn't talked to my mama in twenty-five years. Why don't you and your perverted husband keep pretending we don't exist? Go to the church in your own car."

"Or we can ask the police officer out there on his motorcycle to throw you out altogether," Leslie said.

Paula gasped. "You would never . . ."

Leslie stepped up, the authority in her expression shocking Maxine. "What's the statute of limitations on rape?" Whatever it was, Maxine knew it was long over, but maybe Leslie was banking on Paula not knowing that.

Paula was dumbfounded. "My husband didn't rape anyone."

"I'd be willing to take a DNA test." Leslie's eyes locked with Paula's. "Maybe we can't prove rape. But we can let it all play out in front of a jury and let everybody in the town talk about it. In fact, in case you didn't know, I'm a pretty popular author. I could contact *Essence* and *Ebony* and even the newspaper in Jackson, Mississippi. Everyone would love to hear the story of how I came into existence."

Paula's hands started trembling. She was obviously horrified at the mere thought.

Leslie continued. "Now, if you don't leave my sister alone, you'll be reading about it on the blogs and in your church newsletter before you even get out of the service."

Paula stood glaring at Leslie. Then she looked at each of her nieces before she huffed. "There's a reason I haven't bothered with any of you in all these years. Every one of you are just as awful as your mother." She turned and stomped away. The screen door slammed behind her.

Her exit lifted the heaviness in the room. Maxine was moved that Leslie had come to her defense. "Thank you," she told Leslie.

They stood in awkward silence.

"Well, we better get going," Star finally said. "You know, Mama would have a fit if we were late to her funeral."

Maxine stood, everything inside her wanting to hug Leslie. "Leslie, I'm so sorry. For everything."

Leslie nodded. She didn't say anything. But she did extend her hand toward Maxine. Maxine fought back a tear as Leslie took her hand and led her out to the waiting car.

Chapter 30
Stella

Why was the sun shining? Last night it had thundered and rained and Stella had expected today would be dark and dreary. That was appropriate weather to bury her mother. Not this sun-beaming, beautiful day.

It was almost like Mother Nature didn't want her to mourn her mother. But as she sat here, sandwiched in between Star and Leslie on the first pew in Sweet Home Missionary Baptist Church, Stella knew no matter what the weather was like outside, inside her heart, it was gloomy.

The small church was packed to capacity, which, according to the sign on the wall announcing last Sunday's offering collection of $632, was 500. Stella recognized many of the people, from her mother's coworkers to the woman who did her hair. Black people. White people. Young and old. It seemed like the whole town was here to say goodbye to Pearly Bell.

There were so many things Stella needed to say. That she *wanted* to say, but nothing was coming up. Stella had made the mistake of thinking she could step up and speak at her mother's funeral, but when the time came, not only did she go mute, she was paralyzed in her seat. She knew if she stood, no amount of willpower would force her legs to the front of the church.

Luckily, when Walter called for her and she didn't move, he quickly moved the program along.

"And now, Sister Sophie will come up and pay tribute to Miss Pearly with song," Walter said, motioning toward a young woman wearing a navy dress and donning bright red hair.

As she made her way to the microphone, Stella stared at her mother's casket. The pearl-colored casket was closed, surrounded by wreaths and flowers. On each side of the casket sat two large candles and a 24 x 36 photo of her mother in a pink suit and a large pink hat that dipped down in her face. Stella had never seen that picture, but she instantly loved it.

The young vocalist began singing, and immediately people jumped up and shouted, "Sing, baby!" and "Yes, Sister Sophie!"

Stella resisted turning her full attention to the singer, but eventually, the words gave her no choice.

"I sing because I'm happy . . . I sing because I'm free."

The young vocalist's perfect melodies had Stella swaying as she pushed back the pain in her heart.

Stella's sob could no longer be contained. She buried her face in her hands. Star wrapped her arm around Stella's shoulders and pulled her tight, and together they swayed as the vocalist wrapped up.

". . . His eye is on the sparrow and I know He watches me."

Stella sat, her heart bleeding a river of regrets. Why hadn't she called more? Come back and visited more? Would the sadness she felt now forever corrupt her soul?

Those questions plagued Stella the rest of the service, much of which had been a blur.

Now, as they sat at the gravesite, waiting to lower the casket into the ground, Stella found everything coming back into focus. The minister was speaking, but Stella focused on the decrepit yet elegant chapel just feet from where her mother would be buried. She noted the wall of ivies crawling up the side of the building.

This final resting place would make her mother happy.

"Thank you to everyone who came out to help us celebrate the life of an amazing woman," said the associate minister, who had stepped in so that Walter could be with his wife.

Someone—Stella assumed it was someone from the funeral home—handed each of the Bell sisters a rose as the minister continued talking.

"To Leslie, Star, Stella, and Maxine, your mother loved each of you from the depths of her soul. She was not perfect, but everything she did was done in love and with her heart in the right place," he continued. Though there were about fifty people who had accompanied them to the gravesite, he kept his attention on them. "After our parents die, we take another look at them. We realize all they did for us and gain a new perspective on their lives. As you reflect on the memory of Miss Pearly, take comfort in knowing that she was surrounded by love in life and in death. As you begin your journey of healing, know that you are not alone. You have one another. And you have God."

His words were meant to provide comfort. But as Stella watched Ty with Star, their children behind them, Walter with Maxine, and Nona with Leslie, she felt all alone.

"Ashes to ashes . . ." the minister said, nodding as the gravediggers began turning the handle to lower the casket.

Stella sat in the row of chairs in front of the casket, the rose clutched in her hand, her heart racing with each crank as they lowered her mother into the ground. The minister motioned for the sisters to come to the casket for final goodbyes. First, Maxine and Walter. Then Star, Ty, and the kids. Then Nona and Leslie. Stella didn't know how she found the strength to stand, but she did, and eased to the casket to say a last goodbye to the human being she had always loved most. She gently placed her rose on the casket.

"Mama . . ." she moaned. Stella felt her legs give way first. They felt like putty, unable to hold her up anymore. And she felt her body slipping to the ground. She heard the gasps of her sisters, but then she felt the strong arms keeping her from hitting the pavement.

"I got you. I got you," the voice said.

Stella's eyes rolled into the back of her head and she tried to will herself away from this public spectacle of fainting.

"It's okay. It's okay," he said.

Her eyes fluttered open. "Lincoln?"

"Yeah, baby, I got you. It's okay."

"What, what are you doing here?" Stella stammered.

"I'm here for you. I'm always here for you."

Stella didn't ask any more questions as she threw her arms around his neck and cried.

Chapter 31
Leslie

"My mama is gone."

Leslie mumbled the words. Even though it had been two days since they buried her, it still didn't feel real.

It had been a long week, but they'd managed to settle most of Mama Pearly's affairs. Most of her belongings had been packed up, thanks to Star. Maxine couldn't bear to step foot in their mother's bedroom, let alone pack up her stuff. Leslie and Stella tried to help, but they ended up crying every five minutes, a photo sparking a memory, a piece of clothing sending them into heartache, or their inability to part with belongings.

Finally, after they'd collected the things they'd wanted to keep for themselves, Star shooed everybody out while she finished sorting herself.

"I need to get out of the house for a bit," Stella said. "I'm going to take Lincoln into town and show him around."

Since he'd shown up at the funeral, Leslie had been impressed with the man who Stella had introduced as "just a friend" from Atlanta. The way that man was doting on her, he definitely was more than a friend. Or wanted to be anyway.

As soon as they left, Leslie headed to the back porch, where she'd left Nona about an hour ago. Her wife knew when to give her space, and she'd allowed Leslie that time with her sisters.

"Hey," Leslie said, stepping out onto the porch. "Whatchu doing?"

"Hi, hun. I'm almost finished with this novel. It's amazing." Nona held up the book with the woman standing in front of a massive library collection on the cover.

"You'll have to tell me all about it on the way home."

Nona closed the book and leaned back in the rocking chair. "It really is peaceful here."

Leslie took in the scenery and an assortment of memories engulfed her: Henry Taylor, her mother's handyman installing her a tire swing on that old sycamore tree; the first time Mama Pearly had slaughtered a chicken in front of her, wringing its neck, then chopping its head off. The chicken's body flailed around the yard for five minutes. That had traumatized her for weeks, and sent her sisters into a laughing frenzy. The countless games of hide-and-seek with her sisters. The memories brought a smile to her face. Where had those memories been all this time? Why had she only taken the bad times with her to Houston?

"Any idea who that is?" Nona pointed to a white, four-door Buick that was parked across the street from the house. "There's a man in there. He's just been sitting there the whole time I've been out here."

Leslie peered toward the car, then slowly descended the steps on the porch.

"Leslie," Nona called out.

"It's fine." She waved her assurance. "This is Smackover. Probably somebody is just lost."

The man noticed Leslie coming toward him and he stepped out of the car, staring at her in awe. One look at his espresso skin and Leslie knew exactly who he was.

"What do you want?" she asked, stopping.

Kenny stood on the edge of the property line, like he was fearful that if he sat foot on Mama Pearly's land, she would raise from the dead and shoot him again.

"Can I talk to you?" His voice was feeble, like his frame, which was being swallowed underneath a two-sizes-too-big suit. He was bent over like he was in the early stages of scoliosis. The bags under his eyes were indication of years of hard living. Patches of gray hair adorned both sides of his head, which was completely bald in the middle.

"Talk to me for what?" Leslie was disgusted at the thought that this man was her father.

He shifted but didn't reply.

"What in the world would make you think I'd want to hear anything you have to say?" Leslie asked.

His gaze shifted to the ground, then back up at her. "It's scary how much you look like my sister."

Leslie didn't know what she was supposed to do with that, so she just repeated, "Why. Are. You. Here?"

He let out a heavy sigh. "I just came . . ." He stopped, tucked his hands into his pockets, shifted his weight from one foot to the other, then continued. ". . . I don't know, I just wanted to see you. I'm your daddy."

That made Leslie let out scoffed laughter. "Are you serious? Daddies protect their daughters. They tell jokes, bounce their daughters on their knees, scare off their boyfriends, embarrass them in front of their friends. You're a stranger. To me, anyway. You were a trusted uncle to my sister."

The verbal admonishment made him try to stand upright. He put strength behind his words now. "I know what I did was wrong, but that was a long time ago. And I was hoping . . . Anyway, the Good Lord ain't bless me with no kids, and I was hoping, you know, that me and you could get to know each other. I'm sick; MS," he said. "Don't know how much longer I got on this earth."

She folded her arms again, then raised an eyebrow, as if to say, *What does that have to do with me?*

He continued, "I ain't got no excuse for what I did. I was

young and foolish. Wish I could take it back." He paused. "But then you wouldn't be here, now would you?"

He had the nerve to say that, like it was something she should be grateful for.

"Look, mister, whatever your last name is," Leslie began.

"It's Hayward. You a Hayward."

"No. I'm a Bell. I will always be a Bell." She stopped him before he could say anything else. "You are a man who was able to violate the trust he built with his wife and her family and then walk away without punishment. You were able to cause pain and suffering in a child's life—because make no mistake, Maxine was a child—then move on without any repercussions. The destruction you caused was just a chapter in your life. It was the whole book for me and Maxine."

Her words brought shame to his face. But she didn't care as she continued. "I don't know if you came here expecting to be absolved of your sins. But it's not my place to forgive you. I don't have anything to forgive you for."

"Just don't want you to hate me." His voice was back to being feeble.

"I wouldn't give you that power. You don't mean anything to me," she said.

"It wasn't my fault. Paula said . . ."

She thrust her palm in his face. "Just stop. You're not going to blame this on my aunt. You're responsible for your own actions. You're responsible for raping Maxine. So you need to get right with her and God. Not me. I got nothing for you."

He looked like he was about to protest when his eyes went over her shoulder. She turned and saw Maxine stomping across the yard toward them. Leslie held up her hand to stop Maxine.

It didn't matter, because as soon as Kenny saw Walter a few feet behind Maxine, fury across this face, he took several steps back. "Tell Maxine I'm really sorry," Kenny said before waddling back to his car and taking off.

Leslie turned and headed back toward the porch. She didn't feel how she thought she would feel, meeting her father. There was no hatred. In fact, in that moment, she was grateful that Mama Pearly had decided she was worth living, that Mama Pearly had protected her. And instead of focusing on all that was wrong in her life, for once, Leslie decided to focus on what was right. Seeing Kenny made her realize that fathers were people, and people can sometimes be monsters. There was no playbook to draw from when it came to being the daughter of a rapist. There were books about divorce, about mourning the death of a parent, about dealing with a parent who has been sent to prison for other types of crimes. But no rules on how to handle such a unique position. So she needed to stop trying to figure out how she was "supposed" to process her situation. She knew one thing: she could either accept that uncomfortable truth or deny it completely. There was no halfway.

She decided to accept it. And let it go.

"What did he want?" Maxine asked when Leslie met her in the middle of the yard.

"To apologize to us."

Maxine pursed her lips as she glared in the direction he'd sped off.

"It's up to you whether you forgive him. I don't have room in my heart for him either way," Leslie said.

Maxine's attention turned back to Leslie and her shoulders sank—the anger at Kenny leaving with him.

A momentary silence hung between them. "What about me? Any room to forgive me?" Maxine asked.

Nona watched from the porch, Walter, the yard.

Hate takes too much energy. Try love instead.

As her mother's words swirled in her head, Leslie stared at her sister, then answered her with a hug.

Chapter 32
Stella

For the first time since she'd put her mother in the ground, Stella bore a happy smile. And it was all because of the joy on Lincoln's face.

Lincoln had stepped in from the moment they'd left the graveyard, not leaving her side during the repast. He made sure she wanted for nothing. If she was thirsty, before she could ask for a glass of water, he was there, handing it to her. He'd even contacted her assistant and told her, Superwoman was "taking some time off."

"I can't believe I'm eating a real, live, homemade ice cream float," he said as he dipped the spoon into the glass cup, scooped up ice cream, and slid it into his mouth. He closed his eyes and savored the flavor. "Mmm, just like my grandma used to make."

Stella couldn't help but giggle. "Really? All that over an ice cream float?"

He released a heavenly sigh, then held up a finger to correct her. "A *homemade* ice cream float that's absolutely amazing," he said as they slid into one of the three booths in the front of Adell's General Store.

Stella had taken Lincoln to the only grocery store in town to get a drink, and he'd gone crazy when he saw the soda fountain.

Mr. Adell, whose grandfather founded the store back in 1927, relished Lincoln's excitement and personally made him a supersize float.

"Man, I would've stayed in this place when I was growing up if I lived here," Lincoln said as he pushed another scoop in his mouth.

Stella glanced around, surprised by his reaction. She'd never seen it as anything other than their town store. "Really?"

He pointed around the store. "Come on, now. Can't you see this jewel? Where in Atlanta can you get bait, feed, milk, eggs, T-shirts, feminine hygiene products, *and* a homemade ice cream float?"

She laughed because he was serious. They were interrupted when an elderly woman approached their table.

"Stella?" The woman inched closer. "Why, Stella Bell, that is you."

"Mrs. LeBeurge." The sight of their ninth-grade music teacher brought another smile to Stella's heart. She stood and hugged the woman, who looked as if she had aged every bit of the twenty-four years since Stella was in her class. She had her hair in a tight bun, but it was thin, revealing her scalp. Rouge rested in the wrinkles of her peach skin and the heavy mascara looked like it was weighing down her eyes. She wore a white, lace dress and a rust fur stole, but her voice was proper, like she was teaching an etiquette class.

"It has been years since I've seen you," Mrs. LeBeurge said. "Miss Pearly was so proud of you, said you were down there in Atlanta taking the city by storm." She grew somber as she patted Stella's hand. "I'm so sorry for your loss. We're all going to miss her around here."

"Thank you, Mrs. LeBeurge."

Her smile returned as she looked at Lincoln. "And is this your husband?"

"Not yet." Lincoln winked, and for a change, Stella didn't immediately balk at the thought. Lincoln stood and shook Mrs. LeBeurge's hand. "It's a pleasure to meet you, Mrs. LeBeurge. I'm Lincoln."

Mrs. LeBeurge was smitten as her eyes roamed up and down Lincoln's six-foot-three physique. "Impressive," she said to Stella. "I always knew you would do well for yourself, Stella Bell."

Stella wanted to remind the woman she once told Stella to consider a job at the Piggly Wiggly, but she chose positivity and simply said, "Thank you."

"Well, I really must be going. I retired from teaching five years ago and spend my days caring for Mr. LeBeurge, who is in the last stages of Alzheimer's, and it simply takes its toll on me." She held her hand to her chest, exasperated. "But I love him dearly, so it must be done."

As soon as she walked out the door, Stella and Lincoln exchanged glances and burst out laughing.

"She was a music and drama teacher," Stella explained.

"Well, that was obvious." Lincoln laughed. "And where is she going in a mink stole in August?"

"I know, right?" Stella shook her head. "Coming to the store is probably the highlight of her week."

They settled back in their seats and continued eating their ice cream floats. Stella was grateful for the reprieve from the heaviness of the week. If Lincoln hadn't been here, she probably would've still been under the covers in her mother's bed, overcome with grief.

"This is actually a quaint little town," Lincoln said after a few minutes. "And say what you want, I heard a little pride in your voice as you were showing me around."

She'd taken him by her school, which surprised him that it was a K–12 campus all in one. They'd visited the fishing hole, where she'd gotten her first kiss, and the library, where she spent her summers devouring books.

"Your hearing must be off then, because I'm not proud of this place," Stella said, losing her smile.

"Why do you do that?" Lincoln asked, turning serious.

"Do what?"

"Diminish where you're from?" He shrugged. "There is nothing wrong with wanting something more, but this was the place that employed your parents, kept you safe, healthy, and educated you. It's the place your mom tucked you into bed, and you built memories that will last a lifetime. It's part of your identity. That's nothing to be ashamed of."

Stella weighed his words. She'd been ashamed of her hometown so long that she didn't know how *not* to be. "I don't know. I guess I just always felt bigger than this place."

"And that's okay, but you don't have to erase your past for a different future. This is a wonderful place, especially because I know it lay the foundation for the amazing woman you are today." His smile returned. "Change your perspective. It could change your life." He glanced over to the counter, where Mr. Adell was counting money in the antiquated cash register. "You think he'll make me one of these to go?"

"I'm sure he'd be honored to." Glancing at Lincoln finishing his ice cream float, Stella couldn't help but feel she'd diminished him too—regulating him to nothing more than a good time. But his being there, his love and concern—his ability to encourage her alternative thinking—had her ready to reconsider.

It was time to go. Three weeks before, Stella would've said it was time to "go home," but now she was home. It had taken her mother's death to get her to see that.

Stella and Star had been sitting out back reminiscing ever since Stella and Lincoln had returned from sightseeing.

Nona and Leslie had already hit the road to return to Houston, and Stella and Lincoln had an 8 p.m. flight out of Little Rock, so they needed to get going as well.

"Hey Lincoln," Star said as he peeked out the back porch screen door.

"Hey." He looked toward Stella. "You ready to go?"

"No," she said solemnly. She didn't want this time to end.

"That's okay," he said with a wide smile. "I saw a plot of land down the road. We could get us a double-wide and put it on there and you don't ever have to leave."

Stella playfully groaned. "Uh, yeah, I'll be ready in five minutes."

They all laughed as he said, "Take your time. I'm going to put your bags in the car."

As soon as the screen door closed, Star looked at her sister and whispered, "He's a keeper."

Stella couldn't help but smile. It felt good to have someone take control of her well-being, to be able to share the emotional weight of supporting her and stepping up in ways she didn't expect.

"Did he really Uber from Little Rock?" Star asked.

"Girl, yes. Said he wanted to be able to drive me back. It cost more than the plane ticket."

"Well, he may be just what the doctor ordered for your happiness."

"Sometimes I feel like I don't deserve happiness, especially now. Maybe I'm destined for an unhappy outcome."

Star shook her head. "No, ma'am. That's one of the many tricks that grief plays: it makes you think you don't deserve happiness. You do. We all do."

They sat in silence for a moment until Stella said, "Star, before I go, I just have to tell you again, I really am sorry."

Star held up her hand to stop her. "I told you that was a long time ago. And who knows? I might've gotten to Atlanta and let one of those cute boys from Morehouse turn me out, and I wouldn't have Ty or my beautiful children. So everything happens the way it's supposed to." Her smile turned sympathetic as she took Stella's hand. "That's the thing that you never have understood, Stella. You've run from your life. All your life that's been your MO. You've always wanted something more."

"Is there anything wrong with that?"

She shrugged. "I guess not, but at the same time, sometimes the best things are right in front of you."

"Yeah. Guess I blocked out the good times I had here," Stella said.

"You think?" She motioned around. "This might not be who you are now, but it's your roots, and roots determine how you sprout."

Just as Star finished her sentence, Lincoln peeked around the back.

"No rush, babe, but the car is loaded." He blew her a kiss and walked back to the front.

"Don't miss out on blessings because you can't see that."

"Are we talking about Smackover or Lincoln?"

"Both. You have a good guy right in your face and you can't see it."

Stella sat pondering her sister's words. She hadn't been looking for love, but Star was right. She wanted it. And now she believed she wanted it with Lincoln.

"I don't know what—or who—you're waiting on," Star continued. "Not sure if you think your Prince Charming is going to drop out of the sky with his seven-figure job. Even if he does, something is going to be wrong with everybody." She motioned toward the area where Lincoln had stood just minutes ago. "That man loves you. He seems like he treats you well. And yes, he's rough around the edges, but he seems like he brings you joy. You can't be so busy building a life that you forget to live."

"I like my singlehood." Even as the words left her mouth, Stella had to ask herself if that was really true.

"Tell that to somebody that doesn't know you. All those years of playing dress up with dolls and making them your babies, you can't make me believe that you just lost that desire for motherhood."

Stella was silent.

"Exactly," Star continued. "My point is, you're not going to find the perfect man. He only comes once."

"Are you talking about Jesus?"

Star giggled. "I know. I sound like Mama, right?" That brought a smile to her face. "I'm just saying, sissy, love the life God gave you. Stop trying to create a different one."

"Who are you? And what have you done with my twin?"

"I'm older and wiser. I know love. I've known love with Ty, and trust me, this is happy. When you walk in happiness, negativity can't stay long."

Stella stood and hugged her sister. She welcomed the embrace Star gave her in return. "I forgot how much you bring to my life. I hate that we've missed all this time together," Stella said once they'd pulled apart.

"Well, we have the rest of our lives to make it up. Matter of fact, Cheyenne and the boys can come stay with you for the summer so you can bond. I assure you, Lil Ty will kill all desire for motherhood."

On cue, Jabari came bursting through the screen door, Jordun quick on his heels.

"Maaaaammmmma!" Jabari screamed as he raced past them. "Jordun is trying to kill me!"

Jordun knocked over Star's coffee cup as he chased his brother. "Gimme back my stuff!"

"Ooh. Yeah. I don't know if I'm ready for that," Stella said as she watched them race across the yard.

"You're not." Star laughed as she shook her head, then knelt down to clean up the shattered ceramic cup. "Baby steps."

Stella watched as Jordun tackled Jabari and they began wrestling.

"Um, so you're not gonna stop them?"

"Girl, no. Let them work all that energy out before we hit the road. That way they'll sleep all the way home."

"You've really got this motherhood thing down, huh?"

Star stood and dumped the shattered pieces into a trash can in the corner of the porch. "No, I don't. I just do the best I can and recognize that my good enough is good enough. You'll see when you have kids."

Stella stared out into the yard. "I'm almost forty. I think I missed my window for kids."

"Nope, you still have time, but you'd better hurry. Trust me, you don't want to be sixty chasing after teenagers."

The two of them laughed as Lincoln raced over, pulled Jordun and Jabari apart, and started wrestling them himself.

"I bet Lincoln would make a good father," Stella said as the boys united in their quest to take down Lincoln.

"I bet he would too." Star smiled as she stepped next to her sister. "I guess that means you agree with me that he's a keeper."

"I tap out! I tap out," Lincoln cried as both boys piled on top of him.

Her family had just met Lincoln and he blended right in. The way Jordun and Jabari were giggling and cheering like they'd really defeated Lincoln warmed Stella's heart.

"Twinsie, I think I might have to agree with you. My eyes are open and now I see."

Epilogue
Stella

Stella smiled as she stood at the massive, floor-to-ceiling window that framed the Atlanta skyline. The last time she'd been here, in the Belmont Hotel, not only had she been trying to figure out how Lincoln had received an invitation to the event, but she'd spent half that night trying to find a way to get rid of him.

Tonight was a different story. Lincoln was not only all up in the place, he'd been the one to rent it out.

Stella turned away from the view and glanced across the room, where Star and Ty mingled with some of Star's friends who had flown in for the event. Apparently, Star was in a book club and they'd made this a girl's trip, with all fourteen members attending. She marveled at the life her twin sister had created. In spite of.

In the past six months, they'd honored their mother's wishes and made an effort to see and talk to one another more. It would be years before any of them healed from Mama Pearly's death—if ever. But at least for Stella, each day eased the rawness of her grief and things like this party, time with Lincoln, allowed moments of lightness to find their way back into her life, the way a sunrise creeps around the edges of a drawn window shade. It was not that time would heal her wounds, but it did help shift her perspective.

Stella turned away and strolled to the edge of this little private area in the back of the room. Lincoln had cordoned off this space for her and her sisters, so that they could have privacy, or just have a place where they could take a little reprieve. That was what she needed right now.

She'd been in a state of euphoria from the moment she'd entered the ballroom. There had to have been more than one hundred fresh pink orchids, her favorites, strewn all over the room. She inhaled the scent of fresh flowers the moment she'd first walked through the door. Stella didn't have time to appreciate all of that, though. She'd been rushed by many of the one hundred guests, and she'd mingled and mixed, making her way through the crowd for more than an hour. From local celebrities to some of the players from the Falcons, not to mention all of her friends and work associates, everyone was dressed in their after-five best as they chatted, laughed, sipped champagne, and listened to the jazz quartet that played on the stage.

Even now, as Stella peeked out into the ballroom and watched people chatting while they lined up around the long buffet tables, she had no idea how Lincoln had pulled all this off.

Since her mother had passed away, Lincoln had earned major points by being loving and compassionate, but his stock went through the roof when he'd suggested that she and Star celebrate their birthdays together—at his expense. At first, his offer had made her raise her eyebrows because ever since their relationship began, most of their few out-of-the-bedroom excursions were going Dutch, at best, or picking up the tab all fell on her when he was between events or gigs.

However, the stars had been shining bright upon Lincoln. His private catering business had picked up so much that he'd had to hire two more chefs. And in the six months since her mother had passed, he'd had three serious acting gigs, one that was some top-secret project for OWN that he'd just finished shooting. So even though it had been her instinct to want to pay for this, she'd stepped back when he'd assured her that not only wasn't this a burden, this was something he very much wanted to do.

"Hey beautiful."

From behind her, soft lips pressed against Stella's neck and she inhaled, her nostrils filling with the fragrance of Tom Ford. She spun around and greeted Lincoln with a smile. He said, "You are working that dress."

Looking down at her fuchsia one-shoulder minidress, she waved her hand. "Oh, this thing? Just a little something I threw on." She wiggled her hips, and the dress inched higher up her thighs.

Lincoln leaned away, as if he wanted to get a better look. His eyes shone with appreciation. "I've never heard Chanel described as *little*," he said.

The fact that he recognized her designer was just another indication of how he'd done a full one-eighty since the last time they were here.

Stella smiled her approval at Lincoln's appearance. He looked amazing himself in a black turtleneck, black slacks, and a silver Armani jacket. Another one-eighty.

"When you said you wanted to plan Star's and my birthday party, I never envisioned this." Stella motioned around the room.

Tapping his finger against her temple, he said, "That's because you're always underestimating me." He grinned. "But that's okay. I have a feeling that will stop soon enough."

She tilted her head, wondering what he meant. But instead of asking, she said, "Well, you outdid yourself." She motioned toward the double swan ice sculpture sitting in the middle of the massive buffet, the table covered with all her favorite foods— everything from salt-and-pepper salmon to Jamaican jerk pasta to mini champagne glasses filled with shrimp and grits. "I have a question."

"What?"

"Is that really pink glitter in the ice sculpture?" Her amazement was in her tone.

Lincoln chuckled as he nodded. "I can't take credit for that one.

I told the event planner I wanted your favorite colors—fuchsia, black, and silver—throughout and she ran with it."

Stella was impressed; he'd remembered that? She couldn't even recall when she'd told him that. Surely it had been some random conversation, probably when they'd first started dating and were getting to know each other.

"Jodi was also a big help," Lincoln added.

That was the only disheartening thing about the evening. Jodi's aunt had died suddenly, so her best friend had to rush to her family in San Diego.

But even though she was sad that Jodi would miss the party, Stella had been thrilled that Jodi and Lincoln had found common ground to plan this event. When Jodi and Lincoln had come to her to announce their collaboration on this *grand affair*, she'd been thrilled that they would be willingly working together.

"Two of the people who love you most will do all the planning," Lincoln had told her.

Jodi had added, "That means you have to release that planning gene in you and let us handle it all."

Stella had gone along with them, answered all their questions about her and Star's "must-haves," and then, she'd prayed that one of them wouldn't be calling her for bail money.

"Well, it's all simply marvelous," Stella said, leaning in to kiss Lincoln again.

"It's not every day you get to celebrate your fortieth birthday," he said.

"That *we* get to celebrate." Star's voice floated over their shoulders before they faced her.

Like Stella, she wore a silk, one-shoulder mini-dress, only hers was black, which she insisted on because she'd only lost nineteen of the thirty pounds she'd been working on for this party.

Ty was standing next to his wife, and Stella had to admit he looked great in his black silk shirt and black slacks.

"Yes, that *we* get to celebrate," Stella repeated Star's words as she hugged her twin.

"Thank you making me a part of this day," Star said to Lincoln and Stella.

"I'm just happy we get to do this," Stella said. "It's been a long time since we celebrated our day together," she said as she put her arm around her twin.

Since they'd returned from Arkansas, the two of them had talked at least three times a week. They still bickered about money. But it was nothing like the way they used to. Having her twin back in her life had brought Stella a happiness she didn't even realize she missed. In fact, Star's ability to dive into things that made her happy in order to deal with her grief had been eye-opening for Stella, and why she'd welcomed this party.

Not only did she and Star talk often, all four of the Bell sisters talked via conference call at least once a month. That had actually been Nona's suggestion, when she'd told Stella—in confidence—that Leslie was having a hard time healing and had started indulging in destructive methods, like drinking. Their monthly calls appeared to be good for Leslie, and between that and therapy, Nona said she'd been doing much better these last few months.

"Well, I'm just so happy to be included," Star said, drawing Stella's attention back to the party. "You know there's no way I would've ever had a party like this on our budget."

Ty raised an eyebrow. "What? I could've thrown you a shindig like this if you wanted it." He pointed to the ice sculpture in the middle of the buffet table. "Except for that. Glitter in ice. I don't think I would've thought of that."

They all laughed until Lincoln pointed toward the door. "Looks like your sisters made it."

Star and Stella turned to see Leslie and Maxine standing near the entrance. Stella smiled as she took in her sisters. Maxine, who held onto Walter's arm, wore a peach satin dress, so appropriate for church, while Leslie stood next to Nona wearing a very stylish white pants suit, which would have been appropriate for an interview with the *New York Times*. Stella guessed they'd both misread the part of the invitation that called for after-five chic. A security guard motioned for the four to follow him.

"I'm going to check on something with the event planner, then I'll be right back," Lincoln said as her sisters walked toward their private area.

When the security guard unclasped the red velvet rope and signaled for them to enter, Star squealed, raised her hands above her head, and rocked her hips. "*It's my birthday. It's my birthday*," she said, dancing over to her sisters. "Hey y'all."

"It's *our* birthday," Stella said, walking up.

"*It's our birthday, It's our birthday*," Star continued singing.

"I'm so glad you guys made it."

"We're glad to be here," Leslie said as Nona waved to everyone. "We waited at the hotel for Walter and Maxine so we could all ride together."

"I'm sorry we got here so late, but duty calls," Walter said.

Stella nodded. He'd called and told Stella that he had to preside over the funeral of one of his longtime deacons, so they wouldn't be able to enter the party with her and Star. Walter had been so apologetic, repeating that if there had been anything else he could do, he definitely would have done it.

"No problem, I'm just glad you were able to get Maxine on the plane." Stella turned to Maxine. "How was the flight?"

"It was better than I thought it would be," Maxine said. The way she was clutching Walter's arm, she was acting like she was still on board the turbulent plane. "But it was still rough."

Stella nodded her understanding. Maxine had never been on a plane before, and when she'd first invited her sisters to the party, she'd half-expected Maxine to come up with an excuse. When Maxine had said, "I'll be there," Stella had been more than surprised, she'd been pleased. When Maxine had added, "Thank you for inviting us," Stella had gone from pleased to grateful.

"Hello all," Lincoln said, entering the circle they'd formed. "We've been waiting on you. We have you some VIP seats up front."

"Oooh, VIP," Maxine said, finally relaxing and releasing her grip on her husband. "I feel special."

"You are," Lincoln said. "We have a little presentation, so come on in." He turned to Ty. "You ready?"

Ty nodded, and Star and Stella frowned in tandem, then exchanged glances.

"Maxine and Leslie, can you two make sure my girlfriend and her twin get to their seats?" Lincoln asked.

Maxine's smile was wide. "Of course."

As soon as he and Ty walked away, Maxine raised an eyebrow and stepped closer to Stella. "His girlfriend?" she whispered.

Stella beamed. "Well, yeah," she began, trying to sound all casual. But then the next words poured out of her. "Lincoln and I are officially together. Have been since Mama's funeral."

"You've been with him six months? I thought we stopped keeping secrets." Leslie playfully pushed her sister's shoulder.

Stella shrugged. "It wasn't a secret. It was just under wraps."

"Seems like the same thing to me." Leslie chuckled.

Stella didn't try to hide her adoration as she looked at Lincoln heading to the stage. "Well, you know now," she said. "Last secret. I promise."

They enjoyed a moment before Stella continued, "I really am glad everyone is here to help us celebrate."

Maxine nodded, and the smile she'd worn since she came into the ballroom, faded, just a bit. "I was worried after Mama . . . that we would permanently drift apart."

Stella took her hand. "I know, but a promise is a promise."

"And can you believe Stella paid for this whole party? And didn't complain one time?" Star said cheerfully, breaking the heaviness of the moment.

Maxine and Leslie feigned surprise, and Stella rolled her eyes.

"Well, one reason I didn't complain is because I can't take the credit," Stella said. "This is all Lincoln."

"Aw, that's so sweet," Nona said.

Leslie did a head nod toward the stage. "Lincoln and Ty are shooting us the evil eye, so we'd better get to our table."

The Bell sisters filed out from the back of the room, passing the scores of people standing around the high-top tables in the ballroom. Each of the sisters took their seats, with Walter and Nona seated next to their spouses.

"May I have your attention, please?" Ty said into the mic. "The host has something to say."

"Thanks, man," Lincoln said as he took the microphone. "Thank you all for coming to help us celebrate this fortieth grand affair."

Ty leaned closer to Lincoln so he could speak into the mic. "Yes, I am very happy to celebrate the most beautiful woman in the world."

"Wait a minute," Lincoln said, snatching the mic away. "I have the most beautiful woman in the world."

"Aren't they twins?" someone in the audience called out.

"That honor goes to me," Walter yelled from his seat.

Laughter filled the room.

"Let's just say that honor goes to all the Bell girls." Lincoln chuckled. He turned his attention to Star and Stella. "Can you ladies step up here, please?"

Stella and Star glanced at each other; then they stood and Stella reached for Star's hand as they made their way onto the stage. They released hands but stood in between Lincoln and Ty. Lincoln motioned to Ty, who stepped in front of his wife.

Ty held up his glass. "Star, I've loved you all my life. You are my very best friend and I thank God every day for you. Here's to eighty more birthdays."

"Ohhh, no, I don't think so." Star giggled before kissing Ty.

It was Lincoln's turn, and he held up his glass. "And to Stella, our journey to each other was a little more complicated. But you are the best thing that has ever happened to me. I don't want to do this thing called life without you by my side anymore. I know that I didn't check all your boxes. . . ."

"You do now . . ." she mouthed.

". . . but I'm happy you opened your heart to love again," he continued. "More importantly, that you opened it to love with me." He set down his glass on the floor and reached into his pocket. "And if you would do me the honor," slowly, he moved until he was down on bended knee. He pulled a gold box from his pocket. "I would like to spend forever making you happy."

Now there was a chorus of *Aahs* and gasps filling the room.

"Lincoln, what are you doing?" Stella's eyes widened, shock all over her face.

He ignored her question and simply said, "Marry me."

Stella looked into his eyes and hesitated. Her brain went into analyzing mode, and she thought of all the points: They hadn't talked in depth about marriage. Over the past months, she had moved from *never* to *I can see that*, but were they ready for marriage? Was Lincoln ready? Yes, he'd had a couple of great months, but he was still building his career.

And then, Stella did something she'd never done before—she told her brain to shut up, as she shouted, "Yes!"

She looked down at the gold box and held out her hand for Lincoln to slip the ring on her finger. But then he opened the box and lifted a small blue velvet drawstring bag.

"Wh . . ." she said, taking the bag from him.

"Open it." He eased up off the floor.

Stella smiled as she studied the bag. This was different. She slowly pulled the gold string and the bag fell open to reveal a massive, glistening loose diamond.

Lincoln must've seen the confusion on her and the guests' faces because he said, "You are a one-of-a-kind woman, who deserves a one-of-a-kind ring. This diamond, all four carats, was carefully selected by me. And if you're free on Friday, we have an appointment with Jacob the Jeweler to design the setting, anything you want."

More *awwws* erupted throughout the room, this time accompanied by applause. Stella had no words. She'd imagined a moment like this, becoming engaged to a man she loved, but never this—never a loose diamond.

She clutched the bag for a moment longer, then threw her arms around Lincoln's neck as her guests clapped and shouted their approval.

Star turned to Ty, her hands raised in a questioning manner. "How are you gonna top that?" Star said.

"Woman, please," Ty said, shaking his head and taking a sip of his champagne. "We're already married, with five kids. They're our diamonds."

Star laughed as she hugged her husband, "You're right about that, babe."

"Happy birthday, baby," Lincoln said, his lips meeting Stella's.

Over these past few months, Stella had fallen in love with Lincoln, even though there was a corner of her mind that always questioned whether he was the man for her. But today, as she kissed him from her soul, she knew there was no doubt at all that he was.

"Are you sure you don't want to stay?" Stella asked Nona as they stood in the door of Stella's hotel suite.

The party had wrapped up about an hour before. Walter and Ty had retired to their rooms. Lincoln was still down in the ballroom, making sure everything was cleaned up and wrapped up from the party. Nona had walked back with the sisters to Stella's suite, but after just five minutes, she'd excused herself, saying that she wanted to go back to her room to rest.

"You should stay," Stella said.

"Thank you, but this is sisters' night," Nona said.

Leslie smiled as she kissed her wife. "Good night, sweetheart. I'll be to the room shortly."

"Enjoy yourself, enjoy your sisters." Nona glanced at Stella. "You guys need this."

Stella draped her arm through Leslie's. "She's in good hands. Good night."

Nona smiled her approval as Stella closed the door. She turned to Leslie. "I like her. She seems good for you."

"She is," Leslie said with a smile.

"How are you? Really?" Stella asked.

Leslie's smile spread to her eyes. "I'm good, really. Nona told me she told you about my drinking, so you can stop acting like you don't know."

"I figured you would tell me when you wanted me to know."

Leslie rubbed the back of her neck, as if she was rubbing away the pain of the last few months. "I guess it's easier to self-destruct than it is to practice self-care," Leslie said. "Nona helped me see that the liquor was only clouding my grieving process. She said I had to face the pain directly, and write my way through it. So I wrote a book. It's my first nonfiction on healing."

"I think we all need to read that one," Stella said. "But can I just say I'm happy to see you and Maxine making progress?"

Leslie glanced over Stella's shoulder at Maxine and Star in the living room area of the suite.

"Me too," Leslie said. "We still have some healing to do, but I've forgiven her and Mama. I've been trying to get her to go to therapy with me, but you know she still has that I-take-my-problems-only-to-God mentality."

"That's Maxine," Stella said.

"But let's talk about you," Leslie said, switching gears, and the excitement of the night returned. "Can I tell you how much I love seeing how happy you are? And girl, that proposal! I thought you said he was a broke and struggling chef."

"Mama used to always say *don't count anyone else's money*. She was right," Stella said. "Apparently, that top-secret project he was working on at OWN was a pilot for a new cooking show where he's the chef. It got picked up and he didn't want me to know until tonight."

Leslie hugged her sister. "That's awesome. That's the kind of secret I can live with," she said.

"Indeed it is," Stella said, as they released their embrace. Stella grabbed Leslie's hand and dragged her back over to Maxine and Star. "Come on, let's get Maxine drunk."

"Too late," Star giggled as she pointed toward Maxine, who sat on the edge of the sofa, wobbling. Star had been pumping her full of rum punch for the past hour. She'd kicked off her shoes, hiked up her dress, and pulled her spiral curls back into a ponytail.

"Star, are you s—sure you didn't put anything in this punch?" Maxine said, slurring her words and squinting into her cup.

"I asked if you wanted a little rum in it," Star said innocently. Maxine slowly raised her head in shock. "And I said no."

Star clasped imaginary pearls. "Did you? I thought you said, *Go.*"

Maxine's eyebrow's furrowed and her eyes narrowed.

Stella and Leslie braced themselves for Maxine to go off. Then, suddenly, Maxine smiled; then she chuckled. And that turned into giggles before she leaned her head back and howled with laughter.

"That's a good one!" she roared. "Well, y'all already got me drunk," she raised her red Solo cup, "so fill her up."

Star squealed her delight as she jumped up to refill Maxine's drink.

"Oooh, listen!" Maxine bolted from her seat as the speaker switched songs and started booming Boyz II Men. All four of them stood for a moment, listening as the group harmonized.

"Mama . . . mama, you know I love you."

A mist quickly covered Leslie's eyes.

"No, ma'am!" Maxine said, taking Leslie's hand. "This is Mama Pearly joining our party."

That made them all smile.

Maxine lifted her cup again and sang along. "*Mama . . . mama, you're the queen of my heart . . . Your love is like tears from the stars.*"

She motioned for her sisters to join her. Star joined in first, then she took Stella's hand as she sang. They all turned to Leslie and she added her harmony.

Then, together, they swayed and sang the last lines, "*Mama, I just want you to know . . . .Loving you is like food to my soul.*"

Connect with Us

Visit us online at
KensingtonBooks.com
to read more from your favorite authors, see books
by series, view reading group guides, and more.

Join us on social media

for sneak peeks, chances to win books and prize packs,
and to share your thoughts with other readers.

facebook.com/kensingtonpublishing
twitter.com/kensingtonbooks

Tell us what you think!

To share your thoughts, submit a review,
or sign up for our eNewsletters, please visit:
KensingtonBooks.com/TellUs.